NO WAY UP

Books by Mary Connealy

The
CIMARRON
Legacy
BOOK ONE

NO WAY UP

MARY CONNEALY

BETHANYHOUSE
a division of Baker Publishing Group
Minneapolis, Minnesota

© 2016 by Mary Connealy

Published by Bethany House Publishers
11400 Hampshire Avenue South
Bloomington, Minnesota 55438
www.bethanyhouse.com

Bethany House Publishers is a division of
Baker Publishing Group, Grand Rapids, Michigan

Printed in the United States of America

Library of Congress Control Number: 2016930777

ISBN 978-0-7642-1181-2

Scripture quotations are from the King James Version of the Bible.

This is a work of fiction. Names, characters, incidents, and dialogues are products of the author's imagination and are not to be construed as real. Any resemblance to actual events or persons, living or dead, is entirely coincidental.

Cover design by Dan Pitts

Author is represented by Natasha Kern Literary Agency

16 17 18 19 20 21 22   7 6 5 4 3 2 1

No Way Up is about parents trying to make their children love each other, take pride in the family ranch, and be devoted to each other. Because of this, I dedicate this book to my mom, Dorothy. No, she doesn't own a vast ranch and insist we all live under her roof. Quite the contrary. I think she was FINE with us growing up and moving out of her small farmhouse.

But she's the mother of eight children who have found faith and good lives of our own. We are all accomplished people—perhaps the author, me, least of all. And we all love her because . . . how could we not?

She is the sweetest lady on earth. She's unfailingly generous. She now has eight sons- and daughters-in-law, twenty-eight grandchildren, ten grandchildren-in-law, and thirteen great-grandchildren (I think I counted right, but who knows?).

Mom, along with Dad, raised us with the beautiful legacy of faith, simply by living it themselves and loving us all through the ups and downs.

She'll protest when she reads this, give any credit for how we all came out to us, and speak with wonder of how she could be so lucky to have such wonderful children, as if she had nothing to do with it. That sweet modesty is part of what we all love so much about her.

Thank you, Mom, for the legacy of love.

The steep sides of the pass into the canyon pressed down on Heath Kincaid until he could hardly breathe. Though it was a blustery November day, a sheen of sweat broke out on his forehead. It surprised him because Heath knew mountains, and he knew tight places.

He rode behind Chance Boden, the owner of this vast land grant, and John Hightree, the foreman of the Cimarron Ranch, and two other men brought up the rear riding single file, their aim to fetch the cattle that had gone in here. They passed the busted-down gate Chance had put up to keep cattle out of the rugged, grassless canyon.

"That fence was stronger than the backbone of the Rockies." Chance looked in disgust at the gateposts that just yesterday blocked the entrance. "That cantankerous bull shouldn't've been able to knock it down."

He led his men around the splintered lumber. "Let's make short work of getting 'em out."

Heath was just passing the ruins of the gate when he heard the rumble. Right overhead. Only one thing made that sound.

"Avalanche! Run!" Heath reined in his stallion so hard it reared. In horror he glanced up as he whirled his horse. He saw tumbling rocks knock debris loose.

The rockslide grew, picked up speed. Those ugly rolling stones, raining down the side of the narrow neck of the entrance to the canyon, were heading right for them. Heath's horse neighed in fear and jerked at the reins.

The first rocks pelted them. A sharp stone slashed Heath's temple. The roar grew louder, promising more were coming. As one, the men charged back the way they'd come—out of the bottleneck canyon and away from the vicious hail.

Heath was third in line. Chance Boden and John were now behind him. Bent low over his stallion's neck, Heath looked back to see the rocks pounding down around their heads.

A big one slammed into John's shoulder and nearly unseated him. Chance was barely visible in the dense cloud of dirt just behind John.

Heath burst out of the canyon neck and wheeled his buckskin. The other two cowpokes were just ahead of him. A second later, John charged out of a cloud, blood coursing down the side of his face and from one arm. He reached Heath's side and pivoted. They both watched, gasping for breath in the grainy air.

Nothing.

The biggest rocks were down, but silt and gravel still rained and the passageway was choked with dust.

"Chance didn't make it out!" Heath hurled himself off his stallion. He plunged into the blinding grit. A rock knocked at him and stung, but the worst of the avalanche was over. It didn't matter anyway; he'd be switched if he stood safely back while

Chance might be dying. Chance's horse suddenly appeared out of the dust. Riderless.

The horse nearly trampled Heath. Once he'd dodged the poor critter, he stormed on, stumbling over rubble. The rocks were deeper as he got farther into the pass. He fell over a chunk of granite and landed, tearing his knees and hands. Down low he could see better, and just ahead of him he spotted the sleeve of a blue shirt. Its color stood out against the chalky stone. Extending from that sleeve was a limp, bleeding hand.

"I found him!" He crawled forward and tossed a stone just as John Hightree nearly tripped over him. Heath and John went to work clearing the debris.

The two other cowhands were only a pace behind. It heartened Heath to know he worked with men who'd risk an avalanche to save one of their own.

The four of them heaved rocks, uncovering Chance as fast as they could.

The boss's face was slick with crimson, peeking through the gravel and dirt that coated him. A goose egg rose up on his forehead.

They were all bleeding somewhere. Heath couldn't see if Chance was dangerously hurt or just knocked cold.

Then Heath tossed aside a slab of rock almost too big to lift and saw the brutal wound on the boss's leg. One of the men uttered a harsh oath. Heath spoke silently to the Lord.

Gushing blood. Worse yet, a jagged bone stuck out of Chance's pant leg, just below his knee.

A wound that always crippled—and often killed.

"Mike," John said, taking charge, "get Chance's horse in here. Windy, gather up the rest of the horses. Mike and I will get Chance in the saddle. Heath, you run for town."

The two men vanished into the grit.

"No!" Heath had never disobeyed an order from John in his

life, but this time he had to. "I need to see if he's got an artery bleeding. I've worked with some wounds like this while scouting for the Army at a fort in Montana."

Chance would for sure lose his lower leg. But it was so close to the knee, Heath didn't see how he could tie a tourniquet anywhere but above the knee. But if it didn't get a tourniquet, and skilled medical hands took over, Chance might keep the knee joint, and that made a big difference in a man's life.

Heath whipped his knife out of its scabbard at his waist and cut Chance's right pant leg away. He took precious moments, when he should be tightening a cinch around Chance's thigh, to see if the bleeding had a pulse. If it did, it was life-threatening and a tourniquet couldn't be avoided.

"I don't feel an artery bleeding," Heath said with relief. "I might be able to patch him up, but we've got to clean the wound first. To do that, we have to get him out of this gritty air."

Muttering, not concealing his doubts worth a lick, John picked up Chance's shoulders while Heath got his legs, flinching at the rough handling. They carried him across the stone-cluttered ground into clean air just as Windy came up with all the horses except for Chance's, which Mike had caught and was leading back.

"Lay him down, and then I can clean him up." He and John positioned him. "Get the canteens off the horses. We've got to wash the dirt out of the wound."

Windy, Mike, and John rushed to do as Heath ordered.

Heath prayed for God to guide his hands, because these men were putting their trust in him and he didn't want to fail anyone.

"There's a spring back a couple hundred yards." John handed over the first canteen. "We can get all the water you want."

"Get ready to run for more as soon as one empties. Washing it out could head off infection and that might make the difference between life and death for the boss. And I need something to use for splints. Even a couple of heavy sticks are better than nothing."

Heath hunched over the cruel wound. Dirt and gravel were all through it, even beneath the broken bone. Not a speck of that dirt could stay or Chance would be in a world of trouble.

Ignoring the other men, Heath worked tirelessly on Chance's leg. He didn't know how much water he used or how many times the men ran for more. They had five canteens, and all Heath knew was that when he reached up for more water, it was always there.

Time stretched on. Whether minutes or hours, Heath didn't know. Chance's leg bled until Heath was scared for his boss's life, but he went on cleaning. He remembered the doctor at the fort had carbolic acid on hand to treat open injuries, to stave off suppuration. Heath wished he had some now. Hopefully the doctor in Skull Gulch was a good one who kept up with modern methods.

Finally, Heath couldn't see a single speck of dirt, nor the tiniest piece of gravel. Now he had to deal with the jagged protruding bone. "John, hold down his thigh."

John gave Heath a hard look before he settled both hands above Chance's knee. When John had a firm grip, Heath, his hands coated in blood, caught Chance's ankle and made a ruthless move to straighten the leg. The bone snapped back under the skin.

Chance shouted in pain, the first sign of life.

The cry was horrible, but he was alive.

Having ripped his shirt off his back, Heath turned it clean-side out, folded it with lightning moves, then wrapped the shirt tight around Chance's roughly reset upper shin.

"Did anyone find something to splint this with?"

Two flat pieces of board were thrust into his line of sight. "Perfect."

So perfect he was stunned.

"I found them on the broken fence, Heath," Windy said.

"All of you—give me your shirts." They were handed to Heath one by one, leaving the men dressed in their woolen undershirts. Heath twisted them into ropes of cloth and bound the splints so they wouldn't slip.

"This is tight enough I hope it stops the bleeding, but without cutting off circulation. It's the only chance we have of saving his knee. There just isn't room below the knee and above the break for a tourniquet."

Heath hoped he hadn't missed any filth and was now binding it inside Chance's leg. If he was, infection was guaranteed. It was probably guaranteed anyway.

"Are you done?" Mike asked through clenched teeth.

"Yep."

"Is there more you can do for him, Heath?" John sounded hopeful and skeptical at the same time.

"That doctor in the Army taught me to look for a severed artery, and if none are cut, to clean the wound and use a bandage, because a tourniquet cuts off circulation and everything below the tourniquet will have to be amputated. If an artery is bleeding, you've got no choice. But Chance's break didn't cut through one. On the battlefield I'd do this, then get the man to the doctor. Someone smarter than me has to take over now." Heath was mighty sorry to admit that.

"Go fetch Doc Garner in Skull Gulch. You might be able to tell him things the rest of us can't. Have the doc meet us at the house. And tell Cole and Sadie to get home," John said.

Heath hated the second part of the order. He was to be the one to tell Sadie and Cole the terrible news. They'd always remember him for that. If they decided to kill the messenger, it'd be him they'd kill. But John was not to be disobeyed, not ever, unless a man had a mighty good reason and talked fast.

Heath turned and raced for his horse, glad to the depths of his soul that he'd found the money to buy the fleet-footed, high-endurance quarter horse. The powerful stallion leapt into a gallop from the first pace. Heath jumped over rocks and dodged boulders with one goal in mind—to get to the doctor and bring him to the Cimarron Ranch in time to save Chance Boden, one of the finest men he'd ever known.

It didn't slow him down, but Heath's stomach twisted with regret as he thought of Sadie. Her father might be dying. The very best they could hope for was an amputated leg.

If the broken leg didn't kill Chance, the surgery to save his life or the infection that resulted from it very well might.

And he was the one who had to tell Sadie all of that.

2

The door to her classroom slammed open.

"Sadie, you've got to come fast." Heath Kincaid, one of Pa's cowhands, rushed forward past the rows of suddenly frightened children at the orphanage.

The urgency made Sadie leap to her feet. Her desk chair rolled back and crashed against the blackboard.

"Your pa's been hurt bad."

Without a single question to Heath, who was filthy and bleeding, Sadie looked at the most dependable of her twenty-four students. "Stephanie, find Sister Margaret and tell her I've gone home."

The twelve-year-old dashed out of the room. Another child, almost as steady, was next. "Jeremiah, you're in charge until Sister Margaret gets here."

Heath caught her by the arm. He'd have dragged her out if she hadn't been running as fast as he was. He said, "I hollered at someone to tell Cole to come. They said he'd ridden off to the mines, so they're chasing him down to get him home. No time to saddle your horse; you'll ride with me."

He tossed her onto the horse's back before she could protest—not that she intended to. He was behind her in an instant. His horse was breathing hard, but it was a big, strong stallion. Sadie had noticed the buckskin last Sunday when Heath had ridden home with the family from services. She'd gone home for dinner and had mentioned what a fine horse Heath rode.

The animal looked to have endurance. Pa had spoken of breeding mares to him.

"Pa." The single word escaped her lips.

Heath put the horse to the test. Soon they were away from the Safe Haven Orphanage and leaving behind the little town of Skull Gulch. He leaned forward, pressing her low over the horse's neck, and got every ounce of speed out of the stallion.

"What happened?" Sadie's imagination was running wild.

Close to her ear, Heath answered, "A rockslide came down on your pa. We were out in that canyon past Skull Mesa." Heath mentioned the vast, forbidding mesa with no way up that had given the town its name. Sadie knew well that the pass was a narrow, treacherous spot that led into a rocky land.

"I thought Pa fenced it off to keep the cattle out."

"Big Red knocked the fence down and led some of the cows in. We went in after them and there was an avalanche."

Sadie looked over her shoulder and reached one finger up to touch Heath's face. "You're bleeding."

"We were all in that pass. This is how we all look, your pa the worst of all. John is getting him home. He sent me for the doctor and to get you and Cole home as quick as I can."

John had been working with Pa since before Sadie was born. He went all the way back to when the ranch was owned by Sadie's Grandfather Chastain, her mother's father. John was part of the family. Nearly as much a father to Sadie as Pa.

Over the drumming hoofbeats, Heath went on. "Chance is all busted up." There was a long pause. "I sent Doc Garner

16

running for the CR before I came for you. John wants you and Cole home. Justin too."

"Was Justin with him when he got hurt?" Her middle brother lived on the ranch, the only one of the three of them still at home.

"Nope. Your brother went in a different direction this morning. John ordered me to fetch you and Cole both. He'll send someone for Justin or go himself."

"Pa will be all right." Sadie heard the desperation in her voice. "He's too tough to let a hard trail get the best of him."

Heath didn't respond, and somehow the silence was worse than if he'd agreed . . . or disagreed. But she thought maybe the arms he had around her, guiding the horse, tightened a bit as if he were trying to protect her from what lay ahead.

They were setting a scorching pace. The ranch was ten miles from town, and Sadie often made the ride in about an hour.

They were going to make it in less than half that.

Racing past scrub brush and the towering mesa to the west, Sadie prayed. Working at the orphanage had drawn her closer to God. But to her shame, with fear pounding at her and the urgency of the desperate ride, it had taken until now to pray.

She was asking God to hold her father in the palm of His hand. After long, heartfelt pleas sent heavenward, she felt her spirit calm and grim determination replace her panic. Pa would be all right. They'd do whatever needed doing to ensure it.

Thinking of Ma without Pa was impossible. Chance and Veronica Boden were the most solidly in love couple Sadie had ever known. Not just love either, but respect and hard work toward the same goals. A true friendship. Her parents were united in a way Sadie admired and wanted for herself someday. In fact, she demanded it for herself, which was one of the reasons she'd turned down a lot of offers to marry.

"Tell me how he is." Sadie twisted on the horse to look back. "Don't protect me from the truth."

It wasn't hard to remember Heath with his shining blue eyes. Now they seemed to glow with regret. "I . . . I don't like to say. It's real serious. A badly broken leg."

"You saw his injury?"

"I was there. We were all caught in the avalanche, but your pa was in the most dangerous stretch, so he got hit the hardest." Heath's arm tightened even more, wrapping around her waist, as if she needed someone to hold her together. "I'm hoping and praying that something can be done so that . . . well, sometimes a serious injury turns out not to be quite so bad after there's a closer look."

She felt a harsh shudder shake his whole body. She knew Heath wasn't telling her everything.

"Please, Heath, tell me the whole truth of what happened."

The silence was broken by the pounding hooves, and Sadie braced herself to ask again—however many times she needed to.

"I want to be prepared," she said. "I don't want to run into the house and be unable to control the shock. It'll upset Ma." More silence. Sadie clutched at Heath's wrist, guiding the horse. "Tell me."

Finally, Heath nodded. "The rocks knocked him off his horse, and we had to . . . to . . . he was nearly buried." He fell silent again.

She heard him sigh, long and slow, and she tightened her grip on his wrist, sinking a few of her fingernails into his skin so he'd know she wasn't satisfied.

"Your pa's leg, it's the kind of break where a bone tears out of the skin. It's a mighty rare thing for a man to have a break like that and . . . and keep his . . . his leg. And if infection sets in, well, cutting off his leg might not even save him."

Sadie gasped and glanced back to meet pure compassion, or maybe it was pity. She quit strangling his wrist. Sadie thought of a hundred more questions, but her throat wouldn't work and maybe she didn't want to hear the answers now. Heath wrapped his free arm further around her waist.

She should have demanded he let go. He was too close and it wasn't proper. But she couldn't bear to do it. Couldn't bear not having someone hold her. Then Heath's arm was gone, then back. He pressed a white handkerchief into her hand, and that was the first she knew she was crying.

Her fear and worry and pain were too much to allow her to focus on such a minor thing as tears. She pressed the kerchief to her eyes, and Heath went back to holding her, his big hand spread gently on her belly.

He whispered in her ear, she wasn't sure what. Just snatches of words. "I'm so sorry . . . we're almost there . . . pray for him." Everything he said was jumbled together with soothing murmurs that weren't words.

They thundered on, but for a while Sadie felt as if she'd handed her whole life over to someone else. A man strong enough to do whatever needed doing.

Holding her tight as she wept. Carrying her home.

The stallion's hooves galloped beneath them as Heath did the only thing he could for her. Ride like his horse's tail was on fire. Keep Sadie safe while she cried. Get her home fast.

Seeing her hazel eyes soaked with tears was like taking a tomahawk in the gut.

Her blond hair blew in his face. She'd had it in a neat bun when he'd gone into the classroom, yet it had all sprung free miles ago.

There was a mighty good chance Sadie didn't even know his name. He'd been working on the CR since spring roundup, but she didn't live there, didn't come around much at all beyond

Sunday dinner. He always rode into town for church on Sunday, and any CR riders who went in stayed together, then rode home as a group. There was safety in groups, and even in the civilized West, there were dangers.

But he was one of a crowd and she'd never spoken to him, not a single word. He doubted she'd even noticed him.

But he'd noticed her for a fact. The prettiest little thing he'd ever seen. His boss's daughter, so of course she didn't spend her time around a lowly cowpuncher.

Until now.

Heath regretted bitterly that finally she was going to notice him and remember him for bringing terrible news. She'd always think of him in connection with one of the worst days of her life. And judging by the boss's vicious injury, it was only going to get worse.

He shifted his arm on her slender waist and spoke close to her ear so she could hear him over the pounding hooves. Offering what comfort he could.

Then the ranch came into sight and Heath eased his arm away. They were no longer alone, and holding her so close wasn't proper.

They raced right up to the door.

Heath swung down and lifted Sadie to the ground before she had a chance to dismount on her own. She rushed inside the house. He wondered if that was the closest he'd ever get to the woman who'd been haunting his dreams since the first day he'd laid eyes on her.

Two of the CR cowhands came up and took charge of him. He only now realized he'd gone straight into town and right up to Sadie in his longhandles. And blood-soaked to boot.

Neither of them knew a thing about Chance beyond that he'd gotten home alive.

One man took his horse to cool the animal down. Another

guided him to the bunkhouse, where a bucket of warm water waited for him to wash away this nightmarish day.

All he could think of while he cleaned up and bandaged his meager wounds was the last moment he'd seen Sadie as she ran into the house. Whatever dreams he'd had for Sadie Boden had come too late.

What if she was too late?

What if the long ride into town to fetch her meant she'd never see her pa alive again?

Why had she insisted on moving to town? Why had her work with the orphans seemed more important than her family?

She headed straight to Ma and Pa's big bedroom on the ground floor. She knew he'd be there, but in case there was any doubt, there was a trail of blood to follow.

Sadie saw her pa, unmoving, eyes closed, his face sunken and his cheeks hollow, the doctor tending him. Ma was on the far side of the bed, wringing a blood-soaked rag over a basin of steaming water.

Ma looked up, and so much passed between her and Sadie in an instant it almost sent Sadie reeling backward. Love, relief that Sadie was finally there, terror for her husband, grim determination.

Sadie mentioned none of it. Now was not the time for fussing and tears and hugs. Now was the time to work hard and save Pa.

Doc Garner bent over the bed, working on Pa's leg.

"Mrs. Boden, a clean rag." The doctor snapped out orders as if Ma were his nurse, and Ma responded so quickly Sadie knew she didn't resent it. In fact, she was glad to be of help, glad to obey.

"I'll take orders too, Doc," Sadie offered. But the doctor didn't look up from his work, which Sadie admired.

"Kincaid said he'd tended the wound in hopes of saving the knee." The doctor inspected the wound with single-minded attention. "If we have to amputate—"

Ma gasped. Sadie's heart sank to her boots.

"—having the knee will make a big difference in how hard it is to adjust." The doctor kept talking while he worked, paying no attention to how his words hit. "But there's a chance we can save the whole leg."

With that, Sadie's heart rushed right back up with hope. Heath had said Pa would lose the leg, while the doctor wasn't such a pessimist.

The doctor shook a powder all over the gaping wound. Bloody bandages lay on the bedside table, and the sheets were crimson, but the bleeding looked to have stopped.

"With a fracture treated this well, there's a chance. I know a doctor in Denver who is doing work on broken bones. He'll be able to set it and mend a lot of the torn muscles."

The doctor looked up, his eyes dark and intense. He'd come to treat the children at the orphanage a few times, and she'd never seen this fierce side of him.

"I won't put on a plaster cast because it will have to be removed as soon as we reach Denver and cutting it off will be hard on the limb." He treated the leg with steady, skilled hands. "We need to get him on the train. It's due right after the noon meal and it's getting close to that now. I'll get a buckboard ready. Miss Boden, you wrap another layer of bandages around tight, but not too tight. Be careful not to move his leg. The bone is set and I don't want it to come unset. I need to find a way to keep it from getting bounced around on the wagon. The cloths are clean and all ready to go."

The doctor hurried out of the room.

Sadie rounded the bed. Ma handed her the strips of cloth. Carefully she wrapped Pa's leg. "Ma, did you hear him? He thinks they can save the leg. Heath Kincaid came for me in town, and he made it sound a lot worse than this."

Her temper grew as she thought of how upset she'd been. Heath didn't need to paint things so dark.

"Doc Garner said he's never seen a break tended this well. Usually by the time he gets there, nothing will do but to saw off the leg. Very few people know to treat a break like this."

"So why did Heath sound so grim?" She needed to stop being angry. It wasn't fair and she knew it, but it was like the emotion had broken free and she couldn't rope it and hog-tie it.

Ma's strong hand rested on her shoulder as she finished the bandage. "Don't aim your anger at the man who may have saved your pa's leg, and helped save his life. I won't have it."

It was a bleak order, but it had been delivered with love.

Sadie nodded and straightened from the bed. "What else do we need to do before Pa leaves?"

Ma dunked the rag and wrung it out again, then handed it to Sadie. "Finish cleaning the blood—" Ma paused, swallowed hard—"off his chest as best you can. We're moving him as soon as Doc is ready."

"To Denver?"

"It sounds crazy, but Doc Garner is convinced it's worth a try. It would've been impossible before the train. But now we can get him there and get him proper treatment."

It was true they could make the trip to Denver in a day on the train. A long, hard day. She stared down at her pa, who looked nearer to death than life.

Chance Boden. A vital, brilliant, powerful man. Brought low by a bunch of falling rocks.

Sadie worked on the wounds on Pa's chest while Ma tended and bandaged cuts on his face. All this blood and Ma never flinched from it. Never went pale, never faltered. Ma was just as strong as Pa.

Rosita, their housekeeper, hurried in with another basin of clean water.

"Give it to Sadie and get me more, Rosita. Chance has other wounds to tend."

Rosita set the basin on the small table on Sadie's side of the bed, then placed a hand on Sadie's arm. "*Mi niña*," she said before leaving the room.

Ma and Sadie continued to work over Pa's still form. Finally they had him cleaned and bandaged.

"I've got to pack clothes for Pa and me. Stay with him, Sadie. I'll be gone only a few minutes."

Sadie nodded. Ma gave Pa one long, heartbroken look and then rushed away. Sadie picked up one of his strong, callused hands and pressed it to her cheek, begging God for mercy.

"Sadie."

Her eyes popped open to meet Pa's. Ma should be here, but for now Sadie was alone with the man she loved more than any other on earth.

His eyes sparkled with love. "You're the image of your ma."

"Thank you, Pa. I hope I'm half as pretty."

"What happened to put me in this bed in the middle of the day?"

"Your leg is broken and it's a terrible break. The bone went through the skin. Doc Garner knows a special doctor in Denver. You're going there." Sadie leaned down and kissed him on the forehead with aching gentleness.

"Denver?"

"The break is a kind that often ends with a man . . . losing his leg."

Pa's eyes narrowed in surprise.

"Doc thinks that if we get you to Denver, there's a chance you can keep it."

Rushing on, Sadie said, "The train leaves right after twelve noon and won't be through again for a week. You and Ma are going right now. You'll be in Denver by morning. Doc says there's no time to dawdle with injuries like this."

Ma came bustling in and gasped to see Pa awake. That sound drew Pa's gaze, and the love between them was like a living fire. Sadie had grown up with this love all her life. It had seemed like the connection between her parents was just part of normal life, but right this moment she realized how precious it was.

With all the courage she'd come to expect of her father, he gave a single nod, accepting what was to come. Then he said, "I have to talk to all three of the children."

"There's not time." Ma squeezed his hand tighter.

A sharp shake of his head said he wouldn't be moved. Sadie knew that look, but she also had never seen her mother like this before.

"We are leaving for town in five minutes whether you've spoken to the children or not. You can't stop me from having you carried to the wagon and loaded on that train. We aren't going to miss it."

"Cole had headed out to the mines. He'll be coming fast." Sadie knew it was true. Heath's urgency couldn't have failed to be passed on. "But it'll be a while."

Ma cut in, "Maybe we'll pass Cole on the trail and can speak to him for a few minutes then."

That was unlikely. If he'd gotten down the trail very far, he'd be coming from the west, not the south. Sadie didn't say that, though.

"You mean he'll be coming from *town* when he ought to be here." Pa sounded bitter, as he had hundreds of times before about Cole and Sadie living in town.

"We aren't stopping the wagon for anyone," Ma said bluntly.

"He can ride alongside us and listen, because Justin needs to hear what I have to say. Sadie, I need to explain myself."

A racket in the back of the house drew Ma's attention. "If that's the doctor, you'd better say your piece quickly because we're leaving." With that, Ma turned and left the room again.

Pa looked Sadie in the eye. "I just made this decision a few days ago and I wanted to talk with you about it. Figured to do it on Sunday. Figured I had all the time in the world to explain myself."

"Tell me, Pa." Sadie bickered with her father a lot, but right now she could deny him nothing.

Pa swallowed hard, worry furrowing his brow. "I changed my will. If I don't survive this ride to Denver and whatever quack treatment your ma's got in mind, then you'll know what I've done. But I want you to hear it straight from my lips too, so you'll know I'm serious."

Sadie stopped breathing for a moment. Then she said what she hoped would soothe Pa. "The land is yours to do with as you please, Pa. Whatever your wishes are, we'll abide by them."

"My wish is that you and Cole move back home. I want you to be part of the CR. I want all three of you to make your lives here."

"Pa, I'm close by. My work at Safe Haven Orphanage is—"

Pa's head jerked sideways, refusing her explanation, one she'd made over and over before.

"All three of you are to live here, in this house, for a year. And because I'm hurt, but the will won't be in force yet, God willing, I'm telling you that this begins now. It's supposed to be after I'm dead, so if I live and get back here, we can see about things. But right now, today, I want you all moved home. You can run to town for errands, but you will live here, work here, sleep under this roof. If any one of you moves out without giving it the full year, the land goes to your cousin Mike."

"Mike? You mean Mike Sanders? He's not our cousin. Well, maybe fifth cousin." He was a distant relation on Grandfather Chastain's side, a Canadian who'd wandered into the area years after her grandfather had died and then claimed kinship. "Pa, you can't stand him." What Sadie really meant was that *she* couldn't stand Mike. Nor any of Mike's low-down sons who would fritter away the ranch one foolishly spent dollar at a time. "You've always said he's probably lying about being kin to Grandfather."

"I had to pick someone who'd make you all mad enough to stay here and fight for the land. I want you to imagine your greedy cousin's glee as he kicks all three of you out. I've left it all to him—all my cash money, the mines, everything. If you don't want what I've built, added on to the beginning given to us by your grandfather, then you're free to go build something of your own."

Pa's eyes focused on her. "Justin would fight for the ranch for himself. You, Sadie, I hope you love your brother enough to save it for him. If that's not reason enough, remember this: the moment you move out, all the money for your orphanage ends."

Sadie nearly choked on that threat. Pa loved her, all three of them. She had no doubt. But he'd been hurt when Cole had gone back east to college, then come home, but only as close as Skull Gulch, never to live at the ranch again. Then later Sadie had moved to town.

Though Cole worked hard at the family business, he built a house in town and managed the mine holdings from a place he could call his own. Sadie moved in with him to be close to the orphans who'd so touched her heart.

"I want you here, girl. You can use my money to hire someone for the school, but I don't want you and Cole moving here and then riding to town every day. Cole can do his mine work from this ranch. This land was paid for in blood. Grandfather held it at the cost of his own life. I tried to raise you to see that you are part of a legacy and I've failed. But now I've put things right."

"Pa, you can't rule us like this." Sadie felt her anger flare up. "We're adults. We work hard, and where we live is not for you to—" A sudden sound from Pa cut through her anger and shut her mouth.

"I love you, my precious Sadie girl. Tell your brothers I love them—all of you—more than life itself. It's possible that this very day I will follow your grandfather to the grave, my own blood spilled out and soaked into the soil of the Cimarron. I want you to love your home."

Ma came back in the room with the doctor, who had two cowhands right behind him carrying a door.

"We need to keep you as still as possible, Chance," Doc Garner said. "I'm going to tie you to this door and use it as a sturdy brace on your legs, back, and around your neck."

Pa nodded at the doctor but kept talking to Sadie. "It's not just being gone from the CR, it's arguing with each other. I want you to love each other."

"We do, Pa." Yes, they rubbed each other the wrong way and wrangled their share, especially Cole and Justin, but there had never been a question of their not loving each other.

"And I want you to claim the Cimarron as your legacy and love this land."

Love this land. That was Pa to the core.

"Read the will, Sadie. I want Cole and Justin to know my wishes. But on my honor, you will move home today, right now. If you don't, and I die, the land goes to Mike right now. If I live, then when I get home I'm going to forget the will and invite Mike to come and live here and make legal changes so he owns the place. Make sure your brothers understand I'm serious."

The doctor wrapped something around Pa's neck that made it impossible for him to talk. His eyelids fell shut.

The doctor handed out orders. Ma and the two hands did as they were told as fast as possible. Then, between one heartbeat and the next, they rushed out of the room, carrying Pa on a hard slab of wood.

Ma flung her arms around Sadie. "I know what your pa has done, Sadie. Please, just for his peace of mind, abide by his wishes, at least until we get home, then we can talk more about it. Any part of it you don't understand, the will makes clear. Read it today before anyone leaves the ranch."

Ma raced after Pa, through the kitchen and outside. Sadie chased her to the door. Pa was already loaded onto the wagon. Doc knelt beside him. Ma climbed into the wagon box with Pa. Soon they were off in a cloud of dust.

Sadie stood at the back door of the house and watched the wagon clatter away. One rider galloped ahead, already in the far distance. They were cutting things very close to make the train. Sadie guessed the doctor had sent a cowhand ahead to hold the train even if he had to throw himself on the tracks.

She felt as if that wagon carried her heart, as well as the two people she loved most in the world.

One of whom had just turned her life upside down.

3

Sadie sat at the kitchen table, staring at nothing. Her thoughts were with her parents, her heart beating fast with fear.

A long time had passed before rushing feet drew her notice.

"What happened?" Cole ran in. "Where's Pa?"

"Pa was hurt in a rockslide in the narrow pass south of Skull Mesa."

"But that was fenced off. We knew that trail was dangerous. Why—?"

"Cole!" Sadie had never shouted at her brother in her life. Well, in her adult life. "Don't waste time right now with questions. Let me tell you what happened." She wished Justin would come. She didn't know if she had the strength to tell it all twice. "Pa's leg is badly broken. It's a serious injury, the kind that usually ends with losing the leg."

"No!" Cole strode up to her and crouched in front of her to take her hands.

She was just done telling him about Pa's injury when the front door crashed open and Justin tore into the room, spurs jangling.

"Where's Pa?" Justin must have asked questions as he rode back with John.

"He was in that narrow canyon," Sadie began. Again she told the story of what happened to their pa, filling her brother in.

Cole's voice rose in anger. "Justin, I thought you built a good fence across that canyon."

Blaming Justin when they all knew Pa helped build the fence, and it *had* been a good one.

"Cole, don't start." Sadie only hoped Pa didn't wind up at the Pearly Gates instead of Denver. She had no doubt that Pa was right with the Lord. That didn't mean she wanted him heaven-bound anytime soon. "Let's just take a moment to pray together. We can start by praying Pa gets to Denver safely."

"Don't start?" Cole swept his hat off his head. "Why do you think I moved away from here? No one ever let me start. No one ever ran this ranch right."

He wore a black suit and a matching Stetson. Though he was breathing hard, he always looked clean and tidy. More city than country.

"Not run it right?" Justin strode forward until he stood nose to nose with Cole. "I ought to run a fist through your face."

"Both of you stop it right now." She erupted from her chair and rushed to shove her way between them, disgusted that her brothers might end up punching each other.

They were of a similar height, both dark-haired with dark blue eyes. They looked a lot like each other and strongly resembled Pa. But there the similarity ended. Inside, no two brothers had ever been more unlike each other. The fact that they looked so similar only made their differences more pronounced.

Justin in his dusty brown pants, wearing chaps and spurs, a red kerchief around his neck, a black broadcloth shirt, and black leather vest. His tan Stetson, filthy with sweat, was crumpled and torn. He had a good one for when he left the ranch, but

Justin loved this hat and had worn it for years. He had a quick temper and didn't back away for anyone. And he'd always been quick to throw a fist, especially at Cole.

He wore a tied-down gun and a belt full of bullets. And he was broad in his chest and shoulders from doing hours of hard physical labor every day. His hair was worn long, tied back with a strip of leather. Justin's hands were big and rough and callused.

Cole, five years older, was as different from Justin as night was from day. His finely made suit of clothes. His short hair, always neatly combed. No gun, though Cole certainly knew how to use one. Cole's hands were as smooth as his charm, the nails clean and well-trimmed. Cole liked to talk his way out of trouble. He had an easy smile and the quick language of a trained businessman, which he'd perfected at Harvard while he lived with Grandmother and learned at Grandfather Bradford's side how to run a company. Yet for all his cultured ways, right now Cole looked as uncivilized as a man could get.

"John sent me in here." Heath Kincaid stepped into the room from the kitchen, before Cole could turn and walk out. "He's beyond talking right now."

John was as close to Pa as a brother.

Heath held up a rolled-up piece of parchment paper and pressed it into Cole's hands. "He went into your Pa's office and got this. He gave it to me and said you're all three to listen to how your pa plans to divide this ranch in the event of his death. You're to hear it now, before you leave."

What had John told him? Heath looked like he'd block them from leaving if he had to.

"Let's go sit in your pa's office."

They moved to the office, and Heath headed to the far end of the room and leaned against a windowsill, even though there were places to sit closer to the desk. Apparently he was trying to stay as far out of this as possible. Sadie appreciated that and felt some guilt for the position he'd been put in.

"You've been dragged into family business, Kincaid." Cole extended the parchment back to him. "Can you read?"

"I reckon I can." Heath's lips curled down, as if Cole were holding out a rattlesnake. "This is private family business. I could go get someone who's closer to the family. Maybe Alonzo—"

"No." With surprising fierceness, Cole rejected the name of the CR ramrod, second in command after John. Was he just upset with all that had happened or did he have something against Alonzo? "You're here. Let's get on with it."

Sadie saw Heath swallow hard as he approached the desk. "'The last will and testament of Chance Boden,'" he began.

Heath's voice deepened until Sadie felt it rubbing like gentle sandpaper against her heart.

4

"'To Whom it May Concern . . .'"

Heath had no idea how he'd stepped into this mess. He didn't even know quite why it was a mess. This will split the property between the heirs. The three children were here. So divide it by three and be done with it.

But then why the demand by Chance that it be read immediately? And why did Chance's three grown children look wound up tight enough to snap?

Heath read the will slowly, clearly, and listened as the Boden family gasped.

"'All three of my children will live and work out of the CR ranch house or forfeit the ranch for all three. If any of them leaves for more than a run to town for brief errands or church, or if any of them sets up a place of work away from the ranch, the ranch will be bequeathed to Michael Sanders, third cousin to my wife, Veronica Boden.'"

"Sanders!" Justin surged to his feet. "That polecat? But Pa couldn't abide him or his sons."

"Pa must not have been in his right mind," Cole said, crossing his arms so tight he could have squeezed blood out of a rock. "That's the only reason he'd have left the ranch to Mike. If Pa wasn't thinking right, we can have the will overturned. We need to—"

"Pa told me why," Sadie cut in quietly.

Cole and Justin heard her, though, because they turned on her like a pair of hungry wolves.

She gave a sigh, then looked squarely at her two brothers. "Pa knew we'd all hate the idea of leaving the CR to Mike, even beyond hating to lose it. He knew we'd probably go along with his terms to save the ranch without a further goad. But just in case, he wrote he'd be leaving it all to Cousin Mike if we didn't hold up our end. He knew that was something we couldn't stand for."

"So that's it?" Cole erupted. "Pa's telling us that when his time comes, he plans to rule us from the grave?"

Heath didn't know Cole very well, but he seemed unlike most western men, a cool character who preferred to solve his troubles with words, not with force. Now he looked mad enough to draw his gun and start shootin' . . . if he had a gun. Which he didn't.

Justin moved to the far side of the big room. He started pacing. A man of action. Not one bit happy.

"Cole, it's just a year." Sadie's hands were twisted in her lap. She looked sad, worried, as her eyes shifted between her brothers.

"That's not the point!" Cole jammed all ten fingers deep into his hair. "Pa's been after me to move home since the day I got back from Boston. And now he's found a way to put me under his thumb."

"You're not under his thumb if he's not here," Sadie reminded him.

"He'll be back long before a year is up."

"Well, we want him back, Cole." Sadie sounded angry for the first time. "So that's a good thing."

"Pa loves us all." Justin tried to sound measured, except that Heath could see his color rising. Justin didn't like to hear a word against his pa. "You know he's proud of you, Cole. He said you ran our mining interests better than he could, and he gave you full control over it. Asking you to move home isn't too much—"

"You knew about this, didn't you?" Cole turned on Justin. "You and Pa cooked this up together. You think if you play this right, you can come out as sole owner of the CR."

"That's not true—I'm learning about it right along with you," Justin said, his jaw set. "I'm the one who stands to lose everything if you and Sadie don't rearrange your whole lives to suit Pa's fool plans."

"Losing the mines affects me. Running them is how I earn my money."

"You've got a fancy college degree and could go earn money anywhere. I'm sure, even dead, your grandparents had connections enough to make you the next governor of Massachusetts if you wanted the job."

That turned Cole's face bright red with fury for no reason Heath could understand, but he didn't know about any grandparents. Must be a sore subject.

"Sadie, well, her heart is in the orphanage, not out here. She preferred to move away and leave Ma and Pa and me behind."

While it was covered by temper, Heath could still hear the hurt in Justin's voice. He'd heard that same hurt in his big brother Rafe's voice when Heath told him he was moving on, leaving the family behind.

"The only thing keeping Sadie here is the money for those children she loves. But she could crook a finger and marry some fine man and never look back."

That drew a rude scoffing noise from Sadie. Heath had to wonder what she had against marriage.

"I'm the one who's sunk his life into this land. Losing it would be like tearing off one of my arms. The only way to start over would be to find a job on a ranch as a cowpoke. Save to earn enough to get my own start. And it'd take me years to buy even a small spread. I need you here at home, but with you trapped here too, life is gonna be a misery."

Heath thought that was a lot more reasonable than what Cole had said. But then Justin wasn't being asked to give up the life he preferred.

The two men stared at each other. Breathing hard, their fists clenched. The two were almost mirror images of each other, but they dressed and moved and acted so different that no one would mix them up.

Heath waited and the silence held. He thought of his own pa and how he'd treated his children ill by having a wife in one place and a second family hidden away in another. Heath's mother. Neither woman knew about the other. The old trapper had spent much of his time away from both homes, so no one questioned the long absences. Pa hadn't left a will and he'd shown no sign of caring for his children.

Heath read the final paragraph of the will. "'To the extent God allows, I will love you and pray for you and look down upon you from heaven. Cole, my educated son. So brilliant, so honorable. Justin, my son of the land. Strong of head and heart and back. Sadie, my beautiful girl. The presence of a girl child has brought me more joy than you can know. It is beyond me how a common man such as myself could have three such fine children. You are each more than I've ever hoped to be. I'm so proud of you, I'm near to bursting as I write these words. I want each of you to know I love you.'"

Chance's words were something they would cherish for a

lifetime. And they were lucky to hear them while their pa still lived. Heath would've given a lot to hear "I love you" from Pa, even once. He'd've given a lot to have a single memory that he could linger over and fool himself into believing that Pa loved him. There was nothing.

Heath went on, "'I hope all the trouble my will causes will be well-settled by the time you read this.'"

"Settled?" Cole interrupted. "What does he mean by that?"

"Pa told me he had hoped to talk this all over with us." Sadie had a lacy white kerchief in her hands, and she dabbed at her eyes with it and spoke while looking at her lap. "He made these changes just this week. He wanted to face us with his decisions and, I think, give us a chance to move home without him having to force us. I think if we had, he would've changed his will back."

Justin cut in, "You never gave the CR a chance after you got home from your fancy schooling, Cole. Pa would've never done this if you'd lived here."

"Living here made no sense. My work with the mines requires a telegraph and access to the mail and the train and the bank. Besides that, I have some private business interests that require—"

"Those are just excuses." Justin slashed a hand. "He wanted you to be part of the family again. He felt like your grandmother had stolen you from us. If you'd just moved home for a while after being gone so many years, this never would have happened."

Cole stood and strode away from Justin so as to put some space between them. "Do you know how many job offers I had in Boston? I could have been a wealthy man back there."

"You're a wealthy man here." Justin balled his fists. "And you've always acted like your life back east was so fine and rich. Like the CR wasn't good enough for you to live on. You should have moved home."

"I did move home. I came back to Skull Gulch." Cole closed the distance between himself and Justin like he was done keeping the peace.

"He wanted you here at the ranch. Pa knew your grandmother was trying to poison you against him."

"I saw what Grandmother was doing, what she'd always done. Claim me for herself and bind me to a life under her influence. But I put up with it because I wanted the schooling and I wanted to see a little of the world. But I no more wanted to live under her roof than Pa's. There's no sin in wanting to be on my own."

"If you always planned to come back, why'd you wait until she died? You'd been out of college for years by then."

"Because Grandfather was dead and she was failing in her old age. I couldn't just abandon her. And I was working, building a stake."

"You had a stake right here. While Granny lived, you were content to be her precious pet grandson for the rest of your life."

"I'm no one's pet."

"Did she do this to you too, just like Pa? Offer you an inheritance if you stayed at her side like a trained dog?"

Cole shoved Justin hard. "She was good to me. She loved me and she was dying. It did no harm to stay at her side her final years. She'd named me as her only heir and why not? I was her only grandchild. Staying to comfort her was the right and decent thing to do."

Justin snorted. "Staying to collect your money, you mean."

Cole slammed a fist into Justin's face and knocked him into a table. A lit kerosene lamp went flying and smashed against the wall. Flames whooshed up, fed by the kerosene and the fabric of the drapes.

"Cole!" Sadie screamed and raced for them. "Stop! Justin, no!"

Justin leapt to his feet and dove at Cole, tackling him to the floor.

The fire, fed by splattered kerosene, crawled up the heavy drapes on the only window in the room. Both curtains on the ten-foot window were engulfed almost instantly. Heath hesitated for just one moment. Should he break up the fight or keep the house from burning down around their ears?

He went for the fire while another fist thudded.

"Cole! Justin! Please!" Sadie's high-pitched screaming was almost lost in the crackling fire. Heath yanked the curtains down and stomped on them.

Fire crawled along the floor in a path between the lamp and the overstuffed couch. It'd been splattered with kerosene too, so it'd go next.

"Sadie, leave them!" Heath shouted, stomping the fire frantically. He saw Cole roll, and now Justin was on top, slamming a fist into his brother's face. "Don't let the couch burn."

Heath's heavy denim pants blackened at the hem, and he knew they were seconds away from bursting into flames. Burns were a brutal kind of pain, and fire left terrible scars. Heath had seen his brother Seth's scarred back, so he knew just how bad it could be.

Another line of fire headed toward a basketful of kindling. He rushed to the window and threw it open, reached for the smoldering drapes, ignored his burning hands, and hurled the curtains outside. He shoved his head out the window to make sure he'd heaved the burning fabric far enough to clear the house. No sense starting the outside of the house on fire.

Satisfied, he charged the basket of kindling. He whipped it out of the path of the hungry, crackling blaze and set the whole basket on top of Chance's desk.

With no time to think it out, he tore his shirt off his back and beat at the fire. Sadie had grabbed a small rug and was pounding on the fire heading toward her tumbling, punching brothers.

"Stop punching each other and help us, you two fools," Heath roared. He didn't stop his own combat to see if they heard him. He fought back the fast-moving yellow-and-orange monster and almost had it beat when a sudden dash of ice-cold water landed on his head.

"What?" He gasped and stepped back to see Rosita had just doused the fire and him with it. She'd saved half of the bucketful she'd thrown on him for Sadie's part of this fight. Rosita seemed more careful with Sadie.

"Step back." Rosita must have used that voice in Sadie's childhood, because her obedience was instant. Rosita doused the last of the flames, then picked up a second bucket. Heath looked around, wondering where it was most needed.

Rosita dumped it out with unnecessary force right on top of Cole and Justin.

The shouts separated the two men.

"Both of you—on your feet." Rosita's voice could have commanded a cavalry unit. "If you don't, I promise you I'll throw the *buckets* at your heads next."

Justin swiped his hands across his eyes. Cole shook his head, and water flew everywhere.

"You fight like children while your home burns down?"

"Burns down?" Justin was on his feet instantly, Cole only a step behind.

They blinked at the blackened carpet and the smashed lamp, and both men had the sense to look sheepish.

Heath pulled his shirt back on and found burn holes that showed his woolen shirt beneath enough that it wasn't even decent to wear. Embarrassed to be standing in front of Sadie and Rosita in his longhandles, he tore the charred shirt off in disgust. "You're a pair of fools to fight like that and say ugly words to each other."

Both brothers whirled on Heath and glared at him, their chests heaving. Maybe the next fist thrown would be at him. Well, he'd say his piece, and if they started swinging, he wasn't in any mood to turn the other cheek.

"You have no choice but to live together. Starting today. Your pa says you're to sleep tonight under his roof. That's why he didn't want you riding away before you heard his will. If you leave, ownership of the ranch goes to your cousin Mike."

Sadie looked at her brothers, fearful and sad. She seemed so alone, the only one of the Bodens using her head right now.

Striding over to the desk, Heath moved the kindling box, then rolled up the parchment and set it aside, wishing he were anywhere but here. He braced his hands on the desk and leaned forward, furious. He almost hoped someone swung on him.

"You may not like how he's gone about it, but your pa is a good man. I've only worked here a few months and I already figured that out. If you've known him all your *life*"—he bellowed the word and hammered the side of his fist on the desk—"and haven't figured it out, then you're both idiots. Your father loves you." It was odd to speak of love in all this turmoil, but it had to be said. "In the middle of all your fussing, try to remember he loves you. It may feel like a trap, but nothing could hold you here if you didn't love this land. You're lucky."

"Lucky?" Cole and Justin said the word in unison, crossed their arms, and glared at Heath.

"That's right," said Heath. "I speak as a man whose father *didn't* love him and *didn't* care if he brought his children together. In fact, my pa did his best to keep us all apart."

All three of the Bodens looked at him, maybe startled by the personal statement, but Heath didn't care if he was stepping on the toes of their fancy, rich boots. Suddenly he was furious with all of them, Sadie included.

"You are fools if you don't know what you have in a father's love." Calling them fools made his words worse than they might have been, but he didn't regret a single one of them. "Yes, lucky. Blessed. You're all blessed. And part of that blessing is that, starting right now, you're locked up here at the ranch until one year from today. If you're really that stubborn and selfish that you can't do that for a pa who loves you, then you'll lose everything and you'll all deserve it."

Heath slapped both hands down flat on Chance's desk and stormed from the room, slamming the door behind him.

5

Sadie watched Heath storm out, shocked and oddly thrilled. It took a real man with a heavy dose of courage to speak that way to his bosses.

And Sadie had lived her whole life surrounded by real men. Both her brothers were strong, and her pa as well, and had spines as tough as the Rocky Mountains. All three were hard and smart and decent.

She'd hardly ever met a man who could match them. Heath Kincaid was such a man.

All three of the Bodens could be considered Heath Kincaid's boss, and certainly a word from any of them would send him packing. And if they did, Heath would ride off and find a job punching cattle somewhere else and be a top hand.

That wasn't the real reason Sadie had no interest in seeing him go. But the real reason was murky, and she didn't want to see through the fog just yet. For right now she only knew Heath was good for the CR.

She stood there, watching after him, and wondered how she could arrange to see him again.

"Justin." Cole's much calmer voice turned Sadie's attention. "Living out here doesn't suit me, but I'll do it. I know as well as you that we have no choice in the matter. We have to save the CR."

Heath's fury seemed to have drained the last of the anger from the room.

Justin nodded, scowling. His lip was bleeding and he was soaking wet. "You're not the only one who has to sacrifice for this, you know."

Cole's dark brows slammed down over eyes that were puffy and would probably be black in the morning, his calm broken. "What sacrifice are you making? I'm giving up a house and my independence. Sadie's giving up a job she loves, a job she believes God wants her to do."

Sadie didn't remember agreeing to stay, but neither of her brothers expected any trouble from her. They just assumed she would cooperate. Assumed correctly—but neither of them was worried about what she might decide. She was tempted to do something to scare the life out of them, like saddle up and ride away.

"I'm gonna have to do something as hard or harder than either of you," said Justin.

Cole shook his head. "No, you're not."

"What are you doing that's so hard, Justin?" Sadie faced her brother.

"I'm going to have to live with the two of you!"

Sadie and Cole both took a threatening step forward. Then Justin grinned.

Sadie went from furious to giggling in the twinkling of an eye.

Cole chuckled, then broke out into a full laugh. The three of them laughed so hard, Sadie realized, that it was too hard. Their emotions were wrecked by what they'd lived through today, and as quickly as she'd started laughing, she started crying.

She buried her face in her hands. Strong arms came around her and she looked up to see Cole holding her.

"He does love us, baby sister," Cole assured. "You know how he's always talked of leaving this land as a legacy to us. Heath was right about that being a blessing. It's right to do this for Pa and Ma both. I wonder what Heath went through to make him say such a thing."

Cole met her eyes, then turned to Justin. "Sadie and I are here to stay. Maybe we'll like home so much we'll stay forever, and you won't ever get rid of us."

Justin laughed, but it had a ragged tone. Sadie looked at him. His eyes were moist, yet no tears fell. Or if they did, he could blame it on the bucket of water Rosita had thrown. This was the toughest of the tough men.

Justin extended his hand.

Cole let go of Sadie with one arm so he could shake hands with his little brother.

Seeing their hands entwined made Sadie reach out and rest her hand on top of theirs. "We're united then. To save the CR."

"Yep. Just like Pa wants us to be, the old coot." There was affection in Justin's voice when he said it. "It won't always be easy to get along, but I wouldn't want to live here alone anyway, with Ma and Pa gone for who knows how long."

There was a stretch of silence, and Sadie was thinking, at least for Pa, it might be forever. She suspected they all were thinking the same thing.

Finally Justin broke the silence. "I'm glad you're back."

Her brother sounded sincere, and Sadie realized he really meant it.

❧

Alonzo Deval came running into the room, looking so upset it made Sadie's heart lurch. Had someone else been hurt?

"I just heard about your pa. They said he's been taken away."

Sadie relaxed a bit. Alonzo had become a good friend. His concern helped to dispel what remained of the tension in the room.

"I'm so sorry he was hurt." Alonzo strode up to Justin and grasped his shoulder. Sadie and Cole stepped away to avoid getting run down. Instead he turned sad eyes on them. "He'll heal. Chance Boden is a strong man, and he won't let this get the best of him."

He reached out a hand to Cole, who shook it with a nod. "Thank you."

Then Alonzo turned to Sadie. An uncertain look flashed through his eyes then. As if he couldn't stop himself, he pulled Sadie into his arms and gave her a brief but firm hug.

Sadie held her breath. Alonzo always had a strange effect on her. With his black hair, black eyes, and sharply sculpted face, he was so handsome it was almost startling. But she'd never quite been able to define how she reacted. Was she interested or just able to appreciate his good looks? Somehow it sent a shiver of some deep memory through her, though she had no idea why.

Alonzo had made it clear, in a very proper way, that he would welcome her regard. Even so, she'd kept her distance. Now, however, she quietly let him hug her.

Stepping back, he shook his head. "I'm sorry, that wasn't proper."

Justin slapped Alonzo good-naturedly on the back. They'd become good friends, which was part of why Alonzo had been given the job of ramrod, second in charge after John. He'd even joined the family for Sunday dinner once. He was as good a cowpoke as any on the ranch. He lacked John's years of experience, but he had the speed and strength of youth. He was as tough as a strip of old leather. Another strong man.

"I saw John. He's all torn up about this and he took a few hard hits in the avalanche, too." Alonzo's eyes glinted with worry. "He agreed to go back to his cabin for the day. Which tells me how hard he's taking it. Chance is his best friend."

Much as Alonzo had become Justin's best friend.

Justin would be taking over until Pa returned. John would remain foreman, yet maybe it was time for a new generation to take the ranch onto their shoulders. Alonzo was the right man for that job.

Sadie felt the balance of old against young. Experience against strength. For a moment her whole world tilted.

"I'll make sure things run smoothly outside." Alonzo was burdened with his concern for Pa. "Is there anything else I can do for any of you?"

"Thanks, Alonzo," Justin answered. "You know how things run around here. I'll be back at it soon."

"You okay, John?" Heath had waited a long time, letting himself calm down, before he headed for the foreman's cabin, where he was now standing outside the door.

Besides John, only Alonzo had his own quarters. The rest of them, ten men this time of year, lived in the bunkhouse together.

Roundup was in the spring. They did a big cattle drive in the fall. Right now the cattle they hadn't sold were grazing and the need for hands was slight. Heath had signed on in the spring, and cowpokes were mostly wanderers. So it'd been easy to be kept on over the winter.

Heath almost laughed every time he heard the word *winter* when applied to the New Mexico Territory. Most folks here had no idea what a real winter was.

Hightree swung the door open. He looked grim, and Heath lost every trace of humor. Instead he held up a coffeepot in one hand and had a small pan of stew in the other. "You didn't come to the bunkhouse for supper. I thought you might like some company."

John stood silently for too long, looking from the food to the coffee to Heath. Finally he stepped back and said, "C'mon in. Food sounds good. And company sounds better. I've been alone with my thoughts long enough."

Heath stepped into the small cabin. It had everything a man might need, except a wife and children. But Heath didn't know much about the ranch foreman and thought maybe there was family back along the trail somewhere.

The stove had a fire flickering in its potbelly. The food he'd brought was warm, and keeping it that way was a good idea. The night was chilly, and strong coffee and steaming stew would surely hit the spot.

John quietly set a plate on the table. "You eaten yet?"

"Yep, but a cup of coffee would taste good."

John grabbed two tin cups and set them in place as Heath poured the coffee and put both pots back on the stove. Then John dished himself up some stew, and both men sat at the table in silence while John ate.

Heath nursed his coffee and got himself a refill just as John finished his meal. "This place gonna be all right with Chance away?"

John didn't jump right into saying yes, which Heath took as a bad sign. "Lot of history to this place. It goes way back."

"Boden moved here in the fifties, right?"

"Yep, but it's a lot older than that even."

"Older than the boss? How can that be? Did anyone even live out here besides the Indians back then?"

"The CR is what's left of a huge land grant held in partnership by an old Spaniard named Don Bautista de Val and Francois Chastain. That's Mrs. Boden's pa. He was a French-Canadian fur trader, born in Canada, but he lived on the American side of the border, in the Rockies, most of his life. Bautista was a Mexican citizen. Chastain was riding with Bautista when they found a man cornered by some bandits and saved his life. The man ended up being a powerful man, and he arranged the land grant on the condition that Chastain become a Mexican citizen." John finished his coffee and got up to refill his cup, then topped Heath's off.

"After the Spanish-American War, the Treaty of Guadalupe Hidalgo of 1848 drove the Spanish and Mexicans out. Then the Compromise of 1850 drove the Texans out. All these old land grants predate those border shifts. There were a lot of folks who tried to claim that no one holding a Spanish land grant had any legal standing, especially two Mexican citizens in the United States of America. The New Mexico territorial governor demanded they become American citizens. Bautista was a wealthy, powerful man back in Mexico City. It enraged him to be told he had to give up his citizenship. He walked away from his half of the land and went home. Chastain was born in Canada, then moved to the United States, then down here to what was then Mexico. Becoming American didn't bother him much. So he changed his country for the fourth time in his life and hung on, but he was still a little too Mexican to suit the governor and there was always trouble. And here came Chance." John's face took on a smile. His pride in his boss was clear.

"Chance, an American born and raised, from Boston, Massachusetts, no less, wanted land of his own and had a lot of money to spend. The Don was gone; the trapper looked to be losing everything. And did I mention that Chastain had a beautiful young daughter?"

Heath grinned. "Nope, you didn't mention that."

"Veronica Chastain. I was just a newcomer here. Chance had been here only a little while before Frank Chastain got shot. Señor Frank knew he was dying. He had hopes for Chance and his Veronica, but it was early days and no real courting had begun. He believed a man from Boston could hold the land, so he forced a marriage between them on his deathbed. Although it was a mighty advantageous marriage for Chance, there was no doubt he was interested in Veronica. Cole was only knee-high to a grasshopper and needed a ma. They made a nice family."

"Cole isn't Veronica's son?"

"Not by blood, but you've never seen a ma love a boy so much."

"So having an American in the family helped." Heath nodded. "Makes sense, I reckon."

He had no idea of the politics of Spanish land grants, yet he knew Chance Boden, knew his toughness and how smart he was. Heath could well imagine Chance ending up owning the whole thing.

"Yep. Chance ran the place right with the help of his foreman. That was Sarge. He was a good friend to Señor Frank, and the murder sent him into a rage. He was settled here. Rosita is his daughter. So he'd stay and work a while, then hear some rumor about the man who was believed to have shot Señor Frank, and off he'd go, hunting for the killer. Later he'd be back, reporting what he'd found, which wasn't much. He'd work for a while and then off he'd go again. I liked working here, and Chance and I had become good friends before he got married and became my boss. It didn't take me long to work my way up to foreman."

John paused and cleared his throat. He stared at his coffee, and Heath could tell that the old-timer was remembering all that'd happened today. "A man that savvy . . . brought low by a rockslide."

Heath asked, "How old is Chance anyway?"

"Sixty-eight last spring."

The number surprised Heath; he figured Chance to be a whole lot younger. "You say he's a knowing man, but maybe he's not as sharp as he used to be." Although he seemed plenty sharp to Heath. "He might've pushed himself too hard for someone that old. Maybe Chance doesn't have the skills needed anymore."

"My father," a familiar voice broke in, snapping like a bull-whip, "has more skill than you'll *ever* have."

Heath whirled around and sprayed coffee out of his cup. He stared at the window that framed the furious face of Sadie Boden.

6

Sadie abandoned the window.

To find these two men gossiping about her father, at a time like this, when she'd come to John for comfort? John would need her just as much as she needed him.

Or so she'd thought.

Now they were both going to get a blistering piece of her mind.

The door slammed open, and Heath ran out. He was racing after her; she was racing toward him. They plowed right into each other. He stumbled and grabbed her arms and managed to keep them both upright.

"Sadie, I'm so sorry. We weren't speaking ill of—"

The crack of her hand across his face shut him up. It satisfied her deeply to hit someone. She was starting to have some sympathy for Justin and Cole.

And Heath was handy and had it coming.

"My father has been badly hurt. He's traveling when that will probably make him worse, to see a doctor we know nothing about, and I find you and John talking about him being a washed-up old man."

No, not John. John had been listening, but he hadn't said anything. He'd probably have thrown Heath out in a second if Sadie hadn't come. She had to believe that. She couldn't bear the betrayal if John was gossiping about her father.

"My pa is twice the man you are, Heath Kincaid. Ten times the man. You! Are! Fired!"

Sadie wrenched against Heath's grip. He released her and raised his hands like a man surrendering. "Please, what you heard was—"

"Don't you dare speak to me." Sadie spun on her heel and stormed toward the house.

"You stop right there, young lady."

Skidding to a halt, Sadie was disgusted at herself for obeying John. But he'd been around so long and she respected him so utterly. She whirled to face her old friend. She might just fire him, too.

John's eyes were red, as if he'd been . . . but no. Cowboys didn't cry.

"Sadie, I'm so sorry I hurt you." Heath would just not stop talking, as if she ever wanted to hear his voice again.

Heath pivoted on his boot heel and strode away. Sadie watched him go and something twanged in her chest, a different kind of pain than the worry for her father.

"Sadie," John said and drew her attention away from Heath, who was heading for the corral, probably for his horse. Probably leaving forever.

Good riddance.

"Your pa is about the finest man I've ever known, and I would never say a word against him. I would never sit by while someone else did. We were talking about today. Your pa is as skilled a rider as I've ever known, and he was on his big bay stallion and there's no finer cow pony on this property."

Sadie knew that to be true. That bay was Pa's favorite and had been for years.

"Those two are a hard combination to beat, and they shouldn't have been caught in that avalanche. That's what we were talking about. I'm the one who mentioned it. Heath was just asking questions. We were trying to figure out how a man like your pa didn't hear the first rock fall and get himself through the canyon pass."

John walked up and firmly pulled Sadie to him and hugged her tight. Quietly, he said, "You insult me by believing I'd've let Heath speak a word against him."

Sadie let John hold her until the worst of her burning fury died. Then she eased back and met John's wise gaze. His eyes gleamed against his weathered skin and white hair.

"I just, I need—"

She heard the clatter of hooves and turned to see Heath galloping out of the ranch yard.

Leaving.

Fired.

She'd never see those vivid blue eyes again.

"I shouldn't have fired him. He should have stayed and made me see reason."

"It's all right, Sadie. It's been a day of upheaval and your feelings are all stirred up. Heath was a top hand, but you'll always mix him in with the memory of this awful day. You don't want him around as a reminder, and he may not want to be around if he knows it hurts you. He's too fine a man for that. Let him go. He'll get a good job wherever he stops to hunt work."

"John!" A shout from the barn shifted their attention, followed by the squeal of a furious horse and the dull thud of heels smashing boards. "We need help in here. Quick!"

John scowled at the man, then his eyes went to Sadie. "I won't be long. Wait for me, Sadie. Go on into my cabin, and when I get back I'll tell you more of what happened this morning. I'll tell you how Heath helped save your pa's life."

As John strode away, Sadie watched and wondered.

She'd gone from looking for comfort, to fury, to terrible regret in the space of a few minutes. She knew John was right. It was a day of upheaval. She turned to the west, to watch Heath ride away. Her jaw suddenly clenched. He wasn't going to pay for her irrational behavior. It was an injustice she couldn't let stand.

She ran to the corral and had Pa's big bay saddled and galloping down the trail after Heath within minutes. She might live in town, but she'd been raised a ranch girl and knew her way around.

And this bay was faster by far than the pretty palomino mare she kept in Skull Gulch. A horse, she realized, she'd left behind while she'd ridden in Heath's strong arms.

Heath had gotten her home in time to have a few minutes with Ma and Pa before they left. She'd had time to tell Pa she loved him before he set out. The doctor had spoken of the care Heath gave in tending Pa's leg. Heath had done well by Pa, and she wasn't letting him be punished for her bad temper.

When she kicked the horse, it dug deep and stretched out in a long, powerful stride.

It all came down to Heath being owed an apology, and of course he should get his job back. Sadie had one chagrined moment to remember John's words about Heath's skill. Justin was going to be upset with her if she fired one of his best cowhands for no reason.

He'd definitely support her if she had a good reason.

She didn't.

Which left it to her to chase Heath down and make him listen. As much as she deserved this new aggravation, it was taking all her energy. It'd been a long, hard day.

Heath heard the thundering hooves of pursuit. He turned to see Sadie coming. If she was chasing him down to shoot him, he almost felt like he oughta let her.

Almost.

As he watched her come . . . well, he had eyes as sharp as an Apache tomahawk, but that didn't mean he could believe what he saw. Sadie Boden was riding hard on her pa's stallion, coming right at him. At least that was what Heath suspected. There was nobody else out here.

He turned his horse and rode toward her. Maybe she wasn't coming after him. Maybe she was just going for a wild ride to work out some of her grief.

Skull Mesa loomed behind Heath's back to the west. It was a forbidding place, too rugged to climb. No cattle got up there so no cowpokes bothered to try. It stretched for well over a hundred yards, blocking the view to the west, except where the mountain peaks soared above it.

Maybe she picked this side of the ranch to be alone.

Maybe she thought her pa's horse needed exercise.

Maybe the woman just liked to ride.

He kept his eye on her gun hand just the same, although he didn't see a gun. As she drew near he saw her expression. She was definitely watching him with something other than murder in mind, so he didn't make a break for it. Instead he trotted forward to meet her, and when she saw he was cooperating, she slowed Chance's bay.

They met in the middle of the rugged New Mexico Territory grassland that had made Chance Boden and his whole family rich.

She swung down. "Can I please talk to you?"

Somehow, standing on the ground like that, it was almost like she was looking up and begging—which Heath didn't want.

He dismounted. "Let's walk the horses. I was running mine

too, and he could use a breather." Heath held his buckskin's reins. They were facing the ranch, away from the mesa, away from the west. He walked right up to this beautiful woman. Soon enough he'd have to go on and start over . . . again.

Before they'd gone far, she caught his arm and he turned. They stood facing each other, both horses blowing hard, slowly catching their breath after their fierce gallop.

She'd been chasing after him.

It warmed his heart to think of it.

Finally, as if she'd been gathering her thoughts, she said, "You're not fired. Please don't let my rash words make you move on. John is very unhappy with me for the way I acted."

"You've had a hard day. I don't want to stay around and make it worse."

"Please, can we just forget I fired you? John made me listen to him and I know I acted foolishly."

"Sadie, I think . . ." Heath wasn't sure how to say it. He'd never been much good at talking. Too much of his young life spent alone, he reckoned. "Um . . . I think it might help you if I left."

"No! Why would it help?"

Heath remembered his own anger when his ma died. It only deepened when he learned of his father's betrayal. He'd aimed all that anger on the brothers he'd discovered, even though they did their best to make him family. That wasn't easy when his very existence proved their father a liar and a cheat.

They'd been good to him. They'd taken in a ragamuffin boy and given him a stake in their land because he was as much an heir as they were. But to Heath it'd all felt stolen, and he'd carried anger in his heart that they didn't deserve. In the end he'd left.

"If I stay, I think, deep down inside, you'll always see me as the man who brought you terrible news about your pa."

"And you think I want to kill the messenger?"

Heath reached up, unable to stop himself, and rested a hand on her shoulder. "I think I'd rather leave than live with your low opinion of me. Maybe leaving is the one way I could help."

Sadie shook her head. "That's not true."

Heath watched her closely, lost in her sparkling hazel eyes and the riot of curls that had escaped during her wild ride from Skull Gulch hours ago and now was worse . . . and still she was beautiful. She'd never taken a moment to tidy up.

"I won't remember you with anger. I will remember the hero who knew how to tend Pa's leg and helped save his life. I'll remember the man who held me in his arms while he rode like the wind. I'll remember that you pushed yourself and your horse to the limit to get me to the ranch, and those minutes I had with Pa before he was carried away to the train are precious to me. I will remember you as a good, decent part of one of the hardest days of my life."

And just like that she was crying again.

She should be with her family or somewhere private, give herself peace and quiet and a time to weep.

Instead, after a long, painful day, she'd gone to John. Heath had spoken unwisely, and now she wept and he didn't dare touch her . . . mainly because he wanted to so badly.

He should pull her into his arms, give her shelter and comfort. A woman needed a shoulder to cry on. But a lowly cowhand didn't hug the lady of the manor. He patted her awkwardly until her tears were spent, then dropped his hand. He had a hanky in his pocket, rumpled but clean. He handed it to her, and she wiped her eyes and blew her nose.

"I was rude and you didn't deserve that. John says you're a top hand." Sadie managed a watery smile. "Justin is going to kill me if you ride off."

Heath almost smiled back. He doubted Justin would touch a

hair on her head. "I'll stay until the day I see pain in your eyes at the sight of me."

New tears surfaced and fell on her cheeks. He couldn't resist reaching a hand up and wiping his thumb across the tracks running down her face.

As he looked at her, the mesa rose high behind her. Absently he said, "I feel like that mountain is hovering over our heads." Heath studied the mountain to keep from pulling Sadie into his arms. It stood alone, but beyond it a ways, an entire mountain range stretched. Mount Kebbel was one of them, though Heath wasn't sure which.

Gold found there had made a lot of people rich, the Bodens included.

"I'm from the mountains up north in Colorado. One of the reasons I stopped here to hunt for a job was because"—Heath shrugged, feeling awkward at the emotion welling up in him—"it felt a little like home. I like rugged places. It's beautiful here. I want to go up to the top of Skull Mesa and look across this valley sometime. What's the view like from up there?"

Sadie looked startled. "It's not climbable."

Heath stared at the mesa. "It looks like the sides are sheer, but don't tell me there's no way up. I could get myself up there."

Shaking her head, Sadie said, "I know my brothers and I never got up, and we all tried." She smiled. "None of them knows how many times I tried, and I got higher than any of them. Pa and Sarge tried. John too. Plenty of others have tried. I've lived here all my life and I've never heard of anyone who made it to the top."

"No one? Most mountains call out for someone to scale them just to prove it can be done."

Some of the deep lines eased from her face, and Heath thought he had done right to speak of other things. Normal things.

"I'm a dab hand at climbing." He looked back at Skull Mesa. "Yep. I can get to the top."

"If I'm going to be living at home, with no job and lots of free time, practically in the shadow of that thing, maybe I'll go with you." Sadie turned to stand shoulder to shoulder with him, crossed her arms and looked up at the looming mesa. Heath felt like they were in accord.

"Skull Mesa always makes me think of my family."

Heath grinned. "How is a big old hill like your family?"

"Because the mesa is a fortress, and my pa always preached family sticking together. He liked to think it was the Bodens against the world, a ranch handed down from generation to generation. He called our land the 'Cimarron legacy' and never stopped respecting Grandfather Chastain's efforts to begin it, and that Grandfather's blood had seeped into the soil of this ranch. That's why he hated it so much when Cole came back but didn't live out here at the CR. Pa could never see that Cole coming as close to home as he did was a sign of his love and loyalty. Nope, for Pa it had to be under his roof. Then when I was working long hours at the orphanage and it was just too much effort for me to ride home every night, he didn't like that either. In fact, I think he'd've put up with Cole living in town, but my moving was too much. I've been living in town for less than a year. I'll bet it was when I moved out that Pa started stewing over it, and finally he came up with his plan and changed the will."

"And that's like a mesa?"

"A huge, imposing, beautiful, difficult fortress."

With a laugh, Heath said, "That almost describes my family, too. Especially the huge part, as all my big brothers seem to have a new baby every few years."

"Tell me about your family, Heath. Heaven knows you've heard more than you want to about mine."

Heath felt more relaxed about his past and all he'd ridden away from than ever before. He could tell Sadie and she'd understand. He opened his mouth and saw a glint on the flat-topped mountain. He stopped and focused on that glint.

"You say no one has ever been up there?" he asked.

"No. It's the stuff of legends that Skull Mesa can't be climbed." What it really looked like, what his instincts told him it was . . . "Then who's watching us with a spyglass from up there?"

Sadie peered again at the mesa top. She must have seen it because she asked, "Is that a spyglass or a rifle scope?"

Heath shifted his hold on his horse and dragged Sadie forward so that both horses blocked a direct line to the shiny reflection.

The reflection then vanished. Heath estimated that the top of the mesa was around 150 yards up. And sharp-eyed as he was, he didn't see any movement. Yet there were some rough edges on the mesa and a patch of underbrush, so someone could hide up there. The sides of the mesa, while sheer, twisted in and out like the folds in a heavy curtain. A man could almost step inside the walls at some points. If someone got up there, he could slip his gun through the brush, take careful aim, and be well within rifle range without anyone seeing him.

Heath was a man who trusted his instincts, and that looked like a scope of some kind. A rifle? Spyglass? Whichever it was, someone had found a way to the top of Skull Mesa.

"Let's move out. We're in rifle range." Heath urged her forward, careful where the horses stepped so no one could get a clean shot at them. It didn't take much urging. Sadie hurried forward, as eager as Heath to gain some distance.

He held his breath, sure he was going to hear a rifle shot any second, doing his best to protect Sadie with his body. Moving fast, counting off the steps, the yards . . .

"Who's up there?" Sadie didn't seem to be asking a question so much as wondering out loud.

"And why?" Heath added. "Isn't that mesa part of Boden land?"

"Yep. It's always just been a big stretch of wasted space, but it's ours for sure."

Finally they were out of range. "Let's mount up and make tracks back to the ranch. We need to ask around, see if any of the men have knowledge of someone climbing that mesa."

"You can ask, but I'm sure we'd have heard if someone climbed it." Sadie swung up with such lithe grace, Heath couldn't help but admire her western skills. She reminded him a lot of his sister-in-law Callie, his brother Seth's wife. One tough cowgirl.

Of course, Sadie was twice as beautiful.

"I've heard of mountain-climbing equipment." Sadie urged her horse into a trot. "I'm sure if someone came in with the right kind of tools, they could make the climb, but there'd be no point in hiding it. In fact, most folks would boast about it."

"There's gold on Mount Kebbel. I've heard that often enough."

Sadie nodded. "Cole manages the mines and he's mentioned that more than once."

"Has anyone ever considered there might be gold on Skull Mesa?"

Sadie whipped her head around to stare at the mountain. "If there were gold, it'd be well worth the effort . . . and it'd be kept secret, too."

"Wouldn't scaling a mountain stop someone?"

"I was six years old when they first found gold on Mount Kebbel," Sadie said. "You wouldn't credit the madness. Nothing stops them, Heath. Nothing."

"The only other reason I can think of to climb up there is that it offers a person a good spot to watch over the Cimarron Ranch."

Heath then thought of one other thing: Skull Mesa would

also give a man a real clear view of the narrow canyon where Chance had nearly been killed. Was it possible Chance's accident wasn't at all accidental?

But he didn't speak of that suspicion with Sadie. He wanted to talk to Justin first.

7

As they rode into the ranch yard, Sadie was more aware of Heath beside her than she'd ever been of any man.

Everything that was male in him seemed to awaken all that was female in her. As if she'd been in a deep sleep her whole life . . . until now.

She saw lantern light coming from John's small cabin where it stood just a bit behind the bunkhouse. It had helped enough to talk to Heath that she no longer felt any powerful need to talk to John and decided to leave it until morning.

"Look, every light in your ma and pa's house is lit as if it's welcoming you home."

"Yep," she said dryly. "Whether I like it or not."

"Go on in, let me put up your horse."

Because she was near collapse from the day, and because she didn't think it was wise to spend any more time alone with Heath, she swung down and handed him her reins.

"The doctor told me about how well you tended Pa's leg. Thank you, Heath. Thank you very much."

He nodded. "It was a wonder that I had just the right knowledge in my head."

"How did you learn to deal with a wound like that?"

"I rode with the cavalry for a year, and while it's mostly peaceable on the frontier these days, accidents still happen and there have been a few skirmishes with outlaws. With that many men riding and working, I got to see a lot of ugly things. One of them was working over a broken limb with the bone cutting through the skin. The doctors taught me how to handle it until they could get there. That's what I did for your pa."

"Doc Garner said the man in Denver can sometimes save a leg, even injured that badly."

"I hope he's right. We practiced mighty rough medicine at the fort. I sure hope there are men who can do it better."

"Whether they can save his leg or not"—Sadie shuddered to think of amputation—"the doctor said your treatment was what gives him even a small chance to keep the leg, and you may very well have saved his life. Getting a terrible infection is less likely now."

She reached forward with halting, clumsy motions and took his hand. Not a handshake; she just needed to touch him. "I'm sorry I fired you, and I appreciate you being accepting of my apology. Thank you for coming back. After all you did for us today, you didn't deserve to be treated like that."

"It's all right, Sadie. I understand."

For some reason she really thought he did. She wanted to ask what had made him furious at them for not appreciating their father's love. For offering to ride away rather than stay and be a source of painful memories.

The darkness had fallen and the wind picked up. She needed to go inside, especially because she found herself wanting so badly to stay with him. Their gazes had locked for too long.

He tugged on his hand to get free and even that wasn't hurtful because she saw the reluctance in his eyes. "Good night, Sadie. I'll keep you and your whole family, especially Chance, in my prayers."

"Good night, Heath. God bless you for everything." She strode quickly toward the house before she did something stupid like offer to put up the horses as an excuse to stay with him, an excuse to walk with him right into the privacy of the barn.

Sadie woke up in her childhood bed. It all rushed in. Pa. The wild trip to Denver. The threat Pa had made to cut off the money to Safe Haven and give away the ranch. Her decision, firmly made, that she was home to stay.

Then she thought of one more thing. The glint of light on top of a mesa that had no way up.

Throwing her blankets off, she rushed through dressing. She'd forgotten to tell Justin and Cole. She hurried downstairs to find she'd slept so late her brothers were both gone. Justin, she expected him to work the ranch. But Cole was supposed to work here at home.

Rosita was stirring something at the stove that smelled wonderful, meaty—stew maybe.

"Where's Cole? Isn't he here working?" Fear welled up. Had Cole gotten fed up and left?

"He headed for the mine this morning. He had things to do yesterday that he put off because of your pa."

The Bodens had extensive mining interests on Mount Kebbel, all Cole's to handle.

"And to tell the men at the mine that from now on, they will have to come to the CR if they need to talk to him."

Biting back her worry, she asked, "What can I do to help? What would Ma be doing right now?" Her mother would be sorely missed, and Sadie would do her best to fill Ma's shoes until she got back.

"Before you get to work, you need to eat something."

"I'm not hungry."

"Eat!" Rosita set a plate with two lightly browned biscuits on the kitchen table with a very deliberate slap of ceramic on wood. She added two small dishes, one with a ball of butter and the other with jelly. "You missed both supper and breakfast. I don't want you collapsing."

Sadie took one of the fluffy biscuits because Rosita had that stern tone in her voice that wasn't to be disobeyed. She took one bite and realized she was starving. She'd started on the second one when her hunger eased enough that she had energy to worry.

"Has Ma sent a telegram? Has anyone gone to town to check?" After she asked about her parents, her mouth went bone dry with fear and she thought the biscuit might just choke her to death. "They should be in Denver by now. Surely Ma would send a wire to tell of their arrival. Maybe I should ride to town and check."

Sadie rose.

"Stay there and eat." Rosita jabbed one of her stout, competent fingers at the table, and Sadie rested back on the chair.

"Justin sent one of the men in. He said there'd be more trips in today if there wasn't a telegram first thing. I haven't heard any news, and I'm certain they'd come to the house to let us know what they'd heard."

Sadie caught herself wondering if Heath had gone in. Why not? They'd made the poor man do everything else yesterday. He'd saved Pa, come for her in town, sent the doctor out, rushed a message to Cole. He'd read Pa's wishes and learned about the odd conditions he'd set for his children. Then he'd possibly saved her life a second time by putting himself between her and Skull Mesa—if there'd really been someone up there with a rifle. Honestly, the man had been involved in every moment of yesterday's madness, and all for the good. He was practically part of the family by now.

"Ma would have wired immediately. She'd know we're anxious for news." How were they? Had Pa survived the trip? Her mind stumbled over the awful thought.

"Yes, she would have, *mi niña*, unless they were in a tearing hurry to get your pa to the doctor and she needed to leave his side to send the wire—and refused to. Or she was so worried, she forgot everything except taking care of her husband. Or she thought of it, but it was a long walk to the telegraph office and she didn't want to be away so long."

Wearily, Sadie nodded. "Those are mighty good reasons."

"You may well not hear from her until she's got something to say. So don't twist yourself up fretting when it serves no purpose. God does not want us to waste our time and energy with such things."

As she thought of all the reasons Ma might not have wired, Sadie realized she should have gone along with Ma. One of her brothers would have been fine too, only they weren't on hand when Ma and Pa rushed to the train. If the unthinkable happened, Ma, tough as she was, might have to deal with Pa's death alone in Denver.

Rosita set a cup of milk down in front of her, and it was fortunate because thinking of Ma and even more of Pa had made it near impossible for her to swallow.

Sadie didn't share her thoughts with Rosita, for that would surely earn her another lecture on worrying.

As she struggled to get the biscuit down, she thought of the tales she'd heard of Pa's life before he came to this land. He'd grown up in Indiana when that was the far western reaches of the nation. Sadie knew enough about maps and how far east Indiana was to smile over that.

Then Pa had gone even farther east, interested in a more civilized country. Cole was born there, and Pa's first wife died there.

He'd headed west to start a new life.

Her Ma's life was all intertwined in the stories about Pa. She'd been born out here. She'd married Pa in a ceremony performed on Grandfather Chastain's deathbed.

Sadie's parents were strong, honorable people. They'd torn a living out of a wild land that had been only partly settled by Grandfather Chastain. They'd worked hard and faced danger. It took a rock-solid will to survive such a rugged life. And now Pa and Ma were gone, fighting for Pa's life far away from home.

A hard rap at the back door drew Sadie out of her dark thoughts, and she was grateful for that. It was Melanie Blake, one of Sadie's closest friends, the daughter of a neighboring rancher.

Mel caught her eye through the window in the door and opened it a second before Sadie waved her in. They were close enough friends to barge into each other's houses and know they'd be welcome.

Sadie rose to meet Mel and was pulled into a tight hug.

"We were told your pa was bad injured and your folks left for Denver. I'm so sorry." Mel held her a long time as Sadie felt tears threaten to fall. Her neighbor was a bit older than Sadie—Mel had been in the same grade in school as Justin. But since they'd been grown up, Sadie and Mel had gotten to be good friends. The Bodens and the Blakes had known one another all their lives, so Sadie appreciated Mel coming over to check on her.

They settled at the table together while Rosita set a coffee cup in front of them both along with a slice of warm gingerbread. Rosita checked the cup of milk and saw it was empty. Sadie was glad she'd finished it to spare her being scolded like a child in front of her neighbor. But surely Rosita wouldn't do that?

Oh, who was she kidding? Rosita would scold her and Mel, too. She'd known them both when they were in diapers.

"Have you gotten any news?" Mel asked.

Sadie shook her head. "Justin sent someone to town to check for a wire, but I've heard nothing yet."

"Can you tell me what happened?" Resting her work-roughened hand on Sadie's clenched fists, Mel fell silent. And into the silence Sadie couldn't help but tell her friend everything.

Mel was a much tougher woman than Sadie would ever be. Sadie always felt a twinge of jealousy over that. While Mel rode out with the cattle and was fast with a rope or a gun, went hunting and fishing with her pa—with Justin and Cole too—Sadie had kept to the house. Oh, she'd done a lot of riding and had even gone along on the roundup a few times when she pitched a fit and refused to stay home. But Sadie had been sheltered by Pa and pressured into ladylike ways by Ma. And mostly that was a wonderful thing. But now, when Pa couldn't stand for her to live away from home, she realized all those years of sheltering had led to this. It chafed, and she saw Mel and all her freedom and had to fight that jealous twinge to keep it from blooming into sinful envy.

Justin came into the kitchen. Mel rose and hugged him. It was a short hug, which ended with Mel sharing her kind concern for Pa.

"Justin, do you need me to ride to town and check for a telegraph?"

"Nope. I sent a man in early, and just a few minutes ago I sent another and told him to wait in Skull Gulch even if it takes all day. He'll find me the minute he's back. I'm staying around the ranch today, and I'll bring any news directly to the house."

Sadie frowned. "It's hard to be patient."

"Yep. I'm half mad from waiting."

Mel seemed to realize it was time to change the subject. "Did you get a good price on your cattle in Santa Fe?"

Justin got himself a cup of coffee and a slice of gingerbread and settled in for a visit. He and Mel launched into a long talk about the fall cattle drive. The talk drifted to a busted-up dam on the stream that ran into the Cimarron, dividing their two properties. The dam would be needing repairs while the water was low during the winter months.

Sadie watched the two as they talked. Though she always thought they were a likely match, she'd never seen the smallest spark of attraction between them. She wondered if maybe something could be done about that.

A carriage pulled up to the back door, bearing the elderly maiden ladies who ran the orphanage in town. Sadie went to meet them, thinking it might be a good idea to leave Justin and Mel alone together, though they'd been alone together plenty of times and they usually ended up roping something.

The ladies, Sister Margaret, Sister Louisa, and Miss Maria surrounded her with hugs and kindness, distracting her from thoughts of matchmaking. After their kind greeting, Sadie had to tell them her bad news.

"Sister Margaret, I am sorry to have to tell you, I won't be able to come in and teach anymore. I'm needed here." The three ladies who worked at the orphanage were so gentle and friendly. Sadie knew she would miss their kindly ways.

"We've come to depend on you, Sadie. How will we survive with this burden landed fully on our backs, heavier than ever?" Miss Maria was a melancholy woman, given to dark worries and always predicting a terrible future.

Sadie was used to that and prayed for the woman, but this time it stung that the first words from Maria were about her own woes.

"You are needed by your family now," Sister Margaret whispered, patting Sadie's hand. "We will get along. God will take care of us. Though of course we'll miss you."

Sister Margaret's words helped Sadie to get over her annoyance with Miss Maria. Yet Sadie *had* done a lot of the heavier work for the three much older ladies who managed the orphanage, so Maria was right to worry.

"There will be money provided to hire another worker to take my place—Pa already arranged it—but you'll be left on your own until you can find someone."

Sister Margaret nodded solemnly. "That's very generous of you and your family, dear."

There was alarm on the faces of the other ladies, but Sister Margaret remained her usual serene self. "I have a niece in Omaha who's recently widowed. Reading between the lines of her last letter, I believe Angelique has been left in rather difficult straits. She's the last family I have. I was thinking of asking her to come live with me. I'll write her and send her money for a train ticket. I think she would welcome a new start."

With a sigh of relief, Sadie said, "I hope she agrees to come. And please, let me give you enough money to send a telegraph, and if she agrees, we can send money to a bank in Omaha so that she gets word quickly and can be on her way soon."

"That would be wonderful, thank you. I'll send the telegraph right away."

If Angelique was anything like Sister Margaret, she'd be a perfect fit with the other ladies at Safe Haven. But what to do in the meantime? Maybe Sadie could go in and work for just a short time once a week, do the heavy cleaning and such things. Pa would probably allow it if he understood that she'd left them all shorthanded. Or maybe she could do it and he'd never know. But that wasn't honoring his wishes, and right now she couldn't bring herself to defy her pa.

The back door swung open. "Thanks for the coffee and

gingerbread, Rosita," Mel said. "Bye, Justin." She started to leave, then turned and smiled at the group before her. "Sister Margaret, Miss Maria, Sister Louisa, it's nice to see you again." Mel knew the ladies well. It was a small town, so everyone knew everyone who wasn't a newcomer.

And that's when Sadie had an idea.

"Mel, you asked if there was anything you could do to help, and with all that's . . . that's happened—" Sadie stumbled over what to say, not wanting to go into the particulars—"I have to stay out here at the ranch. I can't work at Safe Haven anymore. Do you think you could go there once or twice a week and help the ladies with the heavy lifting and—?"

"I'd be glad to do that," Mel said, cutting her off. "I should have thought of it myself. I know you need to be here until your parents get back."

"Yes, well, Sister Margaret has a niece who may be taking my job. We haven't asked her yet, but Sister Margaret thinks she'll agree to come. We're hoping only a week or two will pass before she arrives."

Mel went to Sadie and slid an arm across her shoulders. "Don't worry about how long I need to help out. Don't worry about anything. I'll talk to Pa and make sure it's all right, but it's quiet at the ranch right now. This is a good time to keep busy elsewhere."

Mel began talking with the ladies, and they all got along so well that Sadie felt left out. Far too easily replaced. She thought her work at Safe Haven was so vital, but now a woman with true financial need would take her job and her good friend would fill in for her in the meantime. She shook off the feeling of no longer being needed.

Mel headed for her black mare tied to the hitching post, swung up, and rode for home. Sadie invited the ladies to sit and have some coffee.

Sister Margaret very sweetly declined the invitation. "I want to get a wire sent to Angelique right away. I appreciate the offer, but I think we should hurry for home and get on with our planning."

Nodding, Sadie walked the ladies to their carriage. "I'm sorry to abandon you so suddenly, but I'm . . ." Sadie shrugged. She didn't want to air the strange demands her father had made, not even to someone as discreet as Sister Margaret.

Her friends hugged her, then climbed in the carriage and hurried back toward Skull Gulch.

As they left, it struck Sadie that she'd spoken no less than the truth. With Ma gone, there was plenty for her to do. Even Rosita's capable hands couldn't maintain this house. And someone who loved the house and was a member of the family needed to be here making decisions and running things.

For the first time, she was glad that she was back home. It was as if a simple truth had been revealed to her.

She was home to stay.

❧

Angelique DuPree accepted the telegraph with shaking hands. It was the cold making her tremble . . . mostly. But exhaustion and hunger also played a part, and besides, telegraphs always brought bad news. Angelique didn't think she could take yet another blow.

The ragamuffin boy who'd brought it to her stood shifting his weight, watching, wishing. He was hungrier than she was. It twisted her heart, and as foolish as she knew it to be, she reached into her threadbare reticule—once a soft pretty black velvet, but now shiny, the nap worn away—and tipped the boy a penny.

The boy doffed his hat and ran. He knew the neighborhood they were in. He was lucky to get that penny.

Heading up the narrow stairs, every step of the four stories taken in darkness, she hurried to her bitter-cold room and let herself in, as always, careful to lock the door behind her.

A candle, nearly burned to a stub, flickered to life. It was the only heat in the room, and Angelique knew she didn't dare leave it burning long.

Angelique STOP Need your help at once STOP Send wire if agree STOP Will send train fare to First National Bank STOP Love Aunt Margaret

Gasping, Angelique clutched the telegraph to her chest.

Aunt Margaret. Safe Haven Orphanage.

Kind Aunt Margaret. And calling her Angelique too, rather than *Angie*, just as she'd demanded.

Angelique burst into tears. She sobbed until there was no water left to spill, then gathered her wits and started planning. She could afford to send the wire, but it would be with the last coins she possessed.

She doused the candle and opened a tin to draw out her last crust of bread. She kept it tightly sealed or the rats would take it. She could eat only half. It would barely push back her gnawing hunger, yet she needed something for breakfast. She sat on her bed in the dreary boardinghouse. More tears spilled from Angelique's eyes—she hadn't cried herself dry after all. Her tears salted the bread.

When the paltry meal was gone, she whispered into the darkness, "I'm saved. Aunt Margaret, you've saved me."

She lay down on the hard, cold mattress, fully clothed, wrapped in her only blanket. The early-November weather was too cold for her to think of shedding her only dress, or her stockings and shoes. She'd consigned her tattered nightgown to the ragbag months ago. Everything else of her once lavish wardrobe was gone now, taken by bill collectors, along with the house, all of its contents, and any money she had in the bank, which was almost none. All to pay Edward's debts. She had no idea he was in debt until after he'd died.

For the first time in her overindulged life, Angelique had gone to work. And then found out what it meant to labor hard for terrible wages, to eat little, to live among poor folks.

Aunt Margaret would be ashamed of her. Angelique couldn't believe how thoughtless she'd been of her dear old aunt's love. And even now, when Aunt Margaret should have long ago washed her hands of her ungrateful niece, her kindly aunt remembered her and had sensed perhaps Angelique's loneliness, her need.

In the few letters she'd sent to her aunt, she'd tried hard to hide her financial troubles. After the haughty way Angelique—and worse, her mother—had rejected Aunt Margaret when she'd approached them for donations to her beloved orphanage, Auntie shouldn't have had much interest in Angelique or feel any responsibility. But Aunt Margaret was a woman with a forgiving soul and a loving heart. It was natural that she would be the one to give Angelique hope.

Tomorrow she'd be paid, but only if she worked the full twelve-hour shift. How was she to find time to send the telegraph?

She needed that money to feed herself during the train ride.

The telegraph office was only blocks from her work. It might be possible to slip away for a few minutes, long enough to send a wire.

She had to risk it. Because *nothing* would stop her from going to the one woman left in the world whose love she could depend upon.

Nothing.

Sadie longed for a moment alone with her brothers. It would have been fine to have talked to either of them alone, but Justin had gone back to work by the time she came in from seeing the ladies from the orphanage off. And it appeared Cole was gone for the day. She didn't see them again until it was nearly time for supper.

She found them sitting together, talking quietly in Pa's office. Heath was there too, as was John. Sadie wished they'd leave so she could talk with her brothers in private. For some reason, she couldn't bear to sit and make pleasant conversation, so she backed away. She'd just come from helping Rosita, but there might be more to do before the evening meal.

"No, don't leave, Sadie." Cole stopped her. "We need you to join us."

They needed her? She wasn't sure she'd ever heard those words from either of her brothers before.

Justin said, "Heath told us the two of you saw someone on top of Skull Mesa yesterday."

Sadie's gaze flew to Heath. "That's what I came in to talk with you about. I thought you might prefer to hear it without company. Heath knows more about it than I do. But yes, there had to be someone up there. Nothing else would explain what we saw."

"But there's no way up," Cole said. "Justin and I have tried climbing it a few times."

"More than a few," Justin added with a grin.

Sadie smiled but remained silent about the many times she'd tried to climb it. She was quite sure she'd gotten higher than either one of them ever did. Her fine-boned hands could cling to ledges their husky, manly fingers couldn't.

John nodded. "Your pa and I tried to get up there, and I remember old stories of your grandfather wanting to scale that mountain. Most every cowhand around over the years has had a go at it. Of course, we didn't try that hard. Not a lot of time for nonsense like climbing a mountain just because it's there. We tried a few times and then got back to our work."

"I've certainly never been up on that mesa." Sadie couldn't resist looking at Heath. He fit in here with the other strong men. "We couldn't have been mistaken, could we?"

Heath shook his head. "Even if we're wrong and it was a broken piece of glass, then someone had to take it up there."

"A stone?" Cole asked. Sadie could see him thinking. Cole had a fine mind, and he used it to his advantage all the time. He'd done a good job of proving, in a land where muscle ruled, that a sharp mind was to be respected and sometimes feared.

"Iron pyrite maybe." Heath's bright blue eyes shifted between Cole and Sadie.

Justin said, "You mean fool's gold?"

"Or real gold," Heath said, looking amused, as if he knew he might cause trouble.

Sadie wondered if Heath had seen people act like madmen over gold before. She wondered if he could handle what might happen if they found gold on top of the mesa. The Bodens would manage. They'd owned a mining operation for a long time. But Heath might be in for a shock even if he knew there could be trouble; his imagination might not be good enough to brace himself for how bad it could get.

"The shine wasn't right." Heath must have decided there was no excitement coming from his mention of real gold. "It reflected too well, don't you think, Sadie? And it wasn't against the ground, right at the rim of the mesa top. It was higher. My guess is it was a spyglass or a rifle scope, held by someone standing behind some bushes. Someone was up there. Watching us."

Heath looked around the room. "I grew up near this cavern that was so dangerous it made grown men tremble. I got to do a lot of exploring down there. Even though it was a cave underground, there were deep pits and tunnels you couldn't reach without climbing sheer stone walls. I've climbed up and down rock without so much as a toehold. With the right tools I say I can defeat that mountain. If you're willing, I'd like to try. Before last night, I'd've done it just for the fun of it, but someone needs to get up there and find out who was watching Sadie."

Cole said, "I've got to get my office from in town moved out here, and I'm in the middle of some important negotiations with the railroad about shipping ore. I think I'll be tied up until after Christmas at least, but I want in on this mountain climbing. Can you wait?"

"And John and I have to put some time in on the ranch to make sure all the men understand Pa being gone doesn't change anything," Justin added. "It'll be a while before I'm ready, but I'd like to see what kind of tools you use to climb a rock wall. I want you to wait for me, too."

Heath shook his head. "If someone was on that mesa with a spyglass, then he might as well be up there with a rifle. And Sadie was well within range."

"Don't say that. You'll scare Sadie."

"I don't scare that easy, Cole." Sadie glared at her big brother.

Cole ignored her and scowled at Heath. "And why would anyone want to shoot Sadie?"

"No reason I can think of, but why would anyone want to be watching Sadie, or the whole ranch for that matter?"

That got their attention. "I'm just telling you how it struck me. I felt a cold chill up my spine, like someone had a bead on me with a rifle. And even if they didn't, they could have. We got out of range fast, putting the horses between us and the mesa."

"And you between me and the horses, Heath," Sadie was quick to add. "Don't think I didn't notice you put yourself between me and a possible gunman."

Cole and Justin both gave him a look of male understanding, which made Sadie want to yell at them all. She didn't want someone killed because they were protecting her—it made her heartsick to think of it.

"Unless you're willing to order every man on the place to stay a half mile away from the base of Skull Mesa, someone needs to get up there, and they need to do it now."

"We have to use that pasture around the mesa. It's my best winter grass." Justin crossed his arms and slumped in his chair, his eyes narrowed. "There's risk for anyone climbing. It stands to reason someone scaling that mountain will have to be within rifle range. And climbing something that sheer is a slow business. You'd be sitting ducks."

"Nope," said Heath. "Once I'm up against the base, they'll have a hard time taking a shot. They'd have to lean far out and aim straight down. They can't do that without exposing themselves. I propose two people go. Slip up to the mesa before sunrise. Then one can climb partway while the other watches the mesa rim. Then the other can find a good spot on the rock wall and stand guard while the second climbs."

"And that's if whoever is up there is still up there," Sadie said. "If they've come down—and they must, since no one could live up there—then we're at no risk at all. But whether they're up there or not, climbing as a team makes it safer." She thought of all the times she'd tried to scale that blasted mesa on her own. Pa and Ma wouldn't let her climb it, so she'd snuck her way there.

Heath then pulled her thoughts from her childhood misbehavior. "And if someone is up there, they had to *get* up there. I aim to find the path they took and take it myself. If I can't find an easy way, then we're talking about a long, hard climb. I got plenty of rope, but the other things I need will have to be made by the blacksmith in town, and that'll take a while. Then again I might find an easier way and get up fast."

Cole and Justin looked at each other. Then Justin grinned. "I'd really like to climb that old beast. Heaven knows I tried often enough as a youngster."

"I don't think it's a good idea to wait," Heath said.

Cole asked, "Who should we send along with him?"

The men all stared at one another, thinking so hard it was insulting, because of course they never thought of the most obvious person.

"Me," Sadie said a little too loudly. She sounded exasperated.

Justin surged to his feet. "It's too dangerous."

"Nope. You're not going." Cole was one second behind him. "Out of the question."

"Get that idea right out of your head, young lady." John seemed to think he could order her around just like the rest of them.

"None of you get to decide." Sadie stood rather than let the three most important men in her life—not counting Pa, who would be on their side—tower over her even more than usual.

"You've all known me all my life. You know I'm good with a gun. I'm a dependable lookout."

"That's a stupid reason for a woman to risk her life."

"You and Cole have a lot to do, and I'm tending the house with Rosita, but I assure you she won't miss me for a day. I'm not going to sit in here and be a decoration."

Justin strode up to her and bent down until his nose almost touched hers. "You always were reckless."

If he was trying to intimidate her, the effort was laughable. "So then, you should have expected this."

Cole, ever the diplomat, came and circled her shoulders with one of his strong arms. "You aren't a decoration. Running a home is a big job and a noble one. And Ma being gone leaves a sizable gap."

He was absolutely right. Too bad it wasn't going to work.

"Use your sweet talk on someone who will listen, Cole. I'm going with Heath."

She glared at Cole and saw a genial, reasonable expression. It was completely false. That strong arm tightened until Sadie thought she might have to punch her big brother to stop him from crushing her.

"You're not going, even if I have to lock you in your room," John said, and for a second she wavered. Of all the menfolk in the room, John was the one hardest for her to defy. Her brothers were no problem at all.

Cole patted her shoulder—too hard. Justin fumed and issued a few more threats. John gave orders as though he saw it as his sacred duty.

A voice from outside their tense little circle said, "I think she'd be a perfect partner in this search. I'll keep her safe."

The other men turned on Heath as if they were hungry wolves and he a wounded antelope.

Heath grinned and those eyes flashed, making her wonder for the first time if a wild man lurked deep inside him.

Sadie smiled back. He was her new favorite man in all the world. And it wasn't even close to a tight race.

Justin said to Heath, "You're fired."

Heath returned that bad news with another smile. "I don't mind getting fired. It's been that kind of week." Then he looked at Sadie and arched his brows. "And mountain climbing is something a woman can do, I know that well enough. My sister-in-law taught me how."

Heath got ordered off the property.

He refused to go.

Justin called him a trespasser and threatened to beat him senseless.

Sadie gave her permission for him to stay, including staying on as their guest in the bunkhouse. She also impishly invited him to stay in the house since he was fired. He was now more of a friend of the family.

Cole said something about the law and a sheriff and arrest.

"You can't arrest me for climbing a mountain with the owner's permission, Cole."

"Well, I'm the owner and you don't have my permission," Cole shot back.

Sadie raised her hand and wiggled her fingertips. "I'm the owner. I say he can climb that mountain anytime he wants."

He was enjoying himself. He decided to keep making trouble. "You know you should be hollering at Sadie, not me."

She gave him a baleful look that made his smile stretch wider.

"You were all in favor of me climbing that mesa until she said she wanted to come along."

"That's right, Cole." She moved so she stood beside Heath, her arms crossed. "Why aren't you threatening me with jail? And, Justin, you should be threatening to punch me, not Heath."

Justin narrowed his eyes. Heath knew there was a lot better chance that Cole would arrest her than that Justin would punch her. But of course there was no chance of either. Not to her, but they would probably do both to Heath.

"What we need to do is lock you up in your room until you get this blame-fool notion out of your head." John waved his arms in a wild gesture that was nothing like the slow-talking old-timer.

Sadie and Heath stood shoulder to shoulder and faced the two Boden brothers and a fuming John Hightree.

Heath liked teaming up with her.

"It sounds like Sadie's going with or without your permission." He didn't know what was wrong with him, but he was having the time of his life. Maybe he missed his bossy big brothers more than he realized.

Cole accused Justin of handling Sadie all wrong. Justin turned and called Cole a namby-pamby city boy. John started hollering at them both to take their sister in hand.

Sadie spoke to Heath quietly, under the noise. "You've climbed around inside a cave?"

"Yep, I spent a powerful lot of hours underground."

Sadie's eyes widened. "Hours? How big is this cave?"

He'd have answered. He enjoyed that beautiful, dangerous cavern on Kincaid land and would have enjoyed describing it to her.

"I'm going to set your bedroll on fire after you fall asleep on it. That'll stop the nonsense about taking Sadie up that dangerous mesa." John made it much harder to talk and that was a shame, because Heath was enjoying his private little visit with her. He leaned in a bit closer.

"I'll tell you all about it while we're climbing."

"When do we go? Tomorrow morning, bright and early?"

Heath said, "I won't have the supplies I need by tomorrow, but I'm hoping I can find a way up that doesn't require climbing tools. I'd like to head out before sunrise. If I go in the full dark, we can just walk right up to the mesa."

"And that's final," Cole said, breaking into their conversation. Heath wondered what exactly was final, but he figured he could guess well enough.

"I want each of you to give me your word you won't talk about this." Heath gave each of them a hard look. "It's strictly a secret between the five of us in this room."

"Are you giving us orders now, Kincaid?" Justin growled.

"Sure, now that I don't work for you anymore, why not? Don't reckon you'll take orders worth a hoot, but I can still give 'em."

"Then you're hired. And I'm sending you to the line shack on the far side of Mount Kebbel until spring."

"No, you're not. I'm fired and I like it." It was surprising how much he enjoyed defying the Boden brothers and their foreman. In fact, it hit him hard that he wasn't cut out for taking orders. He'd never liked it with his big brothers but figured that was personal.

He was just now figuring out he liked to be in charge. That was the root cause of his leaving the Kincaid spread. No matter how hard he worked, he knew, as the little brother, he'd never really be his own boss. Except now that he knew it, maybe he could find a way to get along with them.

If the Bodens yelled at each other and him and Sadie much longer, he might get his whole life figured out.

"You're staying out of shooting distance of that mesa, and

I don't think you should be outside until we get to the bottom of this." Cole spoke as if it were a law enacted by the Congress of the United States.

Sadie gasped until it was almost an inverted scream. "I'm going."

Cole added, "It's time you calmed down and saw some sense."

"You can't stop me."

"I sure as certain can." Justin glowered at her. "You'll do as you're told and stay to the house like a decent, obedient woman had oughta and that's final."

Sadie had the door open and was outside the second Heath tapped in the hour before dawn.

They'd had to delay the climb several times, but finally today they were going.

He nodded and adjusted the heavy pack on his back. Then, as he touched one finger to his lips, they turned and strode out of the ranch yard.

It had taken longer than she'd hoped to hear from Ma, until at last she sent a telegram saying Pa was being treated by Dr. Radcliffe. He'd been with the doctor for two weeks. They hadn't amputated the leg, though it might still end up that way. Still, the doctor was confident that whatever else happened, Pa would live.

Sadie was glad for the delay because a letter arrived before they left and it was encouraging. Her worry for Pa had been a difficult and constant presence. Now, with Ma's letter, Sadie started to feel like her head was clearing enough to go pay attention to climbing the mesa.

She'd left both her brothers behind, who were wide awake, sitting in the dark, and seething. She ordered them to be completely silent and not light the lantern. Heath wanted nothing to give their departure away.

Cole and Justin had hated that. It was close to the best day of her life.

"Are we—?"

"Shh." Heath cut her off and whispered, "Sound carries in the night."

Which she knew good and well. Slightly embarrassed to be admonished, she walked quickly and quietly toward the mesa. They'd never see a thing short of a blazing fire at this time of night. No sunlight to glint off anything, and because dawn was approaching, the moon had set and the stars, though vivid, provided little light.

Finally they reached the mesa. Heath patted the solid rock as if he were greeting a good horse. He started on the south side and headed along the east, the side visible from the ranch.

"I want to be done with this side before the sun comes up, but in the dark I can't see footprints or a trail of any kind. But I should be able to feel my way up Skull Mesa if I find a climbing spot better than the one Justin told me about."

Matching his whisper, she asked, "Didn't you just tell me we had to be quiet?"

"Now we can whisper a bit. The rock will swallow up the sound." Then he said no more as he ran his hands along the rock wall.

Sadie had no idea what he was up to. Well, of course she knew. He was looking for a way to climb. But since there wasn't one, she saw no way to help him. The dawn was pushing back the dark. Black turned to gray. The swaying winter grass surrounding them, stretching back to the ranch house and for miles in every direction, started to take shape. They'd gone a bit more than halfway around just as the sun rose, so they were now on the west side, farthest from the ranch house, cast in deep shadows. It was a long, slow process because the sides of the mesa were folded in a way that made Sadie think of the heavy drapes hanging in her pa's office. Sometimes the folds in the solid rock were deep enough they stepped into the rock completely. But for all the unevenness, it was a mighty smooth mesa if a person wanted to climb it.

Heath worked quietly, touching as though, even with the breaking dawn, he didn't trust his own eyes, as if searching for something that he'd only know by feel. He stopped just before he got far enough around to step into the light.

He glanced at her, a furrow of worry creasing his brow. "This is the spot Justin said he'd gotten the highest on."

"I always climbed right here, too."

Heath turned back to the rock, then whipped his head around. "You've climbed out here?"

With an unrepentant grin, she replied, "More than either of my brothers. I used to tell Ma I was going for a walk and then come out here. I heard Justin and Cole talk with Pa about how high they'd gotten, and I never told them I'd climbed higher than anyone. I knew Pa would forbid it if he knew."

"Well, aren't you a little scamp, Sadie Boden."

She gave her head a sassy nod. "And I've looked as close all the way around as you have. This is the best way, but I doubt you can make it."

"Best maybe, but there ain't nuthin' easy about it. I'd hoped to find something better. There are a few more yards to explore if we go on around, but I don't want us to be visible to the ranch yard. I reckon we might as well climb here. Justin said he'd sent the men to work in directions away from here. A few men have to stay at the ranch, though, so we're less likely to be spotted if we're on the west side."

His jaw clenched. "I haven't found a single thing encouraging climbing, Sadie. Are you sure you want to come?" Then Heath's eyes slid down her body, and his brows arched high. "Y-you're not wearing a-a-anything."

"Of course I am." Sadie fought a smile.

"No, I didn't . . . I mean, uh, you *are* wearing something, of course you're wearing *something*. It's just your . . . your skirt is *missing*. That is, you don't have a dress on." He jerked his eyes back up to meet hers, cleared his throat. "You do have pants, uh, trousers . . ." He had a faint flush on his cheeks.

She'd managed to embarrass him half to death.

Good.

Heath stared her in the eye so rigidly she could tell it was taking every ounce of his self-control not to look lower.

With a smile, she said, "Ma and Pa both agree I can leave off the skirts when I'm out of town. It's dangerous and foolish to ride in a skirt, especially if I'm working cattle. I suspect that goes double for climbing a mountain. That's different from a sedate ride into church on Sunday morning. Or taking the wagon to town for supplies. I've always worn britches when I was working outside, then I put my dresses back on inside."

Heath seemed to physically rip his eyes away from her. He faced the sheer rock wall. Looking away from her. Determinedly. "It's good sense to not climb this mountain in a skirt. Mighty smart of you, Sadie."

She was tempted to do something like scream just to see how high a man this tense could jump. Maybe they'd get to the top without any climbing at all.

Of course she was supposed to keep quiet.

Still facing away, Heath swung his haversack around and dropped it by his feet. "Justin told me how high he got starting from this spot. I plan to use the chisel when the handholds quit, hoping I can carve places to grip all the way to the top. I ordered some spikes from the blacksmith; they're like nails that weigh a pound apiece. The blacksmith's not done with them, so I'm aiming to manage without them. If I can't, we'll have to try again another day."

He crouched, flipped the pack open, and pulled out a hammer, then a chisel. He had rope around his neck and under one arm.

Sadie looked up and up and up. They were in shadow, yet the daylight was upon them. She knew what they were up against.

"You're a madman. You can't cling to the side of this mountain and chisel at the same time."

Heath pulled the rope off his neck and tossed it on the ground, turned, and grinned at her. His blue eyes seemed to glow in the shadows, and having just called him mad, she thought she saw a flash in his eyes that was untamed, maybe slightly crazy. But no, Heath was a steady hand at all times. Justin had said so. It was the main reason her brothers had let her go off with Heath on this mission.

That and two weeks of relentless manipulation and nagging.

Cole had predicted they'd admit defeat and be home in time for breakfast. Justin thought they'd last until the noon meal. John had grumbled too much to make a guess.

Heath slid a rope around her waist, and she shivered—a warm kind of shiver—to have him so close.

"What on earth are you doing?"

"I'm going up first. You watch where I find handholds and footholds and climb after me. This rope is so if you fall, I can catch you." He gave her another of those wild flashing smiles. "And if I fall, you can catch me."

Sadie snorted to swallow the laugh. "Fine, let's get going."

She didn't mention that she expected to be home for the midmorning coffee break. She'd asked Rosita to make gingerbread.

The sweet young mother looked near collapse.

Angelique knew how that felt.

Being near it herself.

For days she'd dozed, but never really slept. Who could sleep on this clattering, huffing beast? She was filthy, her clothes coated in grit. Her hands were smeared with soot, and she could only assume her face was too. She had shivered her way across the country with a threadbare coat and her single dress. She wore everything she owned on her back. Her only luggage was her weary old black reticule with her carefully hoarded bit of money.

Now she sat, feeling like a victim of some violent storm that would not end. Her eyes barely open, watching someone suffer similar torments, with the added burden of three children to tend.

The train whistle jerked her fully awake. Another town coming up. Finally. A chance to stretch her legs and eat something.

Brakes engaged and squealed. A little boy, twisting in his seat at that moment, pitched face-first toward the squared wooden edges of the train seats. Angelique, from two seats back, dove for the tyke.

The child shrieked. Angelique's shoulder hit the filthy train floor and rammed into one of the metal legs of the bench seats. The boy landed in her outstretched hands. She wrapped her arms around him to cushion his head from the unforgiving wood and iron . . . and hit hers instead, so hard stars exploded behind her eyes.

The mother cried out and stood. The other children began sobbing.

Aching everywhere, Angelique ignored the pain and looked down at a little boy who couldn't be more than four. He cringed and whimpered as if she were going to hurt him, as if he weren't the one who'd come out on top in this dramatic little introduction.

The pint-sized pill probably blamed her for his hitting the floor. Masking her pain—which wasn't too bad since it fit with her general misery—she stood, easing the child to his feet. The mother managed to take his hand and guided the boy to sit by her. With two more children in her arms, Angelique wasn't sure how she did that.

"Thank you so much." The woman's eyes brimmed with tears, and Angelique seriously considered joining her in a good cry. "This wretched train. When will this ride end? Are you all right?"

It was touching that the woman, with all her cares, gave Angelique a thought. A true mother's heart for everyone, it seemed.

Because she liked speaking to someone, rare in a train filled with men, Angelique sat down and faced the mother. Her children were wide awake now and fussing. The little boy crushed himself against his mama. A toddler girl wept and clung in her right arm and a fussing infant squirmed in her left.

Because Angelique had no hope the two older children would want a stranger near them, Angelique said, "Let me hold the baby. You look all in."

Angelique gently took the tiny child and eased her onto her own shoulder without waiting for permission. "What's your name? I'm Angelique."

The mother tried to stop her from this brash kidnapping, but exhaustion slowed her down so much it was a feeble attempt, and Angelique gained possession of what looked like nearly a newborn.

"I won't move out of your sight." Angelique hadn't been around children very much, being an only child herself, and her only schooling came from tutors. She'd hoped for babies when she married, but they'd never come. That was at least partly because Edward paid her very little marital attention.

She hadn't been married long at all before she became grateful for any neglect he might show. He had other women to whom he openly paid improper attention, and Angelique wondered often why the vile man hadn't married one of them.

"I'm Dora Webster."

The infant snuggled against Angelique's shoulder just as the door opened and the conductor came in and shouted, "Next stop, Bennett."

The train whistle blew another deafening blast and set all the children off again. By the time they'd calmed—or as close as they were going to get to it—the conductor had passed into another car with his announcement.

Leaning forward, Angelique said, "I'm glad we're to a town, Dora. It seems like forever since we've had a meal." She thought of her remaining coins. Aunt Margaret had been generous to her so she was well funded, but she intended to give every penny she could hoard back to her aunt or donate it to the orphanage. She'd eat another sparse meal, only she was famished past anything she'd been before, and she'd been hungry many times.

The child sitting beside the mother, the little boy, gave her a wide-eyed look. A moan escaped him, and his hands rested on his stomach as his head pressed into his mother's side.

"We'll just stay on the train," Mrs. Webster said, her voice unsteady, her hands shaking. "I don't want the children to get lost."

Angelique peered out the window at the tiny approaching town, little more than a train station and a few scattered buildings beyond. Getting lost was hard to imagine. She looked back at Dora and noticed how thin she was, her wrists little more than skin over bone, her cheeks sunken. The wide-eyed boy's look had been one of near desperation.

Or hunger.

Angelique had only joined these folks a day ago. She'd seen them climb down off another train and sit at the depot with her.

She arrived there ahead and had already eaten, while the mother had come straight from the train to sit on a bench with her three children, then boarded when Angelique's train pulled in.

They hadn't gone into the diner at that station to eat. Now they weren't going in again.

Angelique could think of only one reason for that. These folks had less than she did.

"For I was hungry and you gave me meat."

The words whispered quietly in Angelique's head as she cuddled the baby and wondered what to do.

"I was thirsty . . ."

"Where are you headed?"

"I was a stranger . . ."

"We are meeting my husband in California. He built a home for us near San Francisco, but I stayed behind until my baby was born." A fond light shone in the mother's eyes. "I miss him terribly."

"I was sick . . ."

Dora looked down at the oldest boy. "We are looking forward to seeing Papa again, aren't we, Son?"

"I was in prison . . ."

Angelique had to admit this train had a prison-like quality. She'd been sentenced for quite some time and would be released from custody when she reached Skull Gulch. Until then, there was no escape. She paused to be thankful no one was naked.

The boy nodded. His silence, his stillness, was unnatural. As little as she knew about children, Angelique knew a boy should be active and noisy.

Unless he was weak with hunger.

Angelique had promised God that if He would deliver her from Edward's cruelty, she would devote her life to her faith. In fact, she'd done more than promise. Even in the midst of her sorrows and long before the cruelty ended, she'd turned her whole life over to the Lord and committed herself to Him, striving to be faithful to His teachings.

Edward had gone, yet new problems presented themselves. She'd done her best to keep her vow through it all. She found it simple to do that now.

Trying for a hearty tone, hoping the woman might believe it came from having plenty, Angelique whispered as if she told a great secret, "Dora, will you please come in and eat with me? I don't want to sit at a table filled with men. I would be glad to buy you a meal just to have your company." Wanting to remember the woman's quiet lie and not hurt her pride, Angelique added, "I will help you with the children so they don't get lost. I would be so grateful if you would let me help."

Her eyes met the young mother's, and both of them knew it was an offer the woman couldn't possibly refuse. Maybe Dora would have refused for herself, but her children were hungry. Tears filled the woman's eyes, though she didn't let them fall.

With a quick nod, she said, "Thank you. That is a kind and generous offer. We accept."

The train slowed, and they stayed busy holding the children so that the rough train with its heavy braking didn't knock them all to the floor.

Once they got into the station house, the woman was so hungry and so occupied with her children, Angelique was quite sure they didn't notice she skipped the meal. There wasn't enough to get three hungry mouths to California, but if Angelique went without, there was enough to get to New Mexico Territory. Maybe Aunt Margaret could help from there. Instead of donating to the orphanage, Angelique would have to ask for more to aid her new friends.

Well, God had called her to the task, and she would not shirk.

Her stomach growled, and she told it to shut up.

10

Heath swung his pack over his neck by its leather straps. He had venison jerky, hard biscuits, and a canteen. He planned on eating on top of the mesa.

He tied the rope between his waist and Sadie's. For some reason, it struck him as very right to be tied to her, which was pure stupid because he was a lowly hired man with a few dollars in his pocket, and she was part owner of one of the biggest spreads in New Mexico Territory.

Not that long ago he'd wondered if she even knew his name. No doubt she had it now.

He grabbed a slim outcropping just a foot overhead. There was a place for a toe at about knee level. He pulled himself up and looked back at Sadie, who stood watching him, arms crossed, as skeptical as any woman who'd ever lived.

"Am I fired or not? Do you remember how we left things?"

Shaking her head, she said, "I reckon you're not fired. But I don't know if Justin will pay you for this day's work. Unless you're back to work by midmorning, of course."

"Why'd you come along if you're so sure we're going to fail?"

He remembered his brother Seth, in one of his crazy moments, asking, *"Do you ever think wild wolves are calling you?"*

Heath had been the man of the family from his earliest memory. That left no time for such foolishness as thinking wolves could talk. But Heath had to admit that occasionally he found deep inside himself a wild streak. A deeply buried, well-controlled core of pure recklessness. That didn't make a man crazy, and Seth wasn't crazy—he was just sometimes way too close to going over the edge. Heath understood now how Seth felt.

And all that crazy had to do with forgetting about this reckless climb with Sadie, and instead dragging her into his arms.

He'd probably end up fired again.

"I mostly came just because I was tired of listening to Justin and Cole order me around." She sounded mighty sassy. "A big part of the reason I went to work at the orphanage was to do something useful with my life. Out here I was never anything but the lady of the manor."

He remembered his ma working their meager land by herself to grow a bare-bones garden. Hunting, milking the cow. Fighting blizzards while she kept body and soul together waiting for her worthless husband to stop by the house. He had a little trouble feeling too sorry for Miss Lady of the Manor.

Thinking it unwise to tell her that, he began scaling. She was about ten feet below him, her eyes fixed on the mesa top, watching for a gunman. She had just enough slack in the rope to give him room to climb while she held tight, or at least as tightly as possible until he secured the next handhold. Once he was secure, she'd close the distance while he looked overhead. Then she'd get a good hold, and Heath would climb again. As if she really did plan to catch him when he fell.

He paused to double-check the rope binding them together. It was solid. He'd done enough climbing in Julia's Cavern—which was how he thought of the place—to know his knots.

"You said you wore those britches and went out to ride and work with your brothers." They looked to be spending long hours together today. He might as well get to know her better.

"My brothers protected me from anything dangerous."

"Not a bad idea. Ranching is rough work. Wicked horns and hooves, rattlesnakes, cougars."

"They were protecting me from sweat, Heath."

He stopped and looked down at her, unable to stop a smile.

Her pretty hazel eyes flashed with irritation. "From getting calluses on my hands. From messing up my hair."

With a short laugh, Heath said, "The more you talk, the more you sound like me."

"Your big brothers wouldn't let you mess up your hair?"

"Not that, not exactly." He laughed again. "But they sure wouldn't move aside and let me run my own land. I wasn't in charge of nuthin' and it didn't suit me. Even though I own a quarter of the ranch, it's just one big ranch. Not four separate ones. Or we ran it like that, anyway, even though it's my name on the deed of my share of the acres. And being the youngest"—extending an arm overhead, he pulled himself up, then reached again—"well, it wasn't ever gonna change."

The lower part of this cliff wasn't real friendly, but it'd have to get a sight worse than this to keep him from reaching the top in short order.

"So I took off. And probably made 'em feel mighty bad." He didn't know how he and Sadie had ended up talking about him. Getting to know her sounded fun. Talking over everything he'd ever done was just a flat-out waste of time. He quit talking before he said one more stupid word.

He climbed for an hour before he found a ledge that was about a foot wide. Time for a rest. He swung up and sat on the ledge, then looked down. Sadie's attention was on the rocks so she hadn't noticed he'd stopped. He reeled in the rope hand over hand until she got to the level of his toes. Startled, she glanced up and her hand slipped.

A tight shriek escaped in the quiet morning.

Hoping she hadn't alerted anyone, Heath hoisted her up. She dangled like a spider on the end of its web for just a few seconds before he quick settled her beside him. And there she sat, not one spidery thing about her.

"Time for a break, boss lady." Somehow he liked her better when he remembered she was his boss—or maybe he liked her in a more normal, friendly way. Being reminded she was his boss helped him not think so much about how pretty she was. Helped a little, anyway.

Whatever mixed-up way he felt, it wasn't salted with the frustration of not being the boss on his own land.

Her cheeks were flushed from toiling up the cliff. Her hair was loose from its bun, and wisps of white-blond curls had escaped to frame her face. And in the middle of all that shone a pair of eyes, gold streaking through brown with hints of green. Eyes so interesting he could look at them all day just to try to describe them better. Except those eyes held the shadows of worry. More than for any other reason, she was here with him to get away from the steady fretting about her pa and loneliness for her ma.

Sadie settled in on the ledge and brushed the hair back from her face. "We're sitting on a ledge about fifty feet up."

Heath looked down. "I think it's more like seventy-five. A long way to fall."

He checked the ledge for signs of crumbling. It was fine. They could sit here in safety a long old time.

"Fifty or seventy-five, it doesn't matter."

"What do you mean?" Heath was startled by her casual remark.

"Once you're past what'll kill you if you fall, what do a few more feet matter?"

Heath said, "True enough." He handed her the canteen, and they both had a drink. "Ready to go?"

Sadie nodded and climbed to her feet. Heath enjoyed the graceful way she moved for a bit too long before he shoved himself up. "We've got another maybe fifty feet of easy going."

"Easy?" Sadie peered down at the sheer rock.

"Yep, compared to the last fifty feet. That's the part Justin says can't be scaled." Heath braced himself to start climbing. "Remember to keep quiet."

Sadie was studying the rock and she turned to Heath. "What's going on here?"

Heath shook his head, confused. "Uh, we're mountain climbing?"

"No, I mean we're talking about someone being up there while we're planning to have to fight for every inch all the way up. If they got up there, so can we. And if where we are isn't climbable, then we're missing something."

The comment froze Heath in place. "You're right." He was silent for a moment before he said, "We're either wrong about there being someone up there or we haven't found the route they used."

Sadie could hear from Heath's tone that he didn't think he was wrong about there being someone up there.

"We didn't go all the way around the base. We were trying to stay away from places visible from the ranch. Maybe somewhere farther on we would have found a better way."

"Justin said he tried dozens of times to climb the mesa, and this spot was the one that got him the highest, remember? If someone came in and cared enough to work their way up, why wouldn't they start here?"

"This was the way I always tried, too. Maybe whoever's up

there at the top did climb here, but they're just better climbers than we are."

"Or maybe there isn't anyone up there after all."

Sadie faced the rock wall squarely and slapped it. "Which means we're completely wasting our time. We might as well admit defeat."

"Sadie, I can climb this mesa. If we don't make it today, I'll get climbing tools and scale it another day."

"But there's no good reason to go up there."

"Finding gold is a decent enough reason."

A furrow appeared on Sadie's brow. "Is that what you're doing this for—to find gold?"

"I don't have much in the way of a thirst for riches. I figure I could be a wealthy man back in Colorado."

"Really? Wealthy?"

"Mighty comfortable at least. I own a nice stretch of land and have a good-sized herd of cattle. I reckon being wealthy means having all I need and plenty I want. And since I've got that already, gold wouldn't change things much."

"I've seen gold change everything."

"Did it change your family?"

Sadie hesitated.

"I'm going to guess that means yes. What happened?"

Sadie seemed suddenly very interested in the rock an inch in front of her face. "I feel like I'm gossiping about my family."

Which meant gold had changed her family for the worse.

"Let's do some climbing," she said.

She sounded so grim, Heath almost flinched. He decided to climb and he sure as certain kept his curiosity about what she was upset about quiet.

He found the first handhold overhead, a notch in the smooth rock about two inches wide with a downward slant to it. He felt crumbling gravel along the top of the notch and brushed it clean.

Most of the places he'd gripped were the same. There was no going fast. Instead it was nothing but slow and careful progress.

Heath had talked this over with Justin in detail and he kept hearing Justin's smug assurance that it only got harder the higher they climbed, until there was no way up at all. And Justin had tried and tried and tried.

It would be a pleasure to make the boss—a man Heath respected greatly—eat his words. And Heath was pretty sure that had to do with his own big brothers and Justin didn't deserve it at all. But it'd still be fun, and he couldn't wait to prove everyone wrong.

About three-fourths of the way up, the rock wall went completely smooth.

"Hold up, Sadie." Heath stopped, looked down and swallowed hard. She was there, sticking with him. There was no doubt in his mind he could get to the mesa top with the right equipment. But he didn't have that equipment. He needed the spikes he'd ordered. He should never have let her come along.

Just as he'd done every few minutes, again he tested the rope binding them. He studied the wall with the skill of a longtime climber. There were lots of little cracks, but from this point on they were thinner than his fingertips. Besides that, the hairline cracks almost all ran up and down, not side to side. They wouldn't work for hands, even less so for feet.

He knew what he had to do, and he hadn't come prepared.

He'd climbed around a lot in Julia's Cavern, that beautiful, dangerous cavern near his family's ranch in Colorado. And he'd gone along when people had come to see it, lured by Julia's books. Both tourists and scientists had made the trip out. Many of them weren't skilled at climbing treacherous walls, and a few, especially the scientists, had pushed into some risky areas. Heath had helped a lot and learned the ways of climbing rocks.

And he knew he could keep Sadie safe—but not today, not

without special preparation. Before he told her the bad news, he looked to his right and realized what he was looking at.

The top of the pass where Chance had almost been killed. He was at the same level with it. Of course, anyone on the top of the pass could be looking right at him, watching him climb.

Yet if he got to the flat top of the mesa, he'd be high enough that no one could see him if he was careful. If someone was on the mesa and watching, he could see who was riding into the narrow gap of the canyon mouth. He could signal to someone on the top of the canyon the exact moment to start a rockslide.

The canyon top there had been swept clear of any loose stones, but what about the other side? The avalanche had come from the west side, which was now clean of stray rocks. But the east side was still studded with them.

He had thought of the view from up here before, but only now as he was looking at it did he realize just what it meant. Two men, working together, could have timed that avalanche just right.

And they could do it again.

Maybe Big Red hadn't even knocked down that fence. Maybe the fence had fallen with some man's help.

With Big Red in the canyon, every man on the ranch knew Chance would go in after him. It was a rugged ride, and Chance wasn't a man to order others to do something he wouldn't do himself. Besides that, Chance took the lead as he always did. Whoever started the rockslide didn't wait for another of the cowhands to get in the way of those rocks. They'd aimed at Chance.

They'd been thinking it was an accident, but in fact it was attempted murder.

Who would want to kill Chance Boden?

He was a wealthy man, and money often drove evil men to murder. But if Chance died, his wife would inherit, then his children. Killing Chance didn't get a dry-gulcher anything.

He needed to talk to Cole and Justin, find out if their pa had enemies. Someone needed to scout the top of that pass and see if they could read sign that the rockslide had been helped along.

With a shake of his head, he remembered what was most important. He needed to get down off this rock. The taste of defeat in his mouth, he looked down. "Sadie?"

She stopped climbing and glanced up at him. "What?"

He swallowed hard. "We've got to go back."

"No!" She'd bullied her way into this climb, and he should have told her no from the start. Because he hadn't, they now had to back down over one hundred yards, every step of it treacherous. And backward was always harder than forward.

Worse yet, Sadie had to lead, at least until they reached the ledge they'd rested on. There was no way for Heath to get past her.

His weak will had put her smack-dab in the middle of danger.

11

"You men help unload our order from that train car." It chafed at Justin to be in town while his sister was attempting to climb a mountain, but there was no way to get men to follow if you didn't lead, and he needed to run the ranch in Pa's absence.

And his stubborn baby sister just would not wait. He should have fired Heath Kincaid a whole lot harder.

Justin had to admit he was real impressed with Sadie's stubborn streak. Muttering to himself, he said, "She reminds me of me."

His boots stomped with hollow thuds on the train station platform, hurrying, trying to cut every minute out of this trip.

His headlong rush broke off when a young woman, wearing a gray dress so faded he could only guess it might've been black at one time, appeared at the top of the platform steps. Messy hair, as yellow as the sun. She quaked like the leaves of an aspen. Her face was as pale as the snowcap on Mount Kebbel.

Behind her, another woman held the quaking woman's arm as best she could. But the second woman had a baby in one arm and she struggled to hang on to the quaky lady in the narrow doorway of the train.

Both women were skinny to the point of being walking skeletons. But the one behind looked sturdier than the one ahead. The one behind also looked very, very worried.

The quaky one stepped down right in front of him, and before he could veer around her, her knees gave out.

Justin caught her and swept her up into his arms. She was so light he knew there wasn't near enough of her. The second woman hurried down with two young children rushing after her, crying and clinging to her skirts. The baby in her arms started wailing, as well.

"She's near starved to death, I think," the second woman said, her eyes filled with tears. "She gave me and my children money to eat. I didn't know, but it must've been the last she had."

"When was this?"

"Three days ago."

"She hasn't eaten in three days?"

"I . . . I don't know. I'm afraid maybe she hasn't. I wasn't paying attention. I did this to her."

"You boarded the train without money for food?"

"We didn't realize how much it would cost. My husband sent me train fare to California, but all the restaurant eating . . ." The woman paused, shook her head, and threw in with her children, crying like the dickens. "I'm so sorry. I wouldn't have taken her last dime if I'd known."

"She walked off the train. I reckon she'll be all right."

"I don't know . . ." The woman's voice broke again, and if this hadn't been so serious, Justin would have been annoyed by all the crying.

"She went to sleep early last night. Then when they called out Skull Gulch, which I knew was her stop, she didn't stir. I had a hard time waking her. I'm not sure when she had even a drink of water. She was too weak to get it herself, and I was too selfish to help."

Justin looked at the woman who was trying to shepherd three children and couldn't describe it as selfish. "I'll get her to a doctor, ma'am. You say she's headed to Skull Gulch. Do you know why? Does she have family here?"

Shaking her head, the woman sobbed, "We spent too much time talking about the children. After such generosity I don't know a thing about her. Angelique. Her name is Angelique."

Justin didn't figure that would help much. "Alonzo!"

The men were busy unloading the train car just like he'd asked. Alonzo left off his work and came over.

"You got any money?"

"Yep. You just paid us yesterday." Alonzo looked about as confused as Justin felt.

"Let's see it."

Alonzo shrugged and pulled a fistful of coins from his pocket. It looked as though the cowpoke had brought every cent of his earnings to town.

"Give it to her. If you had spending plans, find me later and I'll repay you. But first I have to get Angelique here to the doctor."

"You don't need to do that." The woman's eyes went wide, partly with shame, but more with hunger and longing for that money.

"Get this woman and her children to the station diner and tell Willie I'll pick up their meal—and tell him to pack them a big lunch. Then she can use that money you're giving her for the rest of the trip." Pa paid his men well. There should be enough money in Alonzo's hands for the woman and her children to get fat during the rest of their trip.

She kept protesting, but Justin strode away, figuring Alonzo would handle things. He glanced back and saw his hired man slipping a ten-dollar gold piece back in his pocket. Something twisted inside Justin. He'd notice if Alonzo asked for his full salary later.

He headed for the doc with his arms full of woman. John crossed his path. Justin didn't see how John could help noticing the woman in his arms, so he explained what little he knew and told his foreman to make sure the other woman had plenty of money for herself and her children. Justin hurried on. He'd only gone a few steps when Angelique's eyes fluttered open. He stopped, stunned by the beauty of her huge blue eyes, surrounded by dark lashes.

Her face was sooty with smoke from the train's engine. Her hair straggled out from under her tightly fastened bonnet. There was nothing, though, to distract him from those eyes.

He was a moment in thinking to ask, "Are you all right, miss?"

"Aunt M-Margaret . . ." It was all she could manage to say. She sounded as if her throat were bone dry, and if that other woman was right, her stomach had to be so empty it echoed.

"Margaret?" He only knew one Margaret in Skull Gulch and he reckoned he knew about everybody. "Did you say Margaret?"

He only got a nod, and a weak one at that.

"I know Sister Margaret. Are you here to visit her?"

"Yes." She nodded again. "So sorry . . . Nuisance."

He saw her swallow and wince in pain.

"You're not a nuisance at all." Which was not even close to the truth. On the other hand, Justin didn't mind carrying a pretty woman around for a while. "What's your full name?"

She answered, "Websters, the children . . . need help."

He figured she meant the woman who'd been so worried about her. "They're fine. I made sure they had enough money to eat until they get to California."

It seemed that she'd gathered every ounce of her strength to ensure the care of those children, because she went limp in his arms after that. Then she fell asleep maybe, though he doubted it. Women didn't nod off while being carried around in strange towns by strange men. Passed out was more likely. The orphanage was closer than the doctor's office so he headed there. She needed to get inside, out of the chilly wind.

Children's voices sounded from behind the classroom door. "Sister Margaret, come quick!" Justin called loud enough to shake dust down from the rafters. It flitted through Justin's head that he'd been in a big hurry to get home. And he'd been driven by the thought of working hard alongside his men. Now helping this little filly was the only thing that seemed to matter.

Well, he couldn't just leave her collapsed on the station platform, now, could he?

Sister Margaret, the sweet old lady who'd stolen Sadie from the ranch, hurried out into the hall. Her worry about the yelling was gone the minute she saw he carried a woman.

"What's going on?" She came close and was confused for a moment, but then Justin saw her eyes widen. "My sweet Angelique."

Sister Margaret, the mildest woman Justin had ever known, lifted eyes that reminded him of a wounded coyote that had once gone for his throat. "What did you do to her?"

Justin took a step back and tilted his chin down to protect his jugular. "I didn't hurt her. I found her like this."

❧

Aunt Margaret? A voice Angelique hadn't heard for years and a tone that said someone in this world loved her jarred her out of a daze.

"Follow me, Justin. We need to get her to bed right away."

Angelique felt herself being hauled around like a parcel.

"I'm sorry I spoke so unkindly." Aunt Margaret's voice again, such a lovely sound. Angelique would have started crying again if she had a single drop of water to spare in her body. "It was the shock of seeing her hurt. God bless you for bringing her to me. What happened?"

Justin. The man who'd carried her here was named Justin. His hair was too long, he was coated in dust, and yet he was probably so much cleaner than she was it was shameful.

Shameful for her.

"She wasn't harmed, Sister Margaret. I reckon the ride was too long. A passenger with her said she hasn't eaten in days. She weighs next to nothing, so I can believe she's missed a lot of meals. I'll send Doc over before I leave town."

Angelique listened to them discuss her as if she were a child. Or more properly, as if she were an unconscious woman. She wanted to tell them it was just exhaustion, hunger, and thirst. No doctor was needed. But she couldn't muster the energy.

Justin, what a nice name. It sounded like justice, and Angelique could have used some justice back in Omaha. Or maybe what happened was justice. Maybe she deserved it for her own prideful behavior, even though that was only outward. Inwardly she'd been driven by fear.

Soon she was lying on sheets that smelled of fresh air and sunshine. Aunt Margaret was sitting by her on the bed.

"Thank you, Justin. I think a doctor should see her. Come back with him and you can have some of the cobbler we made with the apples and honey you brought in."

"Sorry, but I can't stay. I've been gone from the ranch long enough."

A sniff from Aunt Margaret, like she was annoyed by his reply. "I'll be speaking to your father when he gets back. He's got a lot to answer for, stealing my Sadie from me."

Justin wasn't sure who all knew about Pa's strange orders given to his children. But Sister Margaret clearly knew at least some of it.

A low chuckle. "You lost my sister, but you gained your niece, and it looks like she used her last ounce of strength to get here. So maybe the good Lord has everything in hand, even if it does mean I've got to live with my knothead brother Cole for a year."

"She gained me, too." A cheerful new voice entered the conversation.

Justin turned to see his neighbor and good friend. "Mel, you're working here?"

"Yep, but I reckon I'm fired now."

"We welcome help anytime it's offered, Melanie." Aunt Margaret had a smile in her voice. "Justin, does your father's foolish new rule prevent you from staying long enough to lift Angelique's head up so that she can drink?"

"I reckon not."

"Mel, can you run for some water and pull the broth forward on the stove to heat? Her lips are so cracked, she looks near desperate from thirst. If we could get a drink of water and a bit of broth into her while surrounding her with prayers, it should help restore her."

Footsteps rushed away.

Water? Angelique almost moaned from thirst. If her throat hadn't been so dry, she would have.

That strong arm slipped behind her back once more and lifted her to a near sitting position.

A commotion of someone coming back.

"Easy, miss. Take a drink now." His voice rallied her. A cool glass touched her lips.

"Just a sip, Angelique. Just one small sip." Aunt Margaret tipped water past her lips.

It nearly soaked into her mouth without enough to wet

her throat, let alone get to her stomach. Another sip made her choke and threatened to come up rather than slide past her swollen tongue. Aunt Margaret dabbed at her chin, and Angelique wondered if she had any spit left. What a way to thank someone.

"Ready for another sip, Angelique?"

She nodded.

Another drink went down properly as her insides felt bathed in liquid. Suddenly she was so thirsty she made a compulsive grab for the water. Pulling in a long drink, then another, until the glass was pulled away from her.

"You'll be sick if you drink too fast, my dear, precious girl. Take your time. There's plenty. And I'll skim some broth off the chicken soup. Then if that settles nicely, some bread."

Aunt Margaret gave her more water, and just as suddenly as her thirst had roared to life, she was so full she thought she might cast her belly.

"Brace her up, Justin, so she's sitting. I do think it's mostly exhaustion and hunger. But I sent her money. Why wouldn't she eat?"

Angelique opened her heavy eyelids. With the worst of her thirst gone, the need for sleep crashed down on her.

Justin answered for her. "It sounded to me like a family with young children needed the money more than her. The mother is traveling without her husband and her money ran out. Your niece gave them money days ago. The mother told me she didn't realize she'd taken everything. She was going on to California, so I gave them enough to see them through."

"Thank you, Justin." Angelique finally managed to speak. She saw Aunt Margaret look up, frowning. She looked like a dream of peace in her black habit, with her head covered and her wire-rimmed glasses. Angelique's eyes shifted and she saw the rough-looking, long-haired man again. So rugged. So gentle.

Her husband had been just the opposite, so dapper and well-groomed, yet so unkind.

Her weariness pulled her under.

❧

The feel of that fragile woman was still in his arms. He'd never been that close to any woman, excepting of course his ma and Sadie and Rosita, and he'd never seen one so fragile.

Something roared to life in him when he'd caught her, a need to protect this messy scrap of a woman, although she wasn't short by any means. In fact, her height was part of the reason that her feathery weight had alarmed him.

"I'll go fetch Doc Garner." Justin turned on his bootheel and left the room.

Mel fell into step beside him. "So that's Sister Margaret's niece?"

"I reckon it is. When Sister Margaret spoke of a niece who'd been widowed, I expected a middle-aged lady."

"Sadie worried that the lady coming might be as old as the other teachers and not strong enough to be much help at the orphanage."

"Well, she ain't gonna be much help the way she is, that's for sure."

"We'll fatten her up. I'll stay and help until she's able-bodied and back to her full health." Mel sounded like she was as happy with the work as Sadie had been. Justin didn't see the attraction of caring for a herd of kids.

They seemed like a lot more trouble than cows.

"She can't be more than her early twenties." Justin had already given everything about her too much thought. "Or maybe being as light as a child made her only seem younger."

Whichever it was, she was a very pretty young woman. He didn't see any point in saying that out loud, however.

"I know Sister Margaret was worried about her." Mel frowned in a kind way, as if Margaret's worries were hers, too. "She thought Angelique might be low on money. That's what made her ask her to come out here and help."

"For now, she's gonna be more work than help. I hope she comes around quick." Justin decided then and there he'd check up on the frail Miss Angelique. It was a French name and it reminded him of his ma. He'd make sure the fragile woman was doing well. It was honestly almost his duty because he'd saved her from falling and then carried her to her aunt.

A responsible man took something like that seriously, and Justin considered himself very responsible. He also felt pretty dad-burned heroic. It fed something in him that had been knocked hard when Pa had been hurt. He should have been there; he should have saved Pa.

Somehow catching a falling woman and carrying her to safety, not to mention helping to feed a woman and her children, gave him back his pride.

Which probably made him a prideful fool.

"I'd better get back." Mel distracted him from thoughts of pride and heroics and women in distress, and he was grateful for it. "I just wanted to know what you'd heard from your ma and pa."

Justin had news to share, and he was glad enough to change the subject.

12

"I should have gone to Denver with Ma and Pa," Sadie muttered as she inched backward, fighting down panic.

"What?" Heath drew her attention up.

"Nothing." She needed to keep her thoughts to herself. They had a long way to go, and straight down. It was at less than half the pace of going up, and that had been maddeningly slow. And she needed to not distract Heath.

"What possessed me to want to climb a stupid mountain anyway? Stubbornness? A chance to defy my brothers? More time with Heath? A death wish?"

"Did you say something?" Heath hollered.

"Nope, not a thing." Not a thing that she wanted him to hear. "The gingerbread isn't gonna be warm anymore, and we didn't even get to the top."

"Sadie, did you—?"

"Nothing! I said nothing." She clamped her mouth shut with a disgusted sigh. She was dangling up here by her fingernails, absolutely literally by her fingernails, and it was because of her own foolishness. Climbing this mesa hadn't bothered her a bit when she was a youngster. Which probably just proved that back then she didn't have a lick of common sense.

The sun was high in the sky now. They were in the full light after a morning in shadows. They'd sure as certain missed the midmorning coffee break.

"Your foot is just above the ledge we sat on coming up," Heath called.

That distracted her more than her own muttering, causing her foot to slip. She fell with a sharp shriek. The rope jerked hard, and she dangled and swayed from her belly. A quick glance up showed Heath braced against toeholds, both hands on the rope. How did he cling to the rock with her weight tugging at him? He had to be the strongest, steadiest man she'd ever known.

As he directed her foot, she took a moment to be glad she wasn't wearing a skirt, for he never would have seen past her if she'd had one on.

By the time she reached the ledge where they could rest, her hands were shaking with fatigue, her fingertips scraped nearly raw. Her head was flooded with pure panic and there was a long way to go yet.

Heath was only seconds behind her, as sure as a clinging vine against the rock wall. The man hadn't been boasting when he'd said he was an experienced climber. He sat beside her, and neither spoke for a long time.

Finally she caught her breath and calmed her heart, cleared her fearful brain enough to think straight, and looked to see him staring overhead at the top of the mesa.

"What are you looking for?"

"I've decided there's no one up there, at least not now."

"How'd you decide that?" She noticed one of his fingernails was torn enough to be bleeding and considered how far they had left to go.

"You screamed and no one came and started shooting at us.

That seems like proof enough." He pulled jerky and biscuits out of his pack and handed her a share, and when their hands touched, regret stole his smile away. "I've put you in danger. We've got a long way to go and you're all in."

He didn't say it, but she thought he might be all in, too. Except he probably had deep wells of strength and enough grit to go on, even if his strength was spent.

She struggled to find that well in herself.

They ate for a while and shared Heath's canteen. She felt her spirits revive for the rest of the descent.

He slung his pack over his shoulder as if to go, but she wasn't quite ready yet. She needed just a few more minutes. Without thinking it through, she reached out and took his bleeding hand. "How badly does it hurt?"

His muscles tensed, and she wondered if he'd pull away.

"I've been scraped by a rock before. Pay it no mind."

Studying his hand, she said, "I'd bandage it, but you need your fingers free."

His rugged, scratched-up hand tightened on hers, and she was drawn to his gaze. "I'm sorry I got you into such a tight spot, Sadie. I surely am. I knew I shouldn't let you come on this climb, but I . . ." He looked down at their joined hands.

"You what?"

"I wanted you along." His shining blue eyes locked on hers. "I wanted to spend time with you. And I was so sure I'd show everyone, just crawl right up the side of this mesa with no problem. And there I'd be, on top." He pointed upward. "And you'd be so impressed you might not mind . . . if I kissed you."

Sadie was surprised by his words. Yes, she'd been drawn to him, but she'd never been sure how he felt.

Heath's head dipped, and his lips met hers. A kiss. Her first kiss. It was perfect.

Lips slanted across her mouth. He raised the hands they'd

joined until he laid hers on his shoulder. Then he let go and slid one arm around her waist. So gently, so mindful of where they were. But just as surely lost in the kiss as she was.

Sadie pressed on his shoulders to keep the kiss from getting any deeper. He pulled back.

A cool breeze buffeted them, there where they perched like eagles high above the ground. The sun had strength even this late in the year. The look in his eyes took her away so that neither wind nor sun caught her attention.

"I've liked spending time with you, Sadie. And your family has been good to me. You all have helped me not be so lonely for my brothers. And you've all helped me figure out what I want to do with my life."

"Do you really know?" Sadie perked up. They needed to rest, but her energy was coming from Heath and how interesting he was. She went on, "I thought I knew what I wanted to do, but Pa opposed it and now I'm here, with no idea what comes next."

Heath held her hands in his. "I don't know what I think about your pa running your life the way he is. I know a man wants to protect a woman, and a pa especially wants his daughter to be safe and under his roof until he can turn her over to a husband."

"But, Heath, I—"

"Shh." Heath cut her off gently. "I didn't mean that's right exactly. I just mean I understand it. You probably understand it too, even if you don't agree with it."

He had a point. Begrudgingly, Sadie admitted, "I do understand. Pa has always cared for us with all his heart and all his strength." Shaking her head as if to knock her confusion away, she asked, "You said you know what to do with your life and I interrupted you with my own worries. What do you want to do?"

Heath grinned and seemed to look through her, into the past. "I have three big brothers who are just as bossy as yours, back in a little town called Rawhide, in Colorado."

"It isn't possible to have brothers as bossy as mine."

"Listening to Justin and Cole order you and me around has made me realize how much fun it is to needle them." A chuckle halted his story, then he continued, "I like ignoring their wishes and daring them to fire me. I really like it that I know ranching and I'm not afraid of hard work. I can always find a job."

"That's what John said when I fired you. You'd be able to find another job with no trouble."

With a confident nod, Heath said, "The fun of tormenting your brothers made me see that I left my family because they never let me run my own life. They were so busy taking care of me that they never let me take charge of my ranch, run my own spread. They love me, but they don't see me as an adult who can be trusted."

"Oh, Heath, that's just like what I have here. A family who loves me until I can barely make a move without one of them giving me advice."

"And you love them back."

"I do. I love them all, my brothers, my parents, and I think of John as an uncle. Which makes wanting to strangle them very confusing."

"I miss that Kincaid clan so much." A smile quirked Heath's lips, and he leaned forward and stole a quick kiss. Except he didn't steal it because she handed it right over. "I've been wandering for a couple of years and missing them, but I've never been able to see how I can go back. Until I got to know your family and learned to deal with your brothers. I think I can finally do it. I think I can grab my own ranch by the horns, and even more, handle my brothers without being an ungrateful little pest."

"I could possibly handle my brothers, but what about Pa? How do I get him to let me do the job I love? A job I think God called me to do?" Then, as quiet as a breath, Sadie asked him, "Are you going home, then? Back to Rawhide?"

"Maybe not right away." Heath lifted his uninjured hand and rested it against her cheek, then gave his head a tiny shake. "I think we'd better use some sense and climb on down now, Sadie darlin', before I do something foolish like spend the whole day on this ledge kissing you."

She smiled, and he smiled back with such tenderness that her hands trembled—trembling that had nothing to do with her being tired. Sadie hoped she had the strength left to use her hands and feet, not to mention her mind.

"Are you ready to scamper on down the rest of the way?"

That surprised a laugh out of her, and she shook her head. "Scamper, that's right. We'll just hop on down there."

"I'm eager to get to the part where if we fall, we've got a decent chance of surviving."

Somehow the last part of the descent was easier than she'd expected. Whether Sadie was getting better at it, or that kiss had distracted her from all worries, aches, and pains, she didn't know.

She reached the ground and just kept sinking until she was sitting, her back propped up against the mesa. She'd have gone ahead and fallen over backward if the rock hadn't held her up.

Heath was only moments behind her, landing light-footed right beside her. He focused so completely on untying the rope from his waist that she knew he was deliberately not making eye contact.

Was he displeased with her? Did he think her indecent to kiss him like she did? Was he eager to get back to the ranch before she got any wild ideas that he might have feelings for her?

Then, with a quirk of irritation, she wondered why in heaven's name wouldn't she have such ideas after he'd kissed the daylights out of her?

He finished with his own rope, tightened by the hours of tugging, and crouched to work on hers. She should have done it herself, but she'd been too befuddled.

It wasn't long before he dropped to his knees, and that caught her attention. She looked up and saw he was exhausted. Right up to the limit of his strength. And yet still he was taking care of her. She rested her hands on his where they worked at the knot at her waist.

That got his attention. "Sit down for a few minutes and rest."

After a moment's hesitation, he turned and collapsed beside her, then dropped his head back against the stone and smiled at the heavens. "We made it."

"You were worried we wouldn't?"

He rolled his head sideways and smiled at her. "Nope, I wasn't worried. I was just ready to be on the ground. Climbing is hard work."

Dragging in a couple of deep breaths, he sat up and went back to untying the rope around her middle that bound them together. Finally it came loose. He coiled the rope, dropped it over his head, and slid his arm through.

"I can't believe it took us all day to climb up and down a hundred yards." Sadie took a deep breath and noticed the setting sun. "But I could never be this worn out unless I'd done a hard day's work."

"It was near midday when we turned back, and coming down was a lot slower than going up. We were on that ledge quite a while, too." They sat shoulder to shoulder, and he reached across to touch her chin. "Time well spent, boss."

He leaned forward again, and only moments after wondering if she had behaved decently, she went right back to kissing him.

When they broke the kiss, Heath said, "It's getting dark. I'd better stop this." Which made him kiss her again.

Finally he pulled away, his muscles awkward, as if his mind and body were at war. He shoved himself to his feet. "I'll go scout around the edge. I may come back here at night to see what I can see on the side we didn't explore."

"If Justin never found it in the day, Heath, then you're not likely to find it in the dark."

"Nope. I'll go around the rest of the base, but not for a few days. I think I'm done in for tonight. But having to search in the dark"—he shook his head wearily—"my chances of finding something none of you have after looking for years in full daylight are mighty slim. I think I'm going to have to find this mystery trail by climbing up the hard way and looking down. There's got to be an easier way up there, but it's hidden somehow. With the way the base of the mesa curves in and out, maybe there's a trail that's just hard to recognize as such."

He rested a bit longer before heaving himself away from the rock he was leaning on. "I'll scout around and see if the ranch is settled in for the night. I don't want to head back unless we can go in without being noticed."

Heath left her. Sadie didn't bother to go with him or even stand up. The day had been too hard, and now they had a long walk home ahead of them. She'd save her strength.

The sun had worked its way west and was within minutes of dipping behind the mountains in the distance. Shadows crept nearer, grew longer.

She sat in silence as the day gave way to night.

A boot crunched on the stony ground.

"I think we can head in now." Heath spoke out of the darkness. "The cowpokes are all in the bunkhouse for the night. We might be noticed, but if that happens, well, I've a mind to tell the men I'm sparking you and we were out for a walk."

He reached down, and he must've been rested because he had strength to spare to lift her to her feet. "Would that shame you, Sadie? For it to be known that you're going for walks with one of your cowhands?"

She'd like it so much it reminded her that he was leaving. All the way back to Rawhide, Colorado. And she was trapped here to keep Justin and Cole from losing the ranch and the mines. So it was foolish to waste time thinking of him, and she'd sure as certain better not let him kiss her again.

"No, I'd be proud to be seen with you, Heath. We'll do that if anyone sees us."

She wished he'd said he was truly sparking her. Instead of it being an excuse, she suddenly, fiercely wanted it to be true.

"Let's head in, then." Heath took her hand. Hers were scraped raw and tender, as were his, but he held her with such gentle strength that, right then, at that moment, exhausted and her mind blurred by his kisses, even knowing he was leaving . . . she'd have followed this man anywhere.

13

Heath walked her back and winced when he saw Alonzo Deval standing outside and smoking one of his skinny black cigarettes. The man had noticed them for a fact.

Even from this distance, in the dusk, Heath saw Alonzo draw long and hard on his smoke until the end was as red as the depths of Hades. Then, with a sudden motion, Alonzo tossed it to the ground, stomped it out, spun on his heel, and strode into his house. As ramrod for the CR, he got a house as John did, though Alonzo's was just a bit smaller.

All the cowpokes knew Alonzo spent too much time watching Sadie. Then again, most of them did, Heath included, try as he might to control himself. So he'd never thought much about how Alonzo felt. He figured he knew.

A woman was rare out here, and one as pretty as Sadie Boden was more precious than gold.

But Alonzo looked furious. As if he had some claim on her, or his notions about her were very serious. How far would he go to turn her attention from Heath?

Heath was glad the man had his own house; he wouldn't want to fall asleep with Alonzo in the same room.

"Let's talk to Justin and Cole." Sadie held on to his hand when he'd have left her at the back door. He debated mentioning Alonzo to her but decided to leave it for another time—or never, if possible. He hoped Alonzo just gave up, as any thinking cowhand ought to. As he himself ought to do.

"I'm sure they'll want to laugh at me for failing." Heath couldn't help looking forward to that. And their reaction when he told them that as soon as his spikes were ready, he was going up the mesa again.

He did wish he could figure a way to discourage Sadie from going, yet he didn't hold out much hope.

He went on inside with her. Justin and Cole were sitting at the kitchen table, eating supper. Heath hadn't quite realized it was mealtime. It seemed much later. But considering most of these folks had expected him home for the noon meal, it wasn't too late after all.

Both of them surged to their feet.

"Did you make it?" Justin growled, and Heath knew the man's tone was one of pure envy.

"Nope," he replied.

While a smile twitched his lips, Justin looked disappointed at the same time. The man really wanted to get to the top of the mesa, and to the bottom of this business. But the plain truth was that he wanted to get there himself. And unreasonable as it was, he wanted to get there *first*.

Cole headed for the cookstove. "Rosita's gone to see her sister."

Heath had been here long enough to know this was their usual practice. Rosita would return after Sunday services.

As Cole began dishing up food, Heath saw Sadie gather her strength to help out. He caught her by the arm and guided her to a chair instead.

"We're about done in." Heath sank into a chair beside Sadie.

"That old hill is a stubborn climb. I'll try again after I get the spikes I ordered from the blacksmith."

Heath held up his hands, scraped and bleeding, and under the dirt he saw several fingernails were torn beneath the quick. Which gave him the idea he oughta clean up before he ate. He got up and went to the washbasin.

"Me too." Sadie looked at her hands and followed him to wash up. He finished and toweled his hands, then handed the cloth to Sadie.

"That'll give me time to heal, I hope." He was a weary man and that was that.

"Me too." Sadie took the towel.

Yep, it sounded like she was coming along.

Now that they were both clean, or at least cleaner, their battered hands looked worse than ever. Heath moved back to the table, focused on Justin. He wondered if the boss was going to punch him in the face for letting his little sister get so beat up.

Justin turned to Cole, and Heath saw agreement between them. Probably agreement either to punch or fire him, maybe both. It was kind of nice to see the two half-wits agree on something for once.

Heath was really starting to love these men, and yet they also made him purely homesick.

Cole brought two plates of beef stew over and set one gently in front of Sadie, then slapped the other one down hard in front of Heath. Rosita, who got two days away from her work every week, tended to cook a huge pot of soup or stew or something so they could eat without much trouble until she returned.

He had to talk fast before they could issue a decree, which would set Sadie off again on a nagging spree to get what she wanted.

"How sure are you that that avalanche was an accident?" That was a question bound to distract a man from most anything.

Cole plopped down at the head of the table. "What are you talking about?"

"You saw something out there?" Justin leaned forward, his fists clenched.

"You never mentioned that, Heath." Sadie quit eating to glare at him.

All three of them were paying attention now, firing, fist throwing, and finger pain forgotten.

"I reached a level where I could see straight across from where I was clinging to the side of that mesa, and I saw the top of the slope where the rockslide came down on your pa. Have either of you gone up to check around, make sure that slide was an accident?"

Justin sat at one end of the table, Cole at the opposite end. The table was pushed against the wall, so Heath and Sadie sat side by side. Which boiled down to him being surrounded.

"You think that slide might've been deliberate?" Cole rose slowly from the table. He was leaning past Sadie, so Heath figured the man felt the need to get closer so as not to miss a word—or maybe he just couldn't stay seated.

Heath went on, "We've all talked about what a piece of poor luck it was that a rockslide on that narrow stretch came down at the very worst possible minute, haven't we?"

"It surely was unlucky," Justin said quietly.

"Or it was planned," Heath said. "I have no idea if it was; I just wondered is all. I aim to go up to the top of that canyon first chance I get and have a look around. Setting off a slide like that would leave some sign."

Justin, who hadn't found time to climb the mesa because of all his work, said, "I'm coming with you. We head out as early tomorrow as you did today, Kincaid. *That* pile of rocks we can get to the top of without a problem—there's a decent trail. I'll go with you and say we're getting those cattle out. I'll tell John, but I'm not risking anyone else."

"Except me," Heath said, determined.

"I don't mind risking you."

Heath let a chuckle escape. Being insulted by Justin reminded him so much of Seth, he couldn't stand how much he liked it.

"You're a strange one, Kincaid." Justin acted annoyed that he hadn't pinched Heath's delicate feelings.

"I reckon."

"So I tell John I'm going for the cattle with only you to help. We can get them, too. The avalanche didn't choke the pass all the way off, so we can drive cattle through it still. It won't be raising any suspicions of what we're up to."

"But there are still rocks on one side of that pass overhead. Those could still come down."

"Then you can't go," Sadie said, and rested a hand on Heath's shoulder. "Neither of you can."

"We'll be safe, Sadie. It'd take time to set up an ambush like that. And your pa told the men when he'd be going in there. If someone wished him ill, they'd have had time to plan something." Heath added, "I wonder if Big Red tore down that fence. Might be it was torn down by a more thinkin' kind of critter and the cattle driven in there."

"I don't want the two of you in danger," Sadie said after a moment of silence.

That was honestly a relief to Heath, for her worrying meant she was thinking of only the menfolk going. Still, he figured the woman would insist on coming along.

"But since you're sure it's safe, I'm going with you." Sadie smiled that stubborn smile of hers.

Heath stifled a groan.

"We'd be well advised to hurry through there." Now Cole was going.

"If it's dangerous and someone was after Chance, trying

to make it look like an accident, then there might be a reason he'd be after the three of you, too. No sense all being together in one dangerous spot. Nope, I'll go alone. Cole, go do your mining. Justin, run the ranch. Sadie, you stay inside."

The glares he got from the three of them were identical. Justin and Cole looked alike, while Sadie was more like her mother.

Until now.

Right now he saw the strongest resemblance between these three he'd ever noticed. First time he'd ever realized that *stubborn* could be a look.

"We'll go first thing in the morning." Justin nodded at Cole and a bit more grudgingly at Sadie. Then he turned to Heath. "You're welcome to come along if you've a mind to."

They were all going. He wasn't real surprised, but Heath figured he'd had to at least try and save their contrary hides.

"I'll be waiting with the horses all saddled when you three manage to roll out of bed." Heath left the table and maybe closed the door a bit too hard. He'd just insulted his bosses and walked out on them. But did that get him fired? Nope. Unless he was already fired. He couldn't remember.

He couldn't believe how much he liked these confounded Bodens. There was no doubt in his mind now—he had to return home. He was lonely for his brothers and sisters-in-law and all those cute nieces and nephews.

And that meant he had to leave Sadie, who couldn't come along even if she was of a mind to tie her future to a mangy cowhand, because Chance wanted all his children here under his roof.

Heath was mighty sure there was a Bible verse about that. "A man shall leave his mother and a woman leave her home."

If Chance ever got back here, Heath might just hold a little Bible lesson for the arrogant old man.

In the meantime, there was a mystery to solve, even if solving it meant just proving Heath was worried for nothing. Which he surely hoped he was. Yet the more he thought about how "unlucky" Chance had been, the more he was sorely afraid that what had happened to Chance had nothing whatsoever to do with luck.

14

Sadie, Cole, and Justin rode out of the barn, leading Heath's horse, in the darkest hour of the night, while Heath walked out of the bunkhouse. He stopped to see them all up and ready.

"I knew you'd be trying to prove something this morning." He took the reins from Cole and swung up onto the saddle. "Did you do this to save my poor scratched-up fingers?" Grinning, he fell in beside Cole. Justin took the lead, with Sadie riding beside him.

Heath sure wished Cole would exert himself and insist on leading or at least riding with Justin to be a full partner in being in charge. Then he'd get to ride beside Sadie.

But he strongly suspected her annoying brothers were deliberately keeping them apart.

They'd ridden well away from the ranch in silence before Justin said quietly, "I didn't get you told last night that Sister Margaret's niece arrived in Skull Gulch yesterday."

Sadie perked up. "Angelique? She's here already? That's wonderful. Is she elderly? Will she be able to do most of the heavier lifting?"

"She collapsed in front of me at the train station."

"Collapsed? Is she sick?" Cole rode up on Sadie's other side, and Heath came up beside Cole. They were still keeping her away from him.

"What happened, Justin?" Sadie reached out and grabbed her brother's arm. "She didn't bring something dangerous like cholera or smallpox to town, did she?"

"The story was that she gave all her money to a hungry family on the train, a woman with three little ones, and kept back nothing for herself. She hadn't eaten for as long as three days."

Sadie pressed harder on Justin's arm. "What a lovely thing. She will be the best teacher the orphanage could hope for. I sent money for a ticket and for other travel expenses, but I never dreamed she'd give so sacrificially. I should have sent more."

"The other lady traveling maybe should have had more too, for herself and her children. I think it's more costly than it used to be, and her husband didn't figure it right. Or he just sent all he had." Justin patted her hand.

Sadie looked down and pulled her hand away. Heath could see fingernail dents in Justin's shirt.

"I think Angelique was weak from hunger, nothing more serious."

"Angelique?" Sadie said. "She's French like Mama?"

Justin shrugged. "It sounds French enough."

Sadie's jaw clenched for a time, but she couldn't seem to ever stop talking altogether. "I should be there helping."

"Sister Margaret will fatten her up. And Mel's still helping out. Beyond showing herself to be a mighty generous woman, I barely saw her open her eyes. She fainted right as she stepped off the train and was mostly asleep the whole time."

Sadie frowned. "I have to go in and see if she's all right. I won't stay. I won't help in any way that Pa would object to, but I have to see."

"We can stop in to see her after church tomorrow," Cole said. "Make sure the orphanage has all it needs. I reckon she's little help now, but she'll soon regain her strength."

Nodding, Sadie said, "I don't want to disobey Pa's wishes, not even in spirit. But he would let me visit a sick woman, I'm sure he would, even though she's at the orphanage."

Heath couldn't believe they were wasting time worrying about visiting after church when there might be a murderer around. In fact, if his theory was right, there'd been two murderers. The man keeping watch on the mesa, and the man who set off the rockslide.

"Speakin' of your pa's strange wishes, if someone hurt your pa, would there be any way he knew about the new will? Maybe someone is thinking with Chance gone and you three not that easy about living under the same roof, somehow the ownership of the CR could end up in other hands. If this cousin of yours is as poor a rancher as it sounds, once he took over, the CR would be easy pickins."

They all three looked at Heath.

"Another thing, who knew your pa was riding into that canyon? And how long ahead did they know? If someone knocked down that fence and drove the herd in there, he did it, or I should say *they* did it after they had the trap all set. To know your pa's plans, they'd have to be close. Does that mean our two outlaws are your hired hands? Or at least one of them—he could have a partner hiding out nearby. Whoever drove the herd in there was hoping Chance would go after them, but what if he'd just sent men in and gone another way?"

"Nope, that pass has always been treacherous. Falling rocks is nothing new, though they fall one at a time as a rule. So Pa wouldn't send men to do a dangerous job without going himself. Or . . ." Justin stopped talking, causing all three to look over at him.

"Or what, Justin?"

The silence stretched on. Finally, Justin answered, "Or he'd
send me. He'd have let me go most days, but there was trouble
a far piece out with a herd that'd wandered. Pa lets me travel
the long distances lately."

"Which makes me ask," Heath said, "did the herd you went
after wander on their own or were they driven? That made it
most likely your pa would be in that canyon pass."

"That's a fancy plan, Heath." Cole turned to face the up-
coming pass. "Busted fence, cattle driven in a pass, another
herd run off, two men keeping a lookout. All so they can pick
the right moment to strike. It's hard to believe anyone around
here would plan something so devious."

Hard to believe, Heath thought, but he couldn't help but
wonder.

Justin spurred his horse to take the lead. "Let's keep moving
through here—not fast because the horses have to pick their
way around these rocks, but let's don't take it one second slower
than we have to."

Pushing his horse to a fast walk, Justin headed into the dark
maw of the passage and nearly vanished in the shadows.

Cole made a sweeping gesture with his arm, and Sadie went
next. He looked at Heath and said, "Bring up the rear, Kincaid.
I'll ride after Sadie."

That sounded like the next thing to a threat. Nope, it was
exactly a threat. Cole was saying, *Stay away from my sister.*

Heath let Cole go and kept a straight expression on his face
until he was at the back of the line. Then he grinned. And
wondered about home. If the Bodens weren't in the middle
of so all-fired-much trouble, he'd have set off for home right
this minute. He wondered how Seth's fifteen-year-old son was
doing. Connor had grown up to be a wild man just like his pa,
but with a sensible side like his ma, Callie. He'd always been

Heath's favorite, although he loved all his nieces and nephews. Connor was special because he and the boy had come into the Kincaid family at the same time. Seth had five more sons besides, so Callie sure enough had her hands full.

Heath had been away for going on two years. By now, Ethan's two girls were getting to be marrying age. What if they'd found husbands and moved with them far away? Heath might never see them again. They were beautiful, sweet girls, the spitting image of their fair-haired mother, Glynna.

Ethan and Audra had four more young'uns after the girls, three of them boys, so his family had equal numbers of children. Rafe had four children, two girls as smart and bossy as their ma, Julia, and two sons as stubborn and hardworking as their pa.

And they'd all been mighty good to Heath. He'd surely like to see them again. Now that he knew he could handle his big brothers and demand the respect of running his own spread, he could settle down and be happy in Rawhide.

The shadows wrapped around him and he trusted to his horse more than his own eyes. The other horses had picked their way through, and his buckskin followed along without paying the trail much mind. The light clopping of hooves guided him. Rocks, piled in the middle and scattered here and there, were like barriers warning them not to go on.

The bottleneck pass became a curved trail a couple hundred feet long. Heath reached a spot where he could see the far end. Justin emerged into slightly brighter shadows as day pushed back the night. Sadie appeared next and she was bareheaded so that the meager light gleamed off her pretty yellow hair. Cole was through, then Heath. He took a deep breath, glad they'd made it in, yet knowing they all had to make it out.

"I want to see what's on top of this rock wall first." Justin rode his horse to a sharp uphill slope. He dismounted, rigged a halter to his horse, and tied it to a clump of aspen with a long enough rein that the animal could graze. He loosened the girth on his saddle.

Heath was a pace behind the others, but he was quick about seeing to his horse, then falling in line with the Bodens to climb the hill.

Heath reached the top only to be hit with a chill wind. He hadn't known how sheltered they were during the ride out. Justin crouched, studying the ground. Cole strode to the west. The top of the canyon was the beginning of a solid streak of high ground that built until it could call itself a mountain.

Sadie gazed out in every direction, her coat pulled tight around her. She carefully approached the edge of the pass and peered down at the fallen rocks.

Heath satisfied himself that she was being cautious and then walked on north, trying to figure out where the slide had started. He watched where he stepped so he wouldn't wipe out any footprints left up here, and when he finally looked up, it was to stare straight across at the mesa. Skull Mesa was yards higher than they were. Someone on top of the mesa who came to the edge, and someone on top of this pass, could signal each other easily. Heath wished he could get just a bit higher and see the entire mesa top. Maybe then he could tell if there were signs of life.

Looking around, it was clear they stood on the highest level without going so far west that even a strong spyglass wouldn't let them study that blasted mesa.

"Look at this." Justin's sharp order brought them all to his side. He was hunkered down on a stretch of solid rock that sloped away toward the bottom of the pass just a few steps ahead. "All the dirt and small stones are swept clean." Justin pointed. "These white marks are scratches in the rocky ground. A slide would leave gouges, but this is the very top. No rocks came rolling past here."

The white gashes appeared to be fresh-made.

"That's left from someone working with a pry bar." With a sudden move, Justin surged to his feet and looked Heath in the eye. "You were right. Pa was the target all along."

Cole came up carrying a length of rope. He raised his hand, and a small stick hung from it. "And this is what they used. They loosened the stones, propped them so they were ready to slide, and then when they pulled the rope, the rocks went tumbling down."

"How far back were you when you found that?"

"Back as long as this rope is." Cole raised it high, and Heath saw the rope dragged behind him at least twenty feet. "It's the only one I found; it had fallen into a crack in the rocks. I'll bet there were more, but whoever set off the slide hauled them away. They missed this one."

Sadie lifted one of the few rocks left on top of the canyon with a gasp loud enough to draw their attention. She rose from where she was hunkered down, a piece of paper fluttering in her hand. "I found something that makes all our searching for clues a waste of time."

Heath stepped toward her, Cole and Justin coming just as fast.

"What is it?"

"A note. It says, 'This is a warning. Clear out of this land you stole from Mexico.'"

"It's a threat." Cole took the note from her and studied it. "This sounds familiar, but I can't remember why."

All three of them became bonded by their anger. Heath felt like he was invading a family moment. To give them space to think and talk things over, he turned away and headed for the edge of the wall.

"You can't see the pass right here for a long stretch. The top hangs out so far, the bottom isn't visible. The only way he'd know the exact moment to set off the slide was if someone signaled him." Heath pointed at the mesa. "From up there." A gasp escaped his lips. "Someone's up there now."

All the Bodens spun to look. A long black shape appeared. Heath shouted, "Rifle! Get down!"

The rifle barrel leveled. Heath rushed over to the Bodens and shoved them toward the trailhead, then grabbed Sadie. He ran with her to the trail that would take them out of the line of fire.

The distant crack of gunfire sent Heath hurling forward, tackling Sadie. A ping of metal landed far too close. Heath held Sadie to the ground, keeping her in front of him. Justin appeared on his left and caught Sadie's arm just as Cole slipped past him on the right and caught her other one.

A steady explosion from the long gun sent them sprinting for cover. Justin and Sadie dropped over the curve of the hill. Cole was a step behind, positioned to protect Sadie's back, with Heath on Cole's heels. He saw all three diving for the ground. Heath needed about three more paces to get under cover himself.

He caught sight of a man-sized rock. One more stride before he could jump behind it. As he dove forward, a tearing pain sliced through his left arm. Another impact knocked his feet out from under him. He landed, skidding and rolling, facedown on gravel.

Rough hands grabbed him and hauled him behind the boulder. The gunfire stopped.

Justin drew his gun and fired it at the mesa. But he had a pistol, out of range for something so far off in the distance.

"Don't waste your lead." Cole had his own six-shooter drawn.

"Heath, you've been shot!" Quickly, Sadie rolled him so he was flat on his back, and with a strength that surprised him, she ripped his sleeve open up to his shoulder.

Cole rushed to Heath's side and removed the kerchief from

his neck. Justin supplied his kerchief next as he knelt at Heath's head, staring with worried, angry eyes at the wound.

"Are you hurt anywhere else?" Cole asked.

Sadie wrapped the kerchief tight around the wound.

"No, I think he shot my boot, but it felt like it hit the heel. No harm done."

Justin lifted his hat above the rock, and no one blasted a hole through it. He then peeked out cautiously, rising to his knees to scan the mesa. "Somehow or other, that polecat climbed up there. He's probably running right now because he knows I'm coming." He slapped his Stetson against his knee in anger. "I'm going to get down there in time to catch him." He looked at Cole. "Can you get Heath home?"

Cole nodded. "Yep."

Justin pivoted toward the downhill trail and was gone, running at a breakneck pace.

Without bothering to make Cole work, Heath dragged himself to his feet to find the heel had been shot clean off his boot.

He headed after Justin, then looked down to see two kerchiefs wrapped around the wound. The sight of it made his stomach twist at the same time his battered boot skidded. The combination sent Heath pitching forward. He landed face-first and then slid down the steep trail.

15

Sadie cried out in shock, dove at Heath, and caught his foot. She pulled hard to stop his fall and yanked his boot right off.

She fell backward and landed on her behind.

Her only clear thought was to hang on to the boot. Heath was going to need it.

Cole ran past her and reached for Heath. He was still there but hung up, having grabbed hold of a tiny aspen tree. Cole stretched out to grasp Heath's good arm just as the tree ripped out of the crack in the rocks, then whapped Cole in the face before he could catch him. He kept after Heath, who started tumbling head over heels. Gravel kicked up around him as he scraped and crashed through scrub brush and over every little spike of stone in his path.

Sadie, boot in hand, charged after Heath in time to see him slam against a good-sized outcropping of rock, one of the few still anywhere to be found on the slope.

The jumble of boulders held. Running flat-out, Cole went right on past him, unable to stop.

Heath rolled onto his back, his face bleeding now, his arms

extended at his sides. He stared upward, dazed and only half conscious.

Sadie felt like the lowest form of life on earth. All she'd had to do was think. Heath couldn't be trusted to walk down a mountain on his own, not minutes after he'd been shot. Now he was both shot and battered, the poor man. He'd done so much for the Bodens, including knocking her out of the path of a bullet, then dragging her behind a barrier and shielding her body with his own.

She had to wonder what he was getting paid for all his trouble.

"I'm telling Justin that Heath deserves a raise." Cole came back to her side and frowned down at Heath, shaking his head, breathing hard. "Whatever he's getting isn't near enough."

"I'd think he'd be about ready to ride on at this point." Sadie was mighty sorry about that. But it had to be true.

"Yep," Cole agreed. "Taking care of the Bodens must be wearing him right down to a nub."

"If we'd just been a bit more careful with him, he'd have walked down this slope with some help. Now we're going to have to carry him." That sounded grumpier than Sadie had intended it to. As if she were the one with the trouble. She thought of that note again. The Bodens had plenty of trouble, all right.

"You're not carrying me," Heath groaned. "And there ain't enough money in the world to cover all I've had to do for you Bodens. I'm here because I want to be."

Sadie noticed he didn't look at her when he said that, but then Cole was right here and Heath wasn't thinking clearly.

Cole offered a hand.

Sadie slapped it and said, "Let him sit for a minute, for heaven's sake."

With a narrow-eyed look as if she'd questioned his manhood, Heath reached up. Cole grabbed his hand and pulled him to his feet. It took a lot more effort than Heath probably wanted to admit. Heath's knees wobbled, but Sadie moved fast this time to steady him. She jammed her shoulder under his arm and slipped her hand around his waist. Cole kept a firm grip on him from the other side.

Sadie was determined to hang on to him all the way down to the bottom of the trail.

"Look at the bright side," Cole said, giving Sadie a look that said he didn't like her so close to Heath.

Sadie shook her head at him. "What possible bright side?"

"He slid a long way down. We don't have so far to go with him now."

Then Heath nodded as though it truly was a bright side, the big idiot.

"Do you want to sit down for a bit, Heath?" she asked.

"No, I can make it. Let's go."

Sadie held up his boot. Besides blasting off the heel, the bullet had grazed the entire length of the sole. "How about sitting long enough to put this on? You step on a cactus and you'll be sorry you didn't take the time."

With a nod, Heath picked a nearby rock and sat down. Sadie was too smart to comment on it, but he looked like it was a pure relief to get off his feet.

"I'll help slide it on." She dropped to her knees fast before Cole could shove the boot on instead. Her plan was to take it slow and let Heath's head clear at least a little. She looked up at Cole. "Can you at least dab the blood off Heath's face?"

"He's already got my kerchief around his arm. Dab it off with what?"

Feeling thoroughly annoyed with all men, Sadie tore a strip off her petticoat and handed it over. She didn't tear it any too fast, either.

She quit fooling with the boot and watched her brother's ham-handed doctoring and Heath's grim refusal to say so much as *ouch*. His left temple looked like it'd been run over a cheese grater. The sharply sloping trail hadn't been kind to him.

Finally the men noticed she wasn't working.

"Get on with it, Sadie," Heath growled. "Or let Cole do it."

Her time was up. She finished and stood. She and Cole got on both sides of Heath and eased him to his feet again. Neither one of them let go for even a moment.

"We Bodens aren't taking as good of care of you as you are of us, Heath." She looked up at him just as he looked down and smiled.

"Let's go," he said. His left arm around her shoulder tightened just a bit and could almost be called a hug. "I appreciate that you gave me time to sit a spell. It helped."

The three of them picked their way down the canyon. By the time they reached the bottom, Heath was wobbling. At the first big rock they passed, Sadie guided him toward it. "You can sit while we get the horses."

He nodded, and she thought he looked grateful.

Cole said, "I'll fetch the horses and get your canteen."

"Water sounds good."

The horses stood only a few dozen steps away. Heath seemed to be staying upright all on his own now. Even so, Sadie watched him like a hawk. If Heath started tipping over, she wanted him to end up lying down in a fairly painless fashion.

The kerchiefs on his arm were soaked through with blood, and she noticed his shirt had been torn to shreds. She'd torn a sleeve mostly off when she was tending the bullet wound. There was no saving it, so she ripped the sleeve off the rest of the way.

Folding it haphazardly, she began dabbing at his battered face. No surprise that Cole had done a poor job. "You've taken the worst of it, Heath. Including a bullet for me." Her voice broke.

Heath was patiently bearing her rough medicine, his eyes

fixed over her shoulder, probably so he could pretend that she wasn't poking at his wounds. When he heard the break in her voice, he looked down. All his attention now on her.

"Any man would do the same, Sadie darlin'. I'm mighty glad I was there to protect you."

Cole came up then, leading all three horses, their bridles back in place and the girths tightened on their saddles.

"You protected all of us, Kincaid. Your quick action most likely saved one or more of us, because he never got a shot off while we were unaware. Add in what you did for Pa when he got hurt and all you were asked to do with the reading of his wishes for us. I sincerely appreciate the fine care you've taken of this family."

Heath and Cole looked squarely at each other. Finally, Heath gave his head a short nod. "I find myself uncommonly fond of all of you. I own a ranch up between Colorado City and Rawhide with my three brothers. They've been ordering me around all my life. What you and Justin serve up to me is nothing. In fact, it's almost like I'm home again. The only bad part is it makes me miss my family. So I am happy for any part I had in keeping you all safe. I'm enjoying my time on the CR."

They spent a few minutes ministering to Heath and were just about to help him into the saddle when Justin came riding back.

"I rode a circuit around the mesa, looking for tracks. I could find no sign of anyone climbing down, but I'll bet my best horse on his being long gone."

"Let's get Heath home. He needs a lot more tending."

"Doc Garner is back from riding to Denver with Ma and Pa," Justin said. "I talked to him while I was in town to tell him to see to Angelique. We can send for him. Heath's arm might need a needle taken to it."

Sadie turned to get Heath's horse, but Justin said, "Wait a minute."

"What now?" Sadie scowled at him.

Justin pointed behind her. She spun around, Cole too. And Heath craned his neck to see what Justin was pointing to.

"The cows?" Sadie plunked her fists on her hips. "You want to take the time to drive that herd ahead of us when Heath's been shot?"

"Yep. And Big Red is pawing the dirt, so if we do this right, he'll charge after us and run right through that gap, and the cows will follow. Cole, go see if you can get Big Red to attack you."

Cole turned back. Sadie saw him clench his fists.

"If you start punching him at a time like this, I swear I am going to put cactus needles in your biscuits tonight." Sadie knew she had her fists clenched too, but that was entirely different.

"Big Red's always hated me." Heath started sliding off his perch. "I'll go."

All three of them grabbed him.

Justin said, "He hates everybody, so don't act like you're special. I'll go. You three can all drop behind the cows and push them if they balk at that shadowy pass."

"Somehow, after all we've faced today, that monster bull doesn't scare me one whit." Sadie glared at the big old critter. He had a ten-foot spread of horns. Longhorns didn't grow to be huge animals—a thousand pounds was about right for a full-grown bull—but Big Red was part Hereford, which gave him his color and his name. And he'd never stopped growing. Pa said he weighed two thousand pounds easily.

That was a whole ton of mean.

Justin swung up on his horse and trotted toward the bull. There was no denying that Justin was a mighty fine cattleman, because he handled that old fella with no trouble. He got close enough to taunt him. Big Red charged just as they all knew he would. Justin wheeled his horse and ran, fast enough to keep the bull coming, right into the pass. They vanished. The cows followed after the bull as expected and headed straight out of the rocky canyon. The grass was no good here, with one small spring that trickled with brackish water—enough to keep them alive, but not enough to keep them happy.

"I'll bet my best hat they were driven in. It was all planned by someone," Cole said as he helped Heath mount up.

Sadie swung onto her saddle a beat ahead of Cole. The three of them headed for the pass.

The note came to mind again. *This is a warning. Clear out of this land you stole from Mexico.*

"I thought the day Pa got hurt was the worst day of my life," Sadie said. She let Cole go first, just in case Big Red came back, then let Heath go second so she could see if he was having trouble staying in the saddle.

"And wasn't it?" Heath asked over his shoulder.

She shook her head. "I think our bad days have only just begun."

16

The day had begun bad for Heath and it was mighty early still.

They got out of the pass and immediately saw the cowhands charging for them. Heath figured they'd heard the gunfire. Most of the men were riding the range on the south side of CR land, but these few who were close came a-runnin'.

Somewhat encouraged, Heath held tight to his saddle horn as he studied them, wondering if one of them was the gunman.

Justin took charge. "Alonzo, take a man and shove these cows past the ranch yard and a good distance from this pass."

Alonzo gave Heath's bleeding arm a concerned glance but didn't say anything. He signaled to the closest drover to him, and they fell in behind the cows. Big Red cooperated and showed no signs of going on the attack.

"And you two," Justin hollered at Mike and Windy, "get that fence back up."

"Who was shooting, Justin?" John Hightree was leading the pack. Justin hadn't given him a job. "Heath, are you bad hurt?"

Heath didn't answer. He was in too much pain to assure the old-timer he was fine.

"He's been shot. We need to get him to the house and send for the doctor." Sadie rode up beside Heath, close enough to rest her hand on his back and look him in the eye.

"I'll go." John took off galloping for Skull Gulch.

They rode on in, straight for the house.

"Let me go to the bunkhouse. The doc can come there." Heath was getting in deeper all the time with the family. He kept waiting for the cowhands to complain.

"You're not going anywhere, Kincaid." Cole helped him down so quickly that Heath didn't have time to tell the big galoot he could sure enough get down off his own horse.

"We need to talk while we wait for the doctor." Big Brother Boden swung Heath's good arm around his neck as Justin came up on the other side to help.

Heath would have protested, but his knees were wobbly. As much as he hated looking helpless in front of Sadie, he hated even more the thought of falling on his face again.

They nearly carried Heath into Chance's office, the same room where Heath had read them the bad news about living together. They passed a large mirror in the hallway, and Heath made the mistake of looking at it. He was a mess. A mess with a strip from a lacy petticoat wrapped around his head. Lace dangled nearly to his eyes. He wondered if a man could die of embarrassment.

He was set with surprising gentleness onto a couch.

"I'll go put up the horses and be right back," Justin said, then left the room.

Heath noticed Sadie hadn't come in and felt a pang of neglect. She appeared a minute later with a steaming basin in her hands and cloths tucked under her arm.

"Get his shirt off, Cole."

Heath wrapped his good arm tight around his chest. "I'm not taking my clothes off in front of you, Sadie. You should be ashamed of such improper talk."

She rolled her eyes at him.

Cole said, "He's right. That would be improper, and I won't allow it."

Heath puffed out a breath. "Thank heavens."

With a smirk, Cole added, "One of mine will fit well enough." He rushed out, and Heath heard his footsteps thundering upstairs.

Sadie set the basin on a side table and dropped a cloth in to soak. "We'll wash your face while we wait." She took the frilly bandage off his head, mercifully.

"The bleeding has stopped. Oh, Heath, I'm so sorry you were battered trying to save me."

"I didn't try to save you."

That got her attention. "You didn't?" She sounded hurt, but she began bathing his face anyway.

"I didn't *try*—I succeeded."

That tricked a smile out of her. "Well, that I can agree with."

"And I'd take banged-up bruises from head to toe to protect you, Sadie. I don't regret a single one of them." Heath grinned. "I did dearly love those boots. I'm hoping someone in town can repair them."

"I'll buy you a new pair of boots first thing in the morning, Kincaid." Justin leaned over Sadie's shoulder.

"No you won't."

"Why not?" Justin seemed startled, but then Heath had nearly yelled at him.

"I'll never let you pay me for doing the right thing. That's just shameful."

Justin nodded as if it made perfect sense, as well it should.

Cole was back with a dark gray shirt in his hand. A good color to get stained up with blood.

"Sadie, turn your back." Heath blocked Cole from trying to unbutton.

With a huff of impatience, Sadie dropped the rag in the basin

159

and turned to face the other direction. "Hurry up with it, then. And Cole, you'd better be able to roll up the sleeve on the wounded arm or I'm taking a sharp knife to your shirt."

There was a bit of a tussle because the blood had dried in a few spots around his wound and it hurt to pull the cloth away from his arm. Heath bore it while Justin made quick work of helping him shed his shirt and the red woolens under it. Justin wasn't gentle like Sadie, but then he was a ruthless sort of man.

The new shirt came on, and while they worked on dressing him, he looked at Sadie's back, then past her. She was staring right into a mirror and watching every move he made.

He narrowed his eyes, but she didn't notice at first because she was looking right at his chest in a way that was mighty disturbing.

Finally she looked up and their gazes locked. He scowled at her. She arched her brows and smiled.

Then Cole said, "He's all set, Sadie."

Justin rolled up the sleeve on the arm that needed tending. The shirt was too big so it was easy enough.

It took no patience to sit quietly while Sadie fussed over him, bathing blood off his injured arm and face.

Though Justin and Cole helped at first, there wasn't that much for them to do so they settled into chairs and watched. Rosita brought in a coffeepot, and tin cups dangled from her plump, competent hands.

"What are you doing back, Rosita?"

"The doctor was out with a patient. John told me of the trouble so I came home. He went on for the doctor. Have a cup, then hook the pot over the fire." Rosita set the pot down. "I'll be back with something for you to eat."

She paused as she left the room. The way she studied each of them drew everyone's attention but Sadie's, who was busy fastening a bandage over Heath's arm.

"What is it, Rosita?" Cole asked as he began pouring coffee.

"I saw that piece of paper you left on the kitchen table, Cole."

Rosita must be talking about the note they'd found on top of the canyon pass.

"You all know I have served this family long and I love you as if you were my own children." She didn't wait for them to respond. "I believe it is right to show you something." Her eyes lingered on Cole. "You were told of this when you were very young, Cole, but I doubt you remember it, at least not without being reminded. The rest of you have never heard this. Your parents kept it from you, and I think with the passage of years they have even forgotten it."

"Forgotten what?" Justin accepted the coffee Cole handed him.

Sadie finished with her doctoring and turned to get coffee. She brought Heath a cup and one for herself, then sat beside him on the sofa.

"I am going against your parents' wishes when I show you this. But they are not here and I believe they would show it to you if they could." Her hand slid slowly into the pocket of her apron. She produced a piece of folded paper, yellow with age, bent and cracked at the edges, smeared with some kind of brownish stain.

Cole went to her.

She gave the paper to him. "I feel as if I am letting danger loose on you children."

"We're not children anymore." Cole rested a hand on her shoulder. "Whatever it is, Rosita, we're grown up enough to face it. Besides, our not knowing might only put us in deeper peril."

Nodding, Rosita said, "I will stay while you talk of this. You will have questions." She got coffee for herself and arranged the pot in the fireplace.

Cole unfolded the paper. Heath felt an urge to stop him.

161

Shield all of them from what it contained, though he knew that was foolish. Cole and Justin were both tough men—they'd handle whatever came. But Rosita's dread at showing them this paper was hard to overlook.

Cole read it and began shaking his head as if in disbelief. Finally he looked up. "Where did you get this?"

Not a patient man even on his best day, Justin surged to his feet and went to Cole. He took the paper and read aloud, "'This is a warning. Clear out of this land you stole from Mexico.'" With narrowed eyes, he said, "This is the same note we found at the top of the canyon pass. But this is old."

"When I read the new note," Rosita said, "I had to show you the old one."

"I do remember this," Cole said. "I was four years old, and it was stuffed in Grandfather Frank's shirt pocket. Left there by the man who shot him."

"What?" Sadie jumped up and went to look at the note. Heath didn't bother. He figured they could all read well enough to get it right.

"So whoever set off that avalanche on Chance also shot your grandfather?" Heath asked.

"But that happened thirty years ago," Cole said, staring at the note as though doing so would squeeze more words into view, maybe a signature. "Whoever killed him had to be an adult. He'd be getting on in years, and it's a long time to wait to strike again."

"Maybe whoever wrote this knew about the other note." Justin took it from Cole as if he had to hang on to this bit of evidence. "And since it appears to be a mighty big secret, does that mean he was here back then?"

"He was either here or he knew the man who killed Grandfather and was his confederate." Sadie returned to her chair, every move graceful and feminine, even when she was clearly upset.

"Not much chance a killer would shoot someone as rich and powerful as Grandfather Frank and boast of it—not if he wanted to stay a free man for long. But he might confide in a person or two, enough for the wording of the note to get passed along."

"The land belongs to Mexico?" Cole sat behind his pa's desk as if it were his rightful place. "What in the dickens can he mean by that?"

"Does the land belong to Mexico?" Heath shifted around to try to get comfortable, glad they were thinking about something besides the scratch on his arm.

"No. This land is part of the Treaty of Hidalgo. The boundaries are clear. It was signed away by Mexico over thirty years ago." Cole leaned forward and planted his elbows on the desk.

"I wasn't asking if you were sure of your boundaries. What I'm wondering is if it's possible someone doesn't see it that way?"

"It's very possible," Rosita declared into the middle of the tense conversation. "I know many people here who have always resented the boundary lines cutting them off from what they see as their true country."

"And I know people outside of the state," Cole said, "who are leery of allowing a state into the union that is so heavily populated with Mexicans and Indians. They think we are too foreign to fit in the United States."

"The combination keeps us a territory," Justin went on, "long after other states are welcomed in. New Mexico Territory applied for statehood in 1850 right after the treaty that came out of the Mexican-American War. It's been over thirty years and we're still waiting."

"Some folks may think that gives them a chance to win this whole area back for Mexico."

"I can maybe see someone mad enough back then to shoot your grandfather over this, but why now? If someone was killing mad, why wait thirty years to strike again?"

"Pa," Cole said quietly. "Grandfather was right to force Pa to marry Ma. Pa was a rich man in his own right with powerful friends back east. Killing him wouldn't do anyone any good because he had all his affairs in order and he was a strong enough man to hold the land. Grandfather was too, but he wasn't aware of the danger. Pa was always ready."

Heath didn't think that was enough of an explanation. "When did you find gold?"

Silence settled over the room for a moment.

"It was found in 1866." Justin looked grim. "Right after the war. The rush came about a year later in '67."

"How'd it take a year for the rush to start? Why not right away?"

"Two soldiers found it, but they were in the Army and couldn't stake a claim at the time because they were called away. They came back as soon as they could and got here to find the mountain covered with miners." Justin crossed his arms and paced faster, his eyes unfocused as if he were looking into the past. "Many of them staked claims on our land. Instead of driving them off, Pa managed the claims by taking a cut. Besides that, he ran a mine of his own. He ran it all really well, and when Cole got back he ran it even better."

Justin lifted his coffee cup in a salute to Cole, who smiled. "You're doing a fine job with the ranch too, Justin. Not sure why every once in a while I get the urge to start beating on you."

"I think I drove you crazy when I was a youngster, starting fights you couldn't finish because you were bigger. And now, thanks to that, you're a lunatic. Sorry about that."

Heath had been watching these two scrap since he'd gotten here. But the word amongst the cowhands was that they'd tear into each other, but turn and fight together against anyone who threatened them or anyone in their family.

"The gold rush was a long time after your grandfather died."

The time to think made Heath add, "And starting a rockslide is a whole different way to kill than shooting a man. The man who attacked your pa didn't mean to pass it off as an accident because he left the note. But he didn't lead us up there, which makes me think he wouldn't have minded if we never found out. This assault on your pa was a sneak attack. It sounds like whoever killed your grandfather looked him in the eye."

"Whoever hurt Pa wasn't acting alone." Cole sank into a chair, looking through everyone and everything, trying to figure it out.

"And you've known all this time," Heath said to Rosita, "that Chastain's death had something to do with Mexico?"

"At first, all we thought about was grief and Veronica's sadness and the new marriage. Mr. Chastain had seen his killer, but his thoughts were for his daughter and how to save the ranch for her. He spent his last hours making sure Veronica was safely married to Chance. And he refused to tell who had shot him and asked us to let it go. He said if he told who it was, that would put everyone in danger. But my papa, Sarge, the ranch foreman and a good friend of Mr. Chastain, was too furious. Especially when a young cowhand named Ramone went missing right after the murder. To Papa it was as good as a confession. He started hunting the man. It soon came to light that Ramone was the illegitimate son of Don Bautista de Val, Frank's partner in the land grant."

Heath nodded. "John talked about the land grant the night Chance was hurt."

"We figured the motive for Grandfather Frank's murder was a jealous young man," Cole said, "abandoned by his father and left to work as a cowhand on a ranch he figured oughta be his. He was sweet on Ma, or he acted like he was sweet on her to gain possession of the land through marriage."

Heath said quietly, "Maybe he thought his pa would come

back if he regained the land. Could the return of his father somehow explain the note saying he'd get the land back for Mexico? Maybe when his attack failed, he lost more than a woman and a fortune. Maybe he lost his hope of getting his father back."

Heath had plotted many a wild scheme to get his own father to stay home and be a better family man. None of them had included shooting anybody, however.

"We're wasting a lot of time on guesses." Sadie rose and got the coffeepot and poured everyone another cup. As she filled Rosita's cup, she asked, "Why didn't our parents tell us about the note?"

"Mr. Chastain died asking us not to pursue his killer."

"John told me Ramone was there when Grandfather was killed." Justin thanked Sadie, took the pot, and returned it to the fireplace. "They tracked him to the spot of the murder."

Rosita took a thoughtful sip of coffee. "I have always wondered if rather than kill Mr. Chastain, Ramone instead witnessed his murder. That might have sent him running."

"I also heard there was trouble with the governor, or at least with some of his men." Cole drummed his fingers on the desktop. "I heard Ma and Pa talking. Money passed from Grandfather to Santa Fe, we'd be left alone for a time, and then there'd be trouble and Grandfather would pay again. That ended when Pa took over, and it all seemed settled that an American citizen could retain possession of the grant."

"All that was before there was gold. When that was discovered, this ranch went from a prosperous holding to one of the richest tracts of land in the West." Heath was a man of action, and all this talking was wearing thin. But it was hard to get to work when he had a bullet wound on his arm.

A loud knock at the back door sent Justin out of the room. He returned soon with the doctor in tow.

"We haven't settled much," Cole said with a sour expression.

"Nope," Justin said as he led the doctor in. "But at least now we know there is something to settle."

"And we know to be a lot more careful," Sadie added, looking at Heath's wounded arm. Her sweet concern made him feel like he could flap his arms and fly up to the top of that mesa.

"And now we know there's an easier way to the mesa top. Whoever was shooting had a fast way down." Heath braced himself for more poking and prodding from the doctor. "And I aim to find it."

17

Sadie emerged from church one pace ahead of Cole and Justin. She paused to shake Parson Gregory's hand. "I enjoyed the service."

The kindly man who helped so often with the orphanage took her hand in both of his. "We miss you in town, Sadie. I'm praying for your father and all of you."

"Thank you. We welcome your prayers, Parson."

Sadie felt herself gently but firmly propelled forward. She glanced back to see Justin giving the parson a sincere but brief handshake, with Cole behaving the same. Then Justin caught her arm and pulled her away from the front steps of the church.

"I'm going to talk to the sheriff." Justin saw the town's only lawman across the churchyard. "It's gonna be quick, though. We need to get home and make some plans. Don't wander off."

"But I want to—"

Cole cut Sadie off. "Willa told me there's a letter from Ma at the general store. She said she and Ed would open up so I could get it. Then I need to go to my house and pack crates with paper work I need to run the mines."

"That's fine. That gives me time to—"

"Get the letter, but we don't have time for you to pack crates." Justin pulled on black leather gloves with a hard tug. "We need to get going."

"While you're both busy, I can—"

Heath walked over, already talking, looking as healthy and strong as a man could look after being recently shot. "The blacksmith has my spikes done. I can get to the top of that mesa now. I'm going to the livery with him. Don't head home until I get back. You need riders along in case anyone starts shooting."

"Surely I can take a minute to—" Sadie began.

All three men headed in different directions. They left her standing there, as if she were a well-trained dog who'd stay put until they whistled for her. Men could be a pain in the neck.

Since they didn't actually have her on a leash, something Sadie could only imagine was coming, she went to the orphanage. The men were bright. They could find her when they were ready to head home.

She left the church in a hurry, hoping to get more time to meet Sister Margaret's niece. All the orphans still played in the churchyard, with the faithful teachers Sister Louisa and Miss Maria watching over them. The orphanage had its own Catholic services. A traveling priest came through occasionally, but mostly it was a quiet prayer time with Sister Margaret leading. Sadie had to admit she was eager to meet the mysterious Angelique.

Sadie reached the old adobe building quickly, as Skull Gulch wasn't a big town. She swung open the front door. "Hello? Sister Margaret?"

"Come on back to my quarters, Sadie," Sister Margaret called. Sadie moved to the back of the building. The older lady didn't feel she needed to stop what she was doing and get the door, which made Sadie feel very much at home.

Sadie entered Sister Margaret's rooms and stopped. Shocked.

A painfully thin young woman sat up, with pillows propped behind her back, on Sister Margaret's narrow bed. Sadie glanced at a pallet made up on the floor. It could only mean Sister Margaret had been sleeping there. A twinge of dismay swept through Sadie. She worked hard to lift the burden from all the teachers, and here was Angelique adding more work and Sadie was not here to help.

Angelique looked so frail, Sadie suspected that rather than have nowhere else to sleep, Sister Margaret had chosen the hard floor so she could be near enough to care for the poor, fragile woman.

"Sadie, allow me to introduce my niece Angelique." Sister Margaret made a courtly gesture with one gnarled hand.

"Aunt Margaret, please call me Angie. And Sadie, I'd appreciate it if you would, too."

Sister Margaret's hands came together, almost as if in prayer. "But you said you despised that nickname. You were quite adamant I never call you that again."

"I know, but I was being unpleasant to everyone back then. You most of all, and I regret my unkindness terribly. I miss being called Angie." From Angie's resigned tone, Sadie wondered how many times she'd asked this of Sister Margaret.

Sister Margaret didn't respond. Instead she had a nervous expression on her face. Maybe it was just worry for Angie, but it seemed like more than that. Like she was afraid to say the wrong thing, and somehow her saying the name Angie would be the wrong thing.

Well, Sadie wasn't much worried about trampling on some delicate feelings she could only imagine. "Hello, Angie, it's so nice to meet you. I'm Sadie Boden. I was teaching here but had to quit. I really left your aunt and the other teachers short-staffed. I'm so grateful you were able to come and help out."

Sadie set her reticule and Bible aside and came closer to the bed. "I heard you had a hard trip out here."

"Very hard. But Aunt Margaret is taking such good care of me." Angie managed a weak smile. Dark circles under her eyes looked like exhaustion rather than ill health. "I hope to be out of this bed today and start doing my share of the work."

"Nonsense. Not today, and not any day soon." Sister Margaret walked over to the stove. "You're going to rest and eat good food and regain your strength before you start working."

"But Aunt Margaret, I came out to help. I—"

"Hush now, my sweet girl." Sister Margaret dipped a ladle in a pot of soup that filled the air with the scent of warm vegetables and beef. "Mel said she'd keep right on working until you're ready."

She spoke in her usual gruff-but-kind way—but there was more to it. Sadie could tell Sister Margaret genuinely loved her niece. Margaret filled the bowl and brought it to Angie.

"Prove to me you can sit up and eat a good meal." With a rather loud thud, Sister Margaret set the bowl on a table beside her niece. "That will go a long way toward convincing me you're ready to get to work."

Sadie suppressed a smile. Sister Margaret was using the same voice she used on uncooperative second graders. Underneath the sternness there was affection gleaming in Sister Margaret's eyes, but also worry. It seemed clear that there was some kind of trouble between the two women. Sadie wished she had time to find out what it was, yet she had to head for home and help solve a mystery. If she didn't go soon, Justin and Cole would be here to drag her off.

"It's nice to meet you. Your aunt Margaret has talked of you many times. She was so glad to have the opportunity to send for you."

Angie nodded but didn't speak. Something flashed in her

eyes. Sadie was certain she saw fear. Then, as if Angie knew her expression gave too much away, she turned to her soup, acting as though it held the mystery of life.

Sadie went on, "I miss helping, but I've moved home to my father's ranch for the time being. Mel is an old friend who's filling in."

"She's been a wonderful helper," Sister Margaret said, "but she seems befuddled by the students. She begs the children to behave, and when that fails, as it always does, she snaps out orders. And that just riles them up. I heard her threatening to lasso and hog-tie one of the more unruly little boys the other day."

"So Mel's not a natural teacher, then?" Sadie pressed her fingertips against her lips to keep from laughing.

There was a spark of exasperated amusement in Sister Margaret's face. "Let's just say that Mel is eager to get back to herding something she can understand, like longhorns."

Though it was left unspoken, Sadie heard loud and clear that Sister Margaret was not one bit upset to see Mel head for the range.

"Sadie, let's go!" Justin's voice boomed through the door.

With a smile, Sadie said a quick goodbye to both ladies just as Justin stormed into the room. "We've got to . . ." Justin saw Angie in bed in her nightgown and fell utterly silent. He spun around. "Excuse me. I shouldn't be in here."

Justin tried to leave as fast as he'd come in. But as he stepped toward the door, he glanced over his shoulder and looked again at Angie, then walked straight into the doorframe.

That cleared his head enough he could rush outside. Sadie heard the door slam. He must have been embarrassed because he forgot to nag at her to hurry up, and Justin never forgot to nag.

Shaking her head, Sadie said, "I'd love to stay longer and get acquainted, Angie, but things are terribly stirred up out at the CR right now. I've got to get along."

Sadie gave Sister Margaret a big hug and, with a wave at Angie, hurried out the door. What was going on between Sister Margaret and her niece? And what was it that had Angie so afraid?

"Read Ma's letter, Cole. I don't want to wait until after we eat."

Rosita had gone on ahead of them to the ranch, and they walked inside to a table laden with roast beef and gravy.

"Rosita, you should have waited," Sadie said in dismay. "Today is your day of rest. I'd have helped you."

Rosita slid a pie into the oven and straightened. "I love cooking, *mi niña*. Don't fuss at an old woman who is doing what she loves. Now sit. The pie will be hot out of the oven when our meal is done."

Potatoes, mashed smooth and creamy, waited in a bowl next to the beef. Fresh biscuits were stacked beside a bowl of jelly and a ball of butter. Sadie's mouth watered at the sight of it all. And seeing not one single thing left to do to help get the meal on, she sat down gratefully.

Justin and Cole had insisted Heath and John both join them because they wanted to discuss the latest troubles at the CR. The four of them trooped in, and Rosita sat up to the table, as well. She usually declined to eat with the family, but she and

John had been here when Grandfather Chastain had died. They knew more about this than any of them.

"Eat first," Rosita said. "It is hot now."

While the letter Cole had picked up nearly shouted to her, the savory meal won out, mainly because Sadie hoped they would linger over the letter.

They ate in silence until they'd had their fill. Finally, Cole pulled out the letter, and his expression was almost equally hungry as he fingered the fat envelope.

A smile twisted Sadie's lips. "Go on and read it out loud to us."

He ripped it open and pulled out a thick sheaf of papers. "A good long letter, finally. She's written so many brief notes just telling the basics of Pa's condition."

His eyes slid back and forth as he scanned the papers, and after just a few moments, he looked up at everyone gathered at the table. "It will take a while to read all this, but Ma's first sentence says they believe Pa is going to keep his leg. He may limp, though—"

Justin shouted with relief. Sadie burst into tears. Cole quit reading. His silence was so heavy, Sadie knew it was because he couldn't read more. His throat was swelled with emotion.

Rosita rested an unsteady hand on Sadie's back. She was so much more than a housekeeper to the Bodens. A grandmother, a wise elder, a pair of loving, comforting arms, stern taskmaster with Ma and Pa's full support.

It took a bit, but Sadie pulled herself together and found a handkerchief thrust into her hands. She looked sideways to see Heath, beaming at all of them. He wasn't shouting or weeping or choked with emotion, but he was a happy man.

Sadie matched his smile. "A lot of this is due to your care, Heath. It took fine doctoring and all the prayers we could manage, but your skill right after Pa was hurt made all the difference. I thank God you came to us and were here at our hour of need. Thank you."

Heath gave her a tight nod. His eyes flashed with pleasure at her thanks, but he said nothing else. Many a man would have brushed it aside, talk as if it were nothing. But to say such a thing was to diminish in some ways the miracle that Pa would survive and be whole again.

Cole read a bit more. Ma asked them to continue their faithful prayers for Pa's leg because he had a long journey ahead to reach full strength. She warned of long weeks spent in healing before the leg could be cast in plaster. Until that was done, he dared not move. Pa would stay in Denver until his bone was fully knit together, and then they'd have to see if he could walk without crutches or a cane. They weren't to expect him back until spring. Ma included lengthy details of the doctor's care. She spoke of being taken in by a parson and his wife and living comfortably in their home. Visiting Pa every day and helping with his care filled her hours. Once the bone was fully healed, which would take until after Christmas, Pa might be allowed to leave the hospital if he lived close by and could return often for checkups. Ma was searching for a boardinghouse or a hotel or even a vacant house to rent. But there couldn't be stairs.

She went on sounding lighthearted, nearly giddy with relief and full of high spirits. She asked them each to write back. Letters encouraged Pa and helped her to pass long days of idleness without her beloved home to care for.

They talked over every detail as they savored Rosita's pie. Everything tasted better than it would have without the good news.

Heath had real bad news.

"I'm climbing that mesa tomorrow and Sadie's coming with me. Only Sadie."

He broke up the festive meal.

Everyone at the table turned to him. Not a one of them started hollering. Instead they looked interested, if a little bothered. But there was respect in their eyes that had never been there before. Well, maybe from Sadie, but none of the others. He liked it and decided to enjoy it while it lasted. Good chance Justin and Cole would go back to yelling at him soon enough.

"Why do you want Sadie along?" Cole eased back in his chair, cradling his coffee cup. It was a long way from the way Cole had forbidden it before, while Justin had kept busy yelling at him and firing him.

Heath told them exactly why. He'd been hatching this plan ever since he'd seen that rifle aiming at them from the mesa top. "We leave before sunrise, just like before, but this time you all leave with us—all but John."

The foreman nodded. His part, though it might not seem like it, was as crucial to success as any of the others.

"Are you sure your arm is strong enough?" Sadie snapped a hand up and shoved it almost flat in his face.

Almost like she knew she was questioning his toughness.

"I'm not questioning your toughness, Heath."

He was pretty sure she was.

"I was on the side of that mesa with you. It's exhausting. It took every ounce of strength we had to get as far as we did. And you weren't swinging a hammer, knocking spikes into the mesa wall. We're all eager to get up there, and I'm glad to go with you, but I want you to be ready."

Heath reached up and rubbed his arm, then flexed his muscle and raised his hand high. The swelling was down. The doctor hadn't stitched it because no muscle had been cut. A little lingering pain was easily ignored.

"I can do it." Heath slid his eyes from one to the next—Cole, Justin, John, Rosita, Sadie. He stopped on Sadie. "We go tomorrow."

19

The weight of the spikes was a burden his arm didn't thank him for.

"There's one good thing about that climb we took when we were forced to turn back," Heath called to Sadie, who was tied to him and following faithfully.

"No, there's not." Sadie clung to the edge of the cliff. A quick look down told Heath she wasn't having much fun.

"The good part is we're going twice as fast this time. We barely stopped to rest on that ledge because we scampered right up the side."

"Scampered?" Sadie said it quietly, muttered it, growled it even. He wasn't sure he was supposed to hear, but he had.

"We've reached the part where we couldn't go on. Now we use my climbing skills." It was almost a relief to pull the first spike out of his pack. At least if he hammered it into the stone, he wouldn't be carrying it anymore. Not to mention the spikes would make much more dependable footholds and handholds than the ones grudgingly provided by Skull Mesa.

He positioned the spike, but before he hammered it home,

he paused in the quiet morning air. A breeze buffeted them, thankfully one not strong enough to be dangerous. The top of the canyon pass where they'd found the note drew his attention. Was there someone up there watching?

A bull elk stepped out of the trees. The old boy still had his full rack of antlers, although he would be shedding them soon. Heath thought of the wild critters wandering around his Colorado home and was struck by the similarities between the two places. A herd of cow elk grazed peacefully down the slope from the watchful bull.

Smiling at the beauty of it, he realized no bunch of wild animals would stand grazing if there was a man close by. The elk proved the area was free from intruders.

At least until now. Heath raised the hammer, positioned the spike, knowing he was about to break up the silence and peace of the day.

He slammed the spike home. The ring of metal on metal sent the bull elk bounding toward his cows. They all vanished into the trees.

Heath finished seating the spike, making sure it was as solid as the rock it stuck out of. Satisfied, he continued upward. Slow and steady, he drove the iron pegs until they were anchored deep, then used them for handholds and toeholds.

"What are you doing?" Sadie's voice distracted him, almost knocking him off the cliff.

He hadn't bothered to explain the details of climbing to her. He figured she'd learn from watching. And he didn't have time for a lot of talk now. He had to keep moving, because this kind of climbing was exhausting. He had to get to the top as fast as he could.

"Just keep climbing, Sadie," Heath called down without looking away from his work. "We're going all the way up."

He went back to building himself a ladder in solid rock.

You can't build a ladder in solid rock. Everybody knew that.

At least she knew it because it was so obvious. She hugged up against the side of the mesa and waited for Heath to figure it out.

The hammer blows finally stopped. But instead of Heath deciding this wasn't working and coming back down, he took a few steps higher and started hammering again.

Demanding to know what exactly he'd done was a waste of her breath, so Sadie followed along as she'd been doing all day, only now she was completely focused on Heath. She watched as he worked his way up the mesa.

The spikes he drove into the mountain were solid as . . . well, solid as a rock. They stuck out farther than most of the little ledges they'd clung to, so the going was much faster, even though they had to pause at each new step so that Heath could drive another spike.

Yet he was good at it. A few more ringing blows and up they'd go again.

At last Heath rolled out of sight at the top. Seconds later, his head popped back over the ledge and he smiled down on her. "Come on, Miss Sadie."

Sadie climbed up, the sturdy rope around her middle giving her the confidence to move quickly.

With Heath's strong hands reeling in the rope, she seemed to almost fly to the top. She arrived and scrambled to her feet. And there they stood, facing each other, on top of the unclimbable Skull Mesa. Sadie had gotten here before her brothers.

Grinning like a fool, she said, "This is the biggest accomplishment of my life! It feels wonderful."

Heath nodded. "That it does, Miss Sadie."

"I think I want to climb more mountains."

Laughing, Heath said, "The spirit of an explorer. You'd like the cavern on my land back in Colorado. We should—"

She looked past Heath, and heaven knows what her expression was like but it must've been attention-getting, because Heath stopped talking and whirled around, his gun drawn and cocked.

Then he froze, and the gun lowered. "What is that?"

But of course they both knew what it was. Sadie said, "Someone lived up here."

There was a cluster of what appeared to be ancient buildings, collapsed until they were crumbling, built out of adobe. Battered-looking things, but unmistakably huts. No bigger than that, and yet so ruined she couldn't say what they'd once looked like.

"Looks like this place has been deserted for a thousand years." Heath spoke in a near whisper, like a man might at a cemetery. He was staring at a long-dead settlement of some kind. He started toward the ruins.

They were more mounds of rubble than buildings, but Sadie saw dozens of distinct areas built up. She hurried to catch up with Heath.

"They look ancient." Sadie was struck by the solemnity of the place. When they reached one of the buildings, Heath touched a stack of weathered adobe blocks. Sadie saw a broken piece of pottery and went to pick it up.

"Well, this sure isn't ancient." Heath's voice stopped her in her tracks.

Turning, she saw him crouching by something. She stepped closer to see what he'd found and soon realized it was a tin can. Opened and empty and not a spot of rust anywhere. There were traces of beans in it. The can was only a few days old.

"Someone opened it recently," she said. "Probably that man who was up here with a rifle. But look—there are dozens of cans. He's been up here many times."

"We knew we'd find something like this." Heath studied the whole area, then looked up. His blue eyes flashed wild. "I reckon this is no surprise after our friend started shooting at us."

Rising to his feet, he kept his eyes on the ground and started walking straight for the cliff edge. The flat mesa top was more oval than round, and right here the edge wasn't far away from them. Heath moved with such purpose that Sadie felt the need to hurry after him. She caught up to him just as he neared the edge.

Heath stopped abruptly. "Will you look at that."

"What is it?"

Shaking his head, Heath dropped to his hands and knees, crawled to the edge and peered down. "It's a trail. Come close, but get down. I don't want a strong wind giving you a shove over the side."

She very carefully approached, crawling like an infant. When she got to his side, he smiled and then jerked his head to the spot he'd been looking at.

"It *is* a trail." Sadie frowned at the mystery of it. "How can there be a trail up here, but not one down at the bottom?"

"I wonder if there used to be a trail all the way down. No, that's wrong. I don't *wonder*. There had to be one if folks climbed up here and built homes. What I mean is, look at the rubble at the bottom. That's a rockslide. I think the trail collapsed at the bottom. But if you picked the right spot, maybe a very unlikely-looking spot, you could climb, holding on to ledges, for just a little ways until you gained this trail. It's so obvious from up here. But I don't remember anything noticeable on this side at the base, and I've been around the base several times."

"Should we try to climb down this way?" Sadie asked.

Heath shrugged. "This looks to be easily used for a long way down. And I've got enough spikes left that if we run into trouble, I can use them to help us climb down the rest of the way. Or we'll climb to the top again and go down the way we came up."

"But that man who shot at us was gone fast, because Justin went after him right away. I think we're going to find we can get down the mesa without much fuss." Sadie smiled, and it must have been a crazy smile.

Heath asked, "What's so funny?"

"We've come up the hard way and now we're going down the easy way. I'm imagining what Justin's going to say when we tell him there are now two trails to the top of Skull Mesa, and he never figured out either one of them."

Heath chuckled, then turned and stood, reaching his hand out to help her up. "Come away from the edge. I want to look around for a while before we follow this trail. See what else the old ones who left these houses behind can tell me."

Then all trace of amusement was gone. "And see what I can learn from the tracks of the man who has been watching over Boden land—plotting your father's death, and plotting your and your brothers' deaths, too."

20

They walked to the far side of the mesa and stared down at the ranch yard.

"It's a perfect place to keep watch over our family." Sadie quit talking for a moment. "If that man had wanted to shoot us the other night, we'd be dead."

"Not true. It wasn't our time, and we prove that by standing here fully alive." Then Heath's voice dropped. "It's beautiful, isn't it?"

"Yes, the ranch house is elegant and large without being huge. The bunkhouse and the houses of John and Alonzo are neat and strongly built, with some time given to make them attractive buildings too, even though they're all the same shade of adobe."

Sadie paused, then added, "They're in such a neat row along the southwest side of the yard, but from down there, I didn't realize what a strong defense they are, almost like fortress walls. With the barn beside them, that whole side of the ranch could be defended against an attack. And the hill rising up behind the bunkhouse is another wall. The woodlands and river protect us on the north. The west is open on past this mesa, but the mesa itself takes a big swath out of the possible ways anyone could approach the ranch. My grandfather chose this spot and laid out those buildings, and they've been there my whole life. But I didn't realize until now how wise he was, how much thought he put into this place."

Turning to Heath, she asked, "Is this part of what Pa meant by our legacy? Did he see how thoughtless I was about Grandfather's wisdom?"

Heath just smiled at her. "You don't think like a warrior, Sadie. I doubt your pa was overly upset by that."

They gazed down at the pretty sight for a bit longer, yet Heath didn't want to spend a long time on the mesa top. Justin and Cole would be champing at the bit to find out what was up here.

He trusted them to stay in place, but they'd be mighty grumpy.

Taking back a few bits of proof wasn't a bad idea, so Heath picked up a mostly burned cigarette. A few of the hired men smoked them, but not everyone.

He lingered over a boot print. He was a good tracker, and he'd recognize this boot if he saw it again.

Someone came up here often. There was nothing to make him think anyone lived here or even spent the night. But someone came up here, and had many times. Someone who wanted to keep an eye on the comings and goings at the Boden ranch.

It was hard not to suspect that one of the cowpokes was involved. Heath wasn't sure whoever watched from up here worked for the Bodens, but they had to be talking to one of the hands.

The attack on Chance had been too well-timed.

They set the ambush with the rockslide in place days ahead. They had to. It took time to arrange something like that. They had to be ready before they tore down that fence and herded the small group of cattle into that unwelcoming canyon.

Once the cattle went missing, Chance might've gone after them at any time. When he did mention his plans, someone got the word out. Two men were in place when Chance went in, and it was too farfetched to believe two men were ready to strike all day every day. There had to be someone giving them information.

"You really think one of the men who works for Pa betrayed him?" Sadie stood, watching the ranch yard, as if she could stare hard enough to see the betrayal in a man's heart.

Heath didn't respond. He saw no reason to drive the point home. She knew what he'd say. Betrayal hurt. Heath had learned that at a young age from his own father.

"Let's go on down." He picked up the pack he'd carried and turned to Sadie. Her hurt was painful to see. He couldn't resist offering her some kind of comfort, so he walked to her side and took her hand. "C'mon. We've seen all there is to see. Now let's find our way down the mesa the same way the varmint who shot at us went."

They got to the edge, where Heath tied them together again, then took his first step onto the trail.

It was sharply sloped at first, but soon he could see that someone had cut this path into stair steps nearly as steep as a ladder. It was so old, the steps had worn down to nearly nothing. They worked just fine, however.

They angled into the heart of the mesa. Heath walked on as the gap they were in narrowed into a near chimney until he could reach out his right arm and brush the wall. He wondered just where they would end up. As the space tightened, he found it hard to breathe, like what happened occasionally in the cavern back home. He kept descending, and the narrow cut rounded the gap and went on down like a spiral staircase.

Despite the choking tightness, it was easy to keep his balance with the walls so near. If a man climbed this way a few times, he'd get fast at it. It wouldn't have been hard for that gunman to get to the base of Skull Mesa, grab his horse, and gallop away. But how had Heath missed the bottom of this? How had Justin never seen these obviously ancient steps?

The moment never came when Heath had to resort to climbing. He had gotten used to the steep stairs and was making good time. The stairs emerged into the sunlight as they left the tight gap in the mesa walls. Soon a cliff yawed beneath his feet.

"Whoa." Heath skidded to a stop on the gravel-strewn ladder. His next step was onto nothing. A drop of at least fifty feet straight down to a pile of jagged stones.

Rocks cascaded over the edge and bounced against the wall as they fell.

Sadie bumped into him, and for a few seconds he teetered on the brink of eternity. His arms waved wildly as he fought for purchase.

Life and death warred over him. A gust of wind would be enough to knock him either way.

A rock slipped under his foot, and he lurched forward, falling.

He was yanked back.

Something held him on this side of the Pearly Gates.

Sadie.

Her delicate hands had the strength to hang on. His balance restored, he took two quick steps back, crowding her up behind him. It took a minute, but finally he could breathe again. He hadn't had time until now to be terrified of what had almost happened. If he'd fallen, with the rope tied between them, he'd have dragged her to her death, as well.

He thought of Sadie's words earlier, that they could have died under a man's gun, and he'd brushed it aside. It was not their time. Right now it was taking him a while to find that calm.

"I'm so sorry." She leaned forward and spoke over his shoulder.

A glance back showed worry etched in her brow. Her eyes darkened with sincere regret. Heath would have kissed her if he wasn't afraid of falling off the cliff.

"It cut away so suddenly." He couldn't let her take the blame for their near accident. "I've just been walking along, enjoying the easy way down. Honestly I was daydreaming, thinking of how jealous Justin and Cole were going to be. My carelessness nearly got us both killed."

He turned around carefully. "I'm the one who's sorry. And you saved me, Sadie. Thank you."

And then, dangerous trail or not, she was a step above him, and he looked her right in the eye, then pulled her into his arms and kissed her. It felt so shockingly good. A celebration of survival, the good spirits of being fully alive. He was so deeply moved by the perfection of that kiss, it was a wonder he didn't go tumbling head over heels.

Except he did.

In a distant, reasonable part of his mind, he knew a man didn't fall in love with a woman because she saved his life. That was just foolish.

But something roared to life in him. Something big and wild and reckless that made anything he'd felt for her before—and he'd felt plenty—a pale ghost compared to now.

The kiss broke off when Sadie jerked her head to the side. He'd given her no choice. He'd grabbed her and swooped down on her like a predator.

Now was when she slapped him. Or told him to keep his filthy hands off her. Or sent him down the road with a warning never to come near her or her ranch again.

And why not? He hadn't been fired for a while now.

"Heath Kincaid, this is no time for kissing. I swear you pick times deliberately when we have to stop and get right back to work. A curious woman would wonder if you even really have any honorable interest in me. And if you do, why don't you call on me as is proper and ask me to come out riding with you?"

Which didn't sound like a woman ordering him out of her life at all.

"Sadie, will you come out for a ride with me the very first chance we get?" He found that inner wild man that reminded him of his big brother Seth. "And where hopefully no one will shoot at us?"

Her smile was bright enough to shame the sunlight.

"And when neither of your big brothers is around to watch me like a hawk."

"Uh, Heath." Her smile shrank away.

"Nor John Hightree, who seems to be acting for your pa."

"Heath, we'd better—"

"Nor Rosita, who has the chaperone instincts of a convent full of pistol-packing nuns."

"Justin is watching us right now." She near shouted to get him to shut up.

"He is?"

"Yep, with a spyglass."

Heath turned, and sure enough, there he was—right where Heath had told Justin to position himself to watch for anyone approaching the mesa from the west. "We're not so far away that I can be mistaken about him loading his rifle."

"Nope, maybe we need to figure out how to get to the ground. You might need to run."

"I'm not running away from your big brothers." Heath noticed he'd thrown Cole in. Just because he was staked out on the other side of the mesa didn't mean he wouldn't hear about this. Justin would make sure of it.

Sadie grinned. "I'm glad." Then she arched her brows. "And don't worry, I can save you from both of them."

"I sure hope so."

"John and Rosita will be a bit more trouble."

Heath figured he could handle both of them and the Boden brothers, too. "I'm hoping Justin's heart isn't in shooting me."

"Knowing you got to the top of the mesa and he never did will be almost as much of a goad as witnessing our kiss."

"I'll kind of enjoy teasing him about the climb." Heath quit thinking about Justin then, since he couldn't do a thing about him right now. "And I enjoyed that kiss enough to stare down anyone who says they disapprove, so long as it's not you."

Patting him on the arm, she said, "I very much approve, Heath."

He liked the sound of that. "Let's see if we can figure out how to get the rest of the way down. Then if Justin does decide to start shooting, I can at least not fall to my death on top of being loaded with flying lead."

❧

"This next ledge is almost a sideways cut in the rocks. It isn't even visible from a few feet down or up." Heath was leading them at a snail's pace down the mesa. He called up, "But once I found it, it worked fine. Do you see where it is?"

"I see it. It's no wonder the man who shot at us got down fast."

Heath was about thirty feet from the base when he said, "That's the last place I can find. There's no way down from here; it's as sheer as ice. We're still above the height that will kill us."

"Especially if we land on that talus slide." Sadie was letting him go first, then following when he had a firm place for his hands and feet. She reached his side and looked at him.

"I can lower you down with the rope, and I'll use the spikes to get myself down."

Sadie studied the ledge from where her hands clung to the slot her toes were in. "That will work, but it doesn't explain how fast the man traveled."

"If he had a rope fastened, he could rush right down."

"But then the rope would be hanging there for all the world to see." Peering down, Sadie added, "And he can't possibly jump. Those rocks look mighty jagged, and besides, how does he get up?"

"It's going to have to be the spikes, I reckon." Heath reached for his pack.

"Wait a minute." Sadie ran her hands along the ledge at her feet. "There's something here. It feels like one of your spikes, only it's curved at the end."

Heath crouched and reached past her, brushing her ankle, which made her blush. "It's a hook, hammered into stone just like our spikes."

Heath pulled the rope off his neck and snagged the noose end. "We can just climb right down. I think I'll be able to swing the rope and have it come unhooked." With a frown, he said, "Can our man be a good enough roper that he can toss a loop on this thing from thirty feet down?"

"Either he can or we'll soon figure out what else he does. Let's go. We're still ahead of Justin."

"I'm pretty sure he's setting a pace deliberately to get here the same time we reach the ground," Heath said. "I'd better untie us."

Rather than battle the rope, which was always tough to undo after long stretches climbing, Heath pulled out his knife and, with a quick slash, severed the rope from around his waist. He hooked the longer rope to the hook and said, "You want to go first?"

"Nope, you need the head start."

He grinned as he slid down the rope so fast that she was

purely impressed. She swung herself over the edge and did her best to copy him without falling all the way down.

"Come on down as far as you can," he called. "I'll get to the ground and be ready to catch you."

Sadie didn't bother to mention seeing Justin come riding out of the pass. Her brother had gotten down and found his horse in record time. There was a good chance she wasn't going to get to jump into Heath's arms, and that was just the worst kind of dirty shame.

Heath went on and landed on his feet as nimbly as a cat. He was on the talus slide, and rather than turn and pick his way to safety, he looked up, staying to help her down.

Heath looked behind him. Justin was close enough now that he heard him coming. There was no time to try to save himself now, so Heath, with shocking recklessness, shouted up to her, "Slide down. I'll catch you."

Sadie did as she was told, but when a solid grip landed on her waist, she knew it wasn't Heath who had her.

"Let go. I've got you." Justin had arrived.

Sadie sure hoped he hadn't ridden his horse right over the man she fully intended to marry.

Justin carried her off the rocks, which was just foolish because she could have walked off without a bit of trouble. Then he tossed her up onto his saddle. "Kincaid, get the horses. I'll give Sadie a ride back to the house."

Sadie looked over her shoulder in time to see Heath smirk.

"Before you ride out, take a look at this wall." Heath caught the rope they'd slid down and, with a couple of tries, flipped the rope right off the wall. It dropped, and he coiled it and stared upward. "This wall looks sheer all the way up, but about fifty feet up it folds in on itself. The way the rocks caved in here filled in the bottom of that fold so solid that . . ." Heath shook his head. "I don't quite understand why we can't see it, but it's there."

Justin studied it for a long time. "I can't see it. I see the slide here, but it's not filled in up higher. Looks solid to me."

"Almost like it used to be open and it got slammed closed by the hands of God," Heath said quietly.

They were silent a moment, then Justin said, "Come on in so we can talk it all through before I fire you."

He was talking to her, not Justin, when he arched his brows and said, "I'll be right along."

Justin spurred his horse without giving Heath a second glance.

Once they were out of Heath's earshot, Justin said, "He's nothing but a penniless cowpoke, Sadie. I like him, but he ain't near good enough for you."

Justin was a tough man. He wore civilization very lightly. He was too quick to swing a fist and was wickedly fast with his six-gun, though he'd never had much call to aim it at men.

Long hours of brutally hard work breaking wild mustangs and wrangling thousand-pound longhorns had turned his muscles to corded steel. There wasn't much Justin could lay his back to that didn't give way. There weren't many men Justin could face who didn't back down.

It all came down to Justin being a dangerous man.

Even knowing all that, it was also a fact that he was her big brother. Which made her feel perfectly safe when she swatted him in the back of the head.

His hat nearly flew off, but he caught it and clamped it back on his head. He didn't look overly upset with her. Nor did he apologize for his words about Heath.

"It looks very much like one of the men you and Pa hired at the CR is part of a plot to kill all of us," Sadie told him.

Justin slowed his horse as he turned to focus on her instead of his plans, which, she suspected, were all about how to make Heath sorry he was ever born. He asked with keen interest,

"What makes you say that, especially when I was talking about Heath?"

Sadie leaned closer and looked her brother in the eye. "I just want you to realize that makes you a poor judge of men, so I'm not likely to listen to a word you say."

21

Heath wasn't apt to listen to a word Justin had to say.

Not when there was a killer loose.

To Heath's way of thinking, there wasn't anything more important than what he was feeling for Sadie, but they all needed to stay alive before he could court her. So while it was less important, catching the would-be killer had to come first.

He walked into Chance's office in time to see Cole narrow his eyes, then swing around to glare at Heath.

Justin was nothing but a tale-bearing vermin. It didn't worry Heath, though, because he had the perfect distraction.

"We can climb to the top of Skull Mesa anytime we want. I'd judge it to take about a half hour to hike up, a lot less to come back down. We can start having Sunday afternoon picnics up there if you're so inclined."

Cole and Justin looked to be circling to attack, but that stopped them in their tracks.

"You really found a way up there that easy?" Justin drew near, not a clenched fist in sight. "I saw you get up, but I only spotted you coming down when you got to the part where you had to climb."

"That mesa is high enough, I couldn't see a thing from where I was standing." Cole had the biggest area to watch, the stretch leading from the ranch house to the mesa. Justin was in charge of the west side, not visible from where Cole had stood sentry.

"But then you came up to the edge and disappeared. I thought you'd sat down to have lunch or take a rest. Then all of a sudden you showed up right near the bottom."

"You know how rough the edges of the mesa are," Heath said. "They're mostly sheer walls, straight up and down, but it's not a smooth, round circle."

Justin didn't interrupt, which Heath took as a good sign.

"From up on top, there's a cut that curves back toward the heart of the mesa, then twists around and comes on down. It's a steep slope, but we found a way to walk it. No climbing necessary."

"And then it ends abruptly," Sadie said.

Heath barely controlled a shudder as he remembered just how abruptly. "I figure a man standing on horseback could grab hold and pull himself up to where he can just walk right up the mesa. He wouldn't need any kind of climbing equipment except a rope. We can go back up right now if you want. Plenty of time before sunset."

"I do want to go up. Sadie told me you found plenty of signs up there—a man there recently and what looks like an old village of some kind."

"A village?" Cole blinked. "No one mentioned a village to me."

Yep, Justin had been too busy talking about Heath not being good enough for their little sister. Which was nothing but the plain truth.

"I think that place the trail dropped off must have caved in at some point." Heath could imagine it happening. Rocks tumbled and changed shape all the time. "Maybe a hundred years ago, a thousand or more folks could just walk straight up the side of the mesa. But it's impossible to see from the ground unless you know it's there."

"So how did someone figure it out?" Sadie asked.

"A question I'd really like an answer to." Heath was new to these parts. "You've never heard tales of such a thing? Old myths? Indian legends?"

The Bodens exchanged a glance.

"There are Pueblo folks who live on top of a mesa near here. But all I've ever heard about this place," Justin said, "is that it's unclimbable. That's the myth that has held all these years."

"Well, someone climbed it and did it easily enough to live up there. I'm not talking about our outlaw; I'm talking about whoever had a village up there. There are old huts made of adobe. They're crumbled until only mounds of rubble are left, and brush has grown up through them. If the mounds weren't so unnatural to the mostly smooth mesa top, I doubt we'd have recognized what they are. It didn't have the look of the Mexican builders around here, nor what I know of the local Indians. Whoever lived there were ancient people."

Heath thought of a few old ruins he'd seen in other places. There was a dark canyon in Utah and eerie, abandoned cliff dwellings he'd ridden through called Mesa Verde that had given him chills. No one knew who'd built them. No one knew where those folks had vanished to.

"I think those ruins may be a remnant of some long-dead-and-gone people. And I think they used to walk right up the side of that mesa. Can you imagine such a fortress? They would be invincible. They'd need only to watch over one narrow trail to protect the whole village." Heath fell silent for a moment as he thought of those ancient people, cut off from their home. Much like he'd been cut off from his, except that was by his own choice. "But the trail caved in. The village was abandoned."

Maybe they could have gone on living there, but it was no longer easy. In fact, having a stretch of that trail gone might have scared them. What if the rest of the trail collapsed? Heath didn't worry about such things, because he had his pack with the spikes in it. He could get down if he needed to. But those folks could be trapped up there with no way down. They'd starve to death, one by one, in their fortress.

"But somehow, someone knew." Sadie interrupted his somber thoughts.

That brought him back to the present with a dull thud. "Yes, someone knew the way up. And how is that possible if the only ones who knew are dead and gone?"

"Maybe they're not as dead and gone as we think." Cole's brain was working. That always worried Heath a little. The man was smart, but he didn't think like a western man.

"Rosita, come in here," Cole shouted.

"And just what in the world do you think Rosita can tell you about this?" Sadie asked.

Cole crossed his arms and gave his little sister a sharp look. "Maybe she can't tell me a thing. On the other hand, maybe she can tell me who goes back in these parts a long way. Maybe she knows the ones who tell ancient stories. Twisted-up tales we've never heard before."

Rosita came in, looking worried. As her eyes slid to each one of the Bodens, she seemed to relax. Heath saw how much she loved these three. When she heard one of them shout her name, her first thoughts were of their well-being. Now that she was assured that they were all right, she could calmly handle whatever trouble they faced.

"What is it?"

Sadie moved to Rosita's side. "We need someone who knows the old stories of this area."

"You know I'm Mexican?"

Sadie nodded.

"Well, I have no Pueblo blood in my veins, and those are the folks who have had legends passed down from their distant past."

"But do you know anyone who is Pueblo?"

Rosita had spent her life with the Bodens. Her mother, Consuelo, had been the housekeeper before her. Rosita had married young to a Mexican who'd worked as a hand for the ranch. When he died, Rosita had dedicated her life to the Bodens and had never been connected to an Indian tribe.

"My sister wasn't in the tribe, but her husband's family is Pueblo. Let me talk to her and see who she might know."

"Right now, today." Justin started across the room for the door. "I'll ride in with you."

"No, we can't set out so late. It's a far distance, and if Delfina can find one from her tribe to speak with us, they would not want to do it late in the day. If we set out early tomorrow, our chances of success are greater."

Justin looked like it was rubbing him raw to accept the wait, but he nodded regardless. "We'll go in the morning, then."

"We will need to bring food along. I must prepare." Rosita turned and left the room.

Justin took two steps to reach the door, then stopped so suddenly he nearly skidded.

Cole almost plowed into him.

Instead of moving on, Justin closed the door, turned, and looked at Cole. Then his eyes shifted to Heath. "Before we go, we need to ask you some questions, Kincaid."

"About what?" As if Heath didn't know.

"Just fire him and get it over with," Cole said, crossing his arms. "We've got an outlaw to track down."

Justin matched Cole's stance. The two argued over one thing or another constantly. It was Heath's bad luck that they'd finally found something they could agree on.

Keeping him away from their sister.

Sadie came up beside Heath and took his elbow as if nothing could keep her away from him. "Whatever you're doing, just stop." She stepped forward without letting go of Heath's arm, looking ready to throw herself between Heath and her brothers if necessary.

That made him feel a little low-down, because the man was supposed to stand between a woman and trouble, not the other way around.

But these were her brothers. She could probably handle them better than he could. At least with less punching involved.

Sadie began with Justin. "You told Cole what you saw, Justin, but you couldn't have heard Heath's very proper and respectful request that we begin courting each other. He has done nothing I didn't agree to, and his attentions are welcome."

Hearing her say that made Heath want to drag her out of this room and find somewhere private enough that she could welcome more of his attentions.

"And Justin, I can't believe you would tell Heath he shouldn't spend time with me. He is an honest man, a hard worker, a faithful churchgoer, and he has the courageous heart of a lion.

"Now, if you two are going to stand here and tell me I can't see such a fine man, then I am going to write to Ma and ask her permission. You will recall she was the daughter of a wealthy, powerful landowner who married a cowhand with no ranch and nothing to his name. That would be our pa."

Justin narrowed his eyes. "We know our ma is married to our pa, Sadie."

She sniffed at his interruption. "I suspect Ma will think your opinion is an insult to her and Pa. I think she might very well feel as if every word you speak is a slap in the face."

"She will not," Cole said.

"You know Pa likes Heath. You've seen Heath's loyalty to us. I am not going to put up with any insults to him."

Heath decided he wasn't the one in this room with the courageous heart of a lion.

"I'm not really a penniless drifter, either," Heath said. "I've saved some money, and besides that, I'm part owner of a ranch—"

"We don't want to hear your list of assets, Kincaid," Cole said, cutting him off.

Heath wasn't real sure what an *asset* was, but it sounded like a word Cole hadn't oughta be saying in front of a lady. He'd mention it later when Sadie wasn't right here. "I have asked Sadie to come for a ride or take a walk with me. If you're uncomfortable with that, one of you can come along as a chaperone."

"No, they can't." Sadie glared at Heath.

"Well, I don't want them to come any more than you do, but I thought maybe they'd simmer down if I offered." He looked at the flash of temper in Sadie's eyes and knew how a moth felt when it flew straight into a flame. It was all he could do not to pay her some attention right here and now. "I'd like to speak to Sadie in private for just a few minutes."

"No!" Justin and Cole answered at the same instant.

Heath gave a shrug of one shoulder. It hadn't hurt to ask, but he wasn't real surprised at the response. Still, tormenting the Boden brothers was its own reward.

"Yes, Heath." Sadie smiled up at him as sweet as wild mountain honey. "I'd like a moment, too."

Heath thought of all he could say to goad the two Boden brothers, but he had a moment of maturity, which he probably ought to stretch to more than a moment.

He looked from Cole to Justin. "I know you're trying to

protect your sister from a low-down cowpoke, and I don't blame you at all."

"You are *not* low-down," Sadie gasped out.

Cole looked him straight in the eye. "Heath, it's not that you're low-down, and, well, you're a fine hand and a knowing man and you've helped this family through a hard time. But it's hard for me to believe anyone's good enough for my sister."

"Maybe you're right and I'm not good enough for her. In fact, I should probably move on and leave her to find a worthy man."

Sadie's hand tightened on his arm until he felt her fingernails sinking into him.

"I'm just saying," Cole continued, "I don't know how to go on. If Ma and Pa were here, they'd be in charge of such things. I feel we need to leave this for them. To let you come in here and steal our sister's affections . . . ouch!"

Heath saw Sadie's pointy-toed little boot come back from kicking Cole. She'd aimed high, too. He wore tough leather boots, but she'd gotten him in the knee.

Cole looked to Justin. "Well, you say something then."

"I say let's get to bed. We've got a long day ahead of us."

And that was the most sensible thing any of them had said in a long while.

Heath headed out before he said something that made Sadie kick him as well, like he wasn't good enough for her, and the idea of marriage to her chafed because of her father's foolish wishes that kept her tied to the ranch. And it was hard on a man's pride to come to a rich woman and become wealthy through her.

His cot in the bunkhouse was where he belonged.

22

Rosita packed saddlebags with food while the rest of them made short work of their breakfast.

John knocked on the door, then pushed it open. "The horses are ready."

"Let's ride." Justin grabbed his saddlebag, and the others took theirs and followed him out the door. Justin spoke quickly with John as he mounted up. Someone had to run this place.

As they left the ranch yard, Heath and Sadie side by side, he looked at her and smiled. "We're going for a ride, Sadie girl."

She rolled her eyes. "This isn't exactly what I had in mind."

Heath patted her hand holding the reins. "We'll take another one that's less crowded. I promise."

They were soon moving at a fast pace. Cole reined in his horse so he could drop back to be beside Sadie, then Justin did the same. "Bring up the rear, Kincaid, and watch our back trail."

Heath fell in line behind the Bodens, who now rode three abreast. He saw Sadie try to drop back, but Justin caught her reins and kept her with them. Cole said something Heath couldn't hear. Sadie swatted his arm but quit trying to escape.

Rosita took the lead.

They rode straight through Skull Gulch. Rosita's sister lived by a mesa a far distance to the south called Meseta Blanca.

A few hours later, they finally reached her sister's house.

"Wait outside." Rosita gave the orders just like she owned a huge ranch and all of them worked for her.

Not a one of them disobeyed.

∽✵∼

Delfina came to the door to greet Rosita. She wore a dress with only one shoulder, a long-sleeved shirt under it. She had on leather leggings, held with strips of soft doeskin leather. This was the traditional dress for the Pueblo people, while Rosita wore clothes similar to the Bodens with a few accents from her Mexican heritage. Sadie noticed they wore similar beaded necklaces.

Delfina waved at Sadie, then the men. Rosita spoke quickly in Spanish as she dismounted. Delfina took Rosita's place and rode away.

Rosita said, "Delfina is going to Meseta Blanca. We are to wait here."

Sadie turned in her saddle to watch Delfina ride straight for the almost-vertical wall of the mesa. It seemed to loom over their heads, though it was a mile away at least.

When at last Delfina reached it, she dismounted and tied the horse, and then seemed to walk straight up the rock wall.

"How's she doing that?" Heath urged his horse toward the mesa.

"There is a stairway carved in stone," Rosita answered. "I come and stay with Delfina every weekend, and yet I've only been allowed up that mesa three times in my life. They're very private here."

"Can we go look?" Sadie wanted to see it. Was it how Skull Mesa had been before some part of it caved away? "I don't want to violate some custom and offend the people who live here."

"So long as you don't climb the steps, you will be fine," Rosita said.

Heath started first, his eyes riveted on the mesa. Sadie trotted forward and heard the others coming. They then heard some talk behind them, and suddenly Cole caught up to them on foot and swung up behind Sadie.

He leaned forward and smiled down at Sadie. "I gave Rosita my horse."

Mr. Helpful.

At least he let her ride beside Heath.

"So this is Meseta Blanca." Sadie recognized the name of a village she'd never been near. Pa didn't encourage her riding out into wild country.

Rosita caught up to them, riding Cole's feisty black stallion with complete confidence. "The village of Meseta Blanca is on a mesa many times the size of Skull Mesa. The people of this village aren't known for welcoming outsiders. Delfina will bring an elder down—if she can find one willing to speak to us."

"If there's a village up there," Heath said, "then it's not unusual that they would build on Skull Mesa, too."

Sadie felt her excitement rise. Somehow the top of Skull Mesa had become a mystery that needed solving. If the elders of the Pueblo village knew of the history, maybe they could find out who they'd told.

If they learned who knew, it was a giant step toward finding out who wanted to kill pa and who'd shot at them from the mesa top.

"Delfina said the wise one is very old and tires easily, but he was the trader for the village for years and speaks English well. If he comes, he will come quickly."

They reached the edge of the mesa and staked the horses out to graze as they looked at a stairway so steep it was more ladder than stairs. Steeper than the one on Skull Mesa, but close enough that Sadie knew the same people had built them both.

Meseta Blanca was an ancient village. Though the Pueblo Indians had a warlike past, in recent years—for as long as Sadie could remember—they'd become friendlier people. They weren't nomadic like so many tribes. They built their homes of stone and grew crops. Sadie could see many houses scattered around the base of the mesa. There were cattle and horses, crops growing, and signs of a successful hunt with hides hanging to dry. Quiet people working around the adobe structures that had been built down here.

Sadie looked at the buildings and tried to imagine the ruins at the top of Skull Mesa as being from the ancestors of the Pueblo. Any resemblance was too vague for her to be sure of anything.

She would have loved to climb these stairs and see the village, but instead she waited there on the eastern slopes of the Sangre de Cristo Mountains, along the banks of the Cimarron River.

Water for the Pueblo village must have to be hauled up from the Cimarron to the mesa top. There couldn't be a water source up there, could there? How much work was that? Or did the people come down to get water to cook and drink and bathe with, then climb back up? Whichever they did, the amount of work was staggering.

"Why do they live up there?" Sadie asked.

"Because it's safe," Rosita said. "Their village is impregnable. And with lookouts posted, all the villagers who live down here can be up these stairs in minutes. One man at the top of the stairway can hold off a thousand attackers."

"But they can't get horses up there, so that leaves them vulnerable to thieves."

"No horse or cow can go up, but the Pueblo, armed with arrows, can drive off thieves while never being in danger themselves. It's such a stronghold that defeat is assured, so no one even bothers to attack."

She wanted to ask more questions, a hundred more questions. That was when it struck her that her life had been very narrow. Here this fascinating settlement was so near her home, yet she'd never come here. Pa had discouraged her from leaving the ranch or doing any travel. Now she was almost feverish to climb this ladder, compare this village to the one they'd found on Skull Mesa. And there were other wonders to see. Heath had spoken of a few, but there were more. The Grand Canyon wasn't that far away. There was a train now that went all the way to the ocean. For heaven's sake, her parents had made it to Denver in a single day.

This mesa made her want to see more of the world. Heath had traveled far and wide. She wondered, if he was serious in his courtship, if it led to marriage, would he travel some with her? He seemed mostly determined to return to his own home. And it didn't matter because he'd have to stay here, at least until Pa was satisfied in whatever feverish part of his brain wanted all his children under one roof.

She looked at Heath, who finally tore his eyes away from the steps that seemed to fascinate him as much as they did her. Their gazes locked.

"Are you thinking of the stairway we saw at Skull Mesa?" She had to say something for fear she'd ask him to take her with him when he left, but not go home to his ranch. Ask him to show her the world.

"I am." Heath looked past her to her brothers. "Can you imagine the work it took to carve this ladder out of stone? And what's up there? The buildings on top of Skull Mesa were so crumbled I couldn't get an idea of what they'd once looked like.

I would surely love to go up there and see Meseta Blanca and try to lay that image over the top of the ruins I saw."

Sadie turned to see that spark of curiosity in her brothers' eyes.

"It is impossible." Rosita slashed a hand in the air. Much like when she'd ordered them to ride, they accepted her words as truth.

"You've been up there three times, you said?" Sadie didn't want to give up on whatever she could learn.

"Yes. Their way of building would seem strange to you, but it is their way. The houses are immense, several stories high, with flat roofs. Many families share one dwelling, and there are ladders to climb to reach the upper levels of each."

"Ladders outside? Why didn't they build stairways inside?"

"They didn't because they didn't." Rosita gave Sadie a look that said the question was a waste of time. "There is a good-sized church, and when I was there last, a Catholic priest lived with several other mission folks. This mesa is huge. There is some very sparse farmland up there, but down here they irrigate using the Cimarron."

Sadie tried to imagine it. She had more questions and opened her mouth to ask them.

"Here comes Delfina. And the wise one is with her. Good. I hope he can answer our questions. It's easy to imagine they might know something of that place and have told no one or told very few."

Sadie felt her heart speed up. Maybe instead of more questions, they'd finally get some answers.

The man came first. He hurried down the ladder with agility that belied any great age. He wore leather pants. Sadie had seen the Pueblo men in breechcloths and moccasins a few times. They came to town dressed so, and Sadie had quickly averted her eyes.

To her relief, it looked like in the cooler winter weather the Pueblo men dressed to stay warm.

The man came so swiftly, he left Delfina behind. He leapt the last few feet and landed with catlike grace beside them, kicking up a small puff of dust.

His black hair, streaked heavily with gray, was bound up at the back of his head in some sort of twist. Deep lines were etched in his skin. He was spry, but he was definitely an old man. With unwelcoming black eyes, he studied them. Sadie could see that although he'd agree to meet with them, he was a long way from cooperating.

Justin took a step forward. He spoke a few words Sadie didn't know. Pa had known many native folks. Pueblo mainly, but also Apache and Navajo. He spoke a little of their languages. It appeared that Justin had picked some of it up, too.

After a few words between them, Justin said, "This is Tesuque."

The man's name sounded like *Tee-SOO-kee*.

Justin said their names for the elder. If Tesuque was interested, he didn't show it. Sadie held her breath. Would he deny them a chance to ask any questions? Would he go right back to his mountaintop home? Would he be able to speak English well enough to understand what they wanted?

"Let us go to Delfina's house," the man said.

Delfina reached the ground just as Tesuque spoke.

"My daughter-in-law has promised me her special cake if I speak to you." Tesuque smiled at Delfina with genuine affection. "And Rosita always brings real coffee from town."

Rosita took one of the elder's arms while Delfina took the other. They walked together toward Delfina's house across the rocky ground. The rest of them dismounted and walked a few paces behind.

23

Tesuque ate his cake and drank his coffee with relish. After-ward, he slid low in his chair, a contented man. Delfina added a log to the crackling fire while Rosita rushed to refill his cup.

"Delfina has told me of your questions," Tesuque began. "About the village atop el Caletre Meseta."

"El Caletre Meseta?" Sadie repeated. Then she nearly bit her tongue. It was probably a terrible rudeness to interrupt an elder.

Tesuque smiled with no visible annoyance. "That is the Pueblo name for what you call Skull Mesa. It's a Spanish word, but it means more clearly what your mesa was originally called. It means . . ." Tesuque paused a moment, then his expression eased. "It is like stubborn, only not quite. More like a man who will not give up. A man with . . . with gumption, I suppose you would say. It is said that the folks who lived on el Caletre had to be determined to stay there. It was not an easy place to be."

Sadie nodded, deciding not to interrupt again.

"It's an ancient legend, handed down by the old ones who lived on the mesa. They had a hidden way into the heart of the mountain."

Sadie almost smiled. Tesuque, and no doubt all his people too, had always known a stairway existed. And yet because they'd cut themselves off, those who lived around the area, like her own family, had never heard the legend.

"The men were hunters, and the women tilled the soil. They would come down from their fortress every day, do their work, then return to el Caletre Meseta to sleep. A single man standing guard could fight off an army. Our home here at Meseta Blanca is the same."

Tesuque took a sip of his coffee, then drew a deep breath. "And then one day the Evil Below the Earth shook the world until it split apart. The hand of the Evil One reached up and dragged the stairs into the belly of the earth as if they'd never been. It came during the day, so many were off the mesa top, but the villagers who were trapped on high faced death as their food and water dwindled. They called out to the Creator of All Things.

"Their cries were answered. The Creator came as a great wind, swept them up, and carried them in cradling arms to safety. Though they had carved the stairs and could carve more, they believed the stairs collapsing was a warning, and they feared the Creator would not send the wind the next time, and they would be stranded forever. They found other homes, and many of their stories vanished along with them. But this one remains."

Cole said, "There have been earthquakes here, though they are mostly farther south."

"I've felt one before," Justin said.

To Sadie, the story of el Caletre felt like a myth grounded in truth.

"Do all the Pueblo know of this story?" Heath asked. "I'll bet no one who lives around el Caletre has ever heard it. The mesa is said to be impossible to climb."

"The history is known to the Pueblo, but outsiders have

shown little interest in the words of those native to these lands. Many consider our myths to be the fevered dreams that come from peyote and sweat lodges." Tesuque looked at Heath with cool wisdom.

Sadie knew that if the Pueblo people didn't have real proof of there being truth in the story, they probably would have dismissed it by now. She burned with curiosity. What other old stories were there? What else could Tesuque and other Pueblo folks tell them about the land in which they lived? She was determined that once their current troubles were solved, she'd come back to this place. Tesuque might talk with her more. If he wasn't willing to share more stories, possibly Delfina or her husband knew old tales such as these.

As she thought of Delfina, another notion came to her. "If these stories are passed among your people, who outside your village would know of them? Who comes from here but has entered the world outside Meseta Blanca?"

Tesuque shook his head, but not in dismissal. His expression told her he was looking into the past, pondering, sorting through old memories of who had left the Pueblo village and might have taken the story to someone who'd believe.

Into the silence, Delfina said, "I know of one Pueblo woman. She was of low honor and became the kept woman of a Spaniard. She would have known these stories, and perhaps the Spaniard indulged her and listened. Perhaps he even believed."

"Who is it, Delfina?" Justin's blue eyes sparked with intensity.

"Her name is never spoken among our people, but it is all right to speak the name of the man who lured her away from us." Delfina looked at Tesuque, who seemed as interested as anyone. "A village woman was kept for years by the old Don."

Justin said, "Don? You mean Don Bautista de Val? Frank Chastain's partner in the CR?"

They all straightened. Suddenly it made sense.

"And his son was the man who some believe killed your grandfather," Heath said.

Rosita nodded. "Ramone. I remember him well. He was the old Don's son, born outside of marriage. We only discovered the relationship after Mr. Chastain was dead and Ramone had disappeared."

"Ramone de Val. He ran away the day my grandfather died and was taken into the protection of his father in Mexico City," Sadie said.

"And his mother was a Pueblo?" Cole asked. "She knew the old stories about Skull Mesa? Why didn't we hear about this when we were searching for Ramone?"

"It was no secret," Rosita said. "I knew it. I just never gave it much thought. What did her native ancestry have to do with killing Mr. Chastain?"

Cole and Justin looked at each other.

"Ramone would be an old man by now," Justin said. "After we were shot at, I rode hard to catch the gunman before he got down the mesa. Rushing down that ladder isn't the work of an old man."

Sadie thought of how fast Tesuque had climbed down and she wasn't so sure. She was itching to get back home, to start the search for Ramone. "Could the man who shot Grandfather have also attacked Pa, and shot at us? Is it possible?"

"I'd know him if I saw him, and I haven't," Rosita said. "And there are old-timers in town who would—at least if we warned them to be looking. We need to spread the word."

Cole strode toward the door.

Justin clamped his Stetson on his head. "Let's go find him."

It looked as though her brothers were going to storm out without a word or a backward glance. Which was just rude.

Sadie moved to stand in front of Tesuque. "We are so grateful for your help. Thank you for sharing your stories with us.

I'd like to hear more sometime, to learn about your people. It's wrong that we live so close and know so little about each other. Would you allow me to come back, or maybe you could come to the CR and share a meal with us sometime? Bring your son and Delfina, too."

Tesuque looked at her with his black eyes as if weighing every word. "I do not leave Meseta Blanca often, but I will think on this. Perhaps I will come."

Sadie smiled. "I appreciate that you would even consider it. Thank you for all your help today." Her inviting Tesuque to share more about the Pueblo would be the first step in learning about life outside her ranch and her small town.

~❧~

They were on the trail at a fast clip. The sun hung low in the sky behind them.

Heath heard Cole ask Justin a question about someone he knew living in Skull Gulch. The two were riding hard and talking at the same time. Rosita led the group, all the while focused on the trail.

They were so intent on getting home, or starting their search for Ramone, or someone who was connected to him, they forgot to keep Heath away from Sadie. So he slowed his horse just a bit, figuring he'd get back to town soon enough. She slowed right along with him.

"Can we count this as going for a ride, Sadie?"

Something glinted in her eyes that hadn't been there before. He didn't think it was about Ramone de Val. "Talking with Tesuque made me realize how cut off I've been. I want to see more of the world. Meseta Blanca isn't even far, but I never knew a thing about it. And what's more, I wasn't even interested. Can you tell me about your travels, Heath?"

Heath hadn't really had it in mind to talk about that, but he did like the gleam in her eyes. She looked at him as if he were a great adventurer. Mostly in his wandering, though, he'd worked. He'd signed up somewhere when his money ran low and worked until he had enough to move on. Or if the work and people were enjoyable, he'd stay around longer. But he was always restless. While he never found a place to put down roots, he hadn't really been looking for that. In fact, he hadn't been looking for anything.

And being with the Bodens had helped him figure out why. It was because he already knew what he wanted.

His brothers.

His family.

His home.

He wished Sadie wanted to hear about his home.

Instead she was breathless about Meseta Blanca. She wanted to see it. She seemed to want to see everything.

She was as good as locked into her ranch house for the next year, and when Heath left, he wanted to go back to Rawhide.

It occurred to him then that a curious woman—and Sadie seemed to be real curious all of a sudden—just might be interested in Julia's Cavern. He had to think about how best to broach that subject. Maybe talk of its wonders? Explain more about how he'd learned to climb rocks?

Maybe he could convince Sadie to want to go there to see the cavern. As they rode along in the dusk, he wished he could hold her hand and speak of the wonders of home and encourage her curiosity in that direction. But he had to say it all just right, and despite the perfect setting of this ride, he hadn't thought it out properly. He needed more time. So he decided to change the subject.

"Sadie, did your grandfather's foreman really search for his killer for the rest of his life?"

"No, not all his life. Sarge was Rosita's father, so he'd return often and stay, sometimes for years. But then he'd hear a rumor about Ramone and off he'd go. He never quit wanting justice. And he was more than Grandfather's foreman. They trapped together in the northern Rockies; he and Grandfather were very successful at it. They hung on to their money, while many trappers didn't.

"Ma said Grandfather was looking for a peaceful land where he wouldn't wind up getting killed by someone. He traveled around searching and made it as far as New Orleans. He met my grandmother there, who shared his French blood. Sarge found a wife too, but she didn't want to leave Louisiana, so my grandparents headed west while Sarge stayed behind.

"Grandfather brought Grandmother to this area even before it was part of the United States. He found Don Bautista de Val here with a modest ranch in the middle of Pueblo, Navajo, and Apache country." Sadie stopped and took a breath, looking as if the story was too long but she wanted to tell it all.

"Go on," Heath said, "I'm listening. We've got a long ride ahead."

With a nod, she continued, "The Don was a powerful man. Arrogant." She glanced at Heath. "I only know stories I've been told, but Ma knew him and talked of him some. She said her parents never let her near him. Grandfather and the Don were unlikely partners. The Don was so arrogant that he'd set the Mexican president against him. But no one could deny all the Don's connections. He had come north expecting to be given a Spanish Land Grant, but it wasn't a sure thing that the grant would be forthcoming.

"Then along came my grandfather and grandmother. Something happened, and Grandfather saved the son of a high-ranking official. The president took a liking to him, but Grandfather was all wrong for a land grant. He wasn't Mexican and he wasn't an influential man, beyond having the president's respect. Ma used to tell stories about him and Sarge. Old fur traders, strong, gruff, and barely civilized sometimes, but still fine men. Somehow Grandfather and the Don teamed up. It was the partnership that earned them the grant. Grandfather with his courage and heroism, the Don with his connections. Grandfather had to become a Mexican citizen; up until then he'd been Canadian and American. Switching again in exchange for a few hundred thousand acres wasn't one bit hard."

"So they got the grant," Heath said.

"Yep," Sadie replied. "And then Sarge's wife died giving birth to their first child. He left the city and found Grandfather and his massive landholding. Sarge became foreman, but soon he was like family. More a partner than a hired hand. Pa always saw it that way, except there was no way to get Sarge a legal stake in the land. He didn't seem to mind. They called it the de Val-Chastain land grant. You've heard how when the Mexicans ceded this land to America, there was trouble and the Don went home in a fury. Well, Grandfather became American and kept half the grant. There was now a New Mexico Territory, and the governor took the other half. And for a while he seemed content with that."

Heath said, "And when he wasn't content any longer, that's when your grandfather met the thoroughly American Chance Boden."

"That's right. Along came Pa, as American as the *Mayflower* and the Boston Tea Party all wrapped up together. He hadn't been here long when Grandfather got shot and was dying. He demanded my pa marry my ma in order to save the ranch. Grandfather refused to tell anyone who'd shot him, though it was clear he knew. We found out about Ramone's connection to the old Don right after the murder."

"He was de Val's son with the Pueblo woman?"

"Yep, and Ramone ran off as Grandfather lay dying. To many, it was as good as a confession. Grandfather didn't want his killer caught and said it would put anyone hunting the man in too much danger. And with the land now in fully American hands, he believed there wouldn't be another attack."

"And now you think Ramone is back?"

"Well, he killed before."

"Maybe, but . . ." Heath said absently.

"You don't believe it?"

Heath shrugged. "You don't know for certain if Ramone killed him. You said your grandfather was having trouble with the governor, didn't you?"

"Yes, but why would Grandfather cover for the governor?"

"To send you after the governor's man would put you in terrible danger. He might have believed he secured the land, then kept his secret to protect your ma. You said all his thoughts were for her and getting her married—that all fits with protecting her."

"So Ramone's ma having knowledge of how to climb Skull Mesa might not mean she's the one who passed on the secret, and Ramone might have nothing to do with this?"

"All I know is if Ramone is *not* the killer, then Sarge spent his life looking in the wrong place. And if the governor—or people working behind his back but using the power of his office—was behind this, well, they never followed up on stealing the land after your grandfather died. Doesn't that prove it isn't about politics? It has to be Ramone."

"But whoever is behind the current trouble has to be linked to the past somehow," Sadie said. "That note proves it. And if so, why now? Why reappear and pick up on trouble left behind thirty years ago?"

"That I just don't know," Heath admitted. "But it might be linked to finding gold on Mount Kebbel. Gold is a mighty good reason to cause trouble."

Heath saw Skull Gulch ahead and figured Cole and Justin were only minutes away from coming to their senses, meaning his ride with Sadie was nearly over and they'd wasted it trying to solve a crime and talking about things that had happened decades ago.

Sadie nodded. "They found gold there, the first strikes anyway, right after the Civil War. Why wouldn't they have acted then?"

"Maybe there was an honorable man in the governor's seat at the time. Maybe new folks became in charge, not so honorable as in the past." Heath hoped all this jawing got to the bottom of who'd attacked them. But he kinda hoped they'd talk about more personal things.

"And maybe they know the stories, or maybe Ramone has been drawn into some kind of conspiracy. And they're using him, hoping he'll end up the scapegoat so that they can get their hands on a fortune in gold."

Cole twisted in his saddle real sudden-like, then reined in his horse so that Heath and Sadie caught up to him fast.

Justin figured it out and was only a couple of paces behind.

"A conspiracy is mighty hard to arrange," Heath said, "especially between a middle-aged man in Mexico City and the political crowd in an American territory. Let's don't make this more complicated than it already is."

The Boden brothers were upon them, and Heath raised his voice for them to hear. "So we get to town and we split up."

The sun had fully set now, but to Heath's way of thinking they still had some time and he didn't want to let another day go by.

"We question the folks in town about Ramone. Maybe we find someone who remembers him or his ma. If she was mixed up with that rich old Don and had a child with him, folks will sure enough remember it."

Cole shifted his eyes between Heath and Sadie as if he'd

like to start yelling, only he didn't see anything to get ahold of and yell about. "Agreed." Cole seemed to give up on yelling in order to focus on crime-solving. "The menfolk can go on alone. Sadie, you can either come with me or wait for us at the orphanage, whichever you want."

Heath saw the turmoil in Sadie. She wanted to hunt, yet she missed the orphanage. She glanced at him, and he thought for a second that maybe she'd come along on the search.

"If it helps you decide, little sister, you're not riding around with Heath. But I'd be glad to take you with me."

Sadie's lips curled into a smirk. "I'll go to Safe Haven, thank you. I've missed the children, and I've no interest in having a babysitter."

Justin snickered.

Cole gave a satisfied nod. "Then let's start. We want to talk to anyone connected to the Pueblo tribe who's heard the story about the mesa. It had to be someone who mixed with them and, considering the tribe's private ways, there couldn't be that many. Don't forget to ask about Ramone's mother."

Rosita had pulled up at the edge of town, and when they reached her, she told them the Pueblo woman's name. She re-membered her well.

"And ask about any Mexican who's over fifty years old, some-one new around here. Maybe we can find Ramone just by learn-ing who's new around these parts."

"That's a whole passel of folks, Cole." Justin sounded doubtful.

Cole admitted that to be the plain truth. They rode off in different directions. Heath glanced back a couple of times, wishing Sadie would defy her brothers and come along with him. Instead she trotted straight for the orphanage and swung down. Every move she made looked like she was eager to get back to work.

Heath realized this was what she'd do when her year of living at home was up. If her pa let her go, she'd go back to working at a job she loved and felt called to. If that annoyed her pa, Chance had probably better stretch his rules out for another year. He could hold ownership of the CR over their heads for the rest of his life.

And if things went on with Sadie as he hoped they would, then Heath was trapped here with her. Yet he wanted to go home and mend things with his brothers. The more he hung around with Justin and Cole, and saw the lengths a good father went to in keeping his family together, the more he wanted to find a way to live and work with his own family.

He saw his part in the troubles. In fact, the fault was almost all his. Yes, his big brothers were bossy, but only a kid would let that bother him. A man needed to take charge of his own life, be confident in his own skills, and take whatever advice he wanted and ignore the rest without letting it bother him overly.

He was finally man enough to do that. Now he wanted to get home and prove it. But he wasn't going anywhere so long as the Bodens were in danger.

24

Sadie walked into the Safe Haven Orphanage and found Angie up and bustling about in the bright lantern light of the kitchen.

"I see you're feeling better." Sadie was relieved. "I'm sorry I haven't been in to check on how you're doing."

Angie took the last stack of dishes off the long tables where the children were served their meals. "I'm much better, yes. I mostly just needed rest and a few good meals." With a warm smile, she set the dishes by a basin of sudsy water.

"You're still as slender as a reed, but don't worry—Sister Margaret will fatten you up. You look happy, too." Sadie grabbed a dish towel and began drying while Angie washed.

"I am."

The youngsters did chores, being very much a part of keeping the place running smoothly, just as children in any family would help out. But the days were long, and by early evening they were worn down. Sister Margaret had set the hour before bedtime as a time of quiet prayer and reading. The older children read to the younger ones after they were all in their nightclothes and ready for bed.

Sister Margaret and Sadie had always helped them prepare for bed, and afterward Sadie did the dishes as Sister Margaret arranged small reading groups, then came in to help finish tidying up. Now Angie was hard at it in Sadie's absence.

"I'm doing the job you used to do." Angie looked sideways, up to her elbows in dishwater, and blushed. "Aunt Margaret speaks so highly of you. I'm hoping I can begin to teach with your skill. I have a lot to learn."

Margaret stepped into the kitchen and said, "You're doing wonderfully, Angie."

Sister Margaret hadn't called her niece Angie the last time Sadie was here. Hopefully that was a sign they were getting on well. She'd been at this job for many years and, due to her age, Margaret desperately needed the help.

Which made Sadie think of something. She was standing right next to a woman who'd lived near Skull Mesa for years. And the ladies who helped her were also longtime residents of the area. "Are Maria and Louisa here tonight?"

The two ladies always cleaned the schoolroom and set everything in order for the next day of school while Margaret and Sadie were busy cleaning up the kitchen.

"Yes, of course," Margaret said. "They should be done with their chores soon. Can you stay long enough to share a cup of tea with us?"

"Oh, yes. I'd love that." Sadie finished wiping the last pan.

Maria and Louisa came in only moments later. Sadie was glad to see them, because she was going to find the two ladies and drag them in here if they hadn't shown up.

They all sat together at one of the tables in the dining area, each holding a steaming cup of fragrant tea.

"I have some questions concerning events around here nearly

thirty years ago. During the time my father first settled in the Skull Gulch area and Grandfather Chastain was killed. Were any of you here then?"

Sadie's heart sped up as she realized that instead of being sent off to behave while the big, strong men solved the crime, she might be the one talking to the best possible people to help them get to the bottom of what happened so long ago.

All three ladies nodded. "I well remember your pa and little Cole," Sister Margaret said. "Such a sweet child."

"Do you remember Don Bautista de Val? He left before my pa came into the country."

"Yes," Margaret answered, "he was a regal man. Not exactly friendly, though he was generous to the orphanage. He helped us financially when we were just getting Safe Haven started. Of course, later he boasted about it to everyone. But I always tried to remember his generosity when he passed me on the street, nose in the air, as if I were unworthy of his notice."

Nodding, Sadie turned to the other ladies. "Do any of you remember a scandal involving a Pueblo woman who was the Don's companion? She had a son, and that son was a suspect in my grandfather's murder."

The ladies glanced nervously at one another.

Sister Margaret swallowed hard. "We know of it, Sadie, but we mustn't lapse into gossip."

"I wouldn't ask except that the child, the Don's son who was born on, let's say, the wrong side of the blanket, may have returned to Skull Gulch."

A gasp escaped from two of the ladies. Angelique leaned forward, clearly caught in the tension.

"Do you think he might have come back to cause more trouble?" Sister Margaret asked, running a hand along the high collar of her faded work dress.

Should she tell the ladies about her climbing Skull Mesa?

Should she mention the accident that hurt her pa wasn't accidental? Or that someone had recently shot at her? These weren't facts widely known.

Before she could decide, Maria straightened and cleared her throat, drawing everyone's attention. As if she had to physically force the words from her mouth, she said, "I know much about this."

"You do?" Sadie watched every nuance of Maria's expression.

"Yes." Maria looked at Sister Margaret and waited.

Margaret nodded. "It's time for the truth, Maria. Be assured that you will always have a home here."

"What?" Sadie was shocked to hear that Maria had a secret so dark, she might fear Safe Haven would be closed to her if it became known by the community, regardless of her years of service. Sadie took a firm grip on herself, resolved to be silent and let Maria speak.

"Thank you, Sister." Maria's eyes lowered. "I know of this because I am . . ." Maria took a shaky sip of tea. "I am Ramone de Val's sister."

Despite her best efforts, Sadie gasped. She quickly clamped her mouth shut.

Maria looked up, then went back to talking into her teacup. "*Mi madre* died shortly after the terrible business with Ramone and Señor Chastain. I was an outcast because of my mother's choices and stayed strictly to my home. The Don was also my father and I had no hope of a decent marriage, and no interest in a life like my mother had lived. When Mama died, I came here to the Safe Haven Orphanage. I was already an adult woman, nearly thirty years old, far too old to be considered an orphan. But to avoid an unsavory life, Sister Margaret took me in and let me be one of the teachers. It would never have been allowed in a regular school. But here, with only orphans, there were no outraged parents to complain. And the need was great."

"What about Ramone?" Sadie couldn't resist asking.

After a long moment of hesitation, Maria said, "Ramone is here. I have seen him."

Sadie clenched her fists. "The man accused of killing my grandfather is nearby?"

Maria looked sharply at her. "My brother is no murderer. He is a man of gentle heart. But recently the Don died, and Ramone is bitterly *furioso* that he was left nothing and cast out. He served Padre long and well and became the next thing to a slave to a father who had a twisted view of love. There were children within the Don's marriage, and they were remembered while Ramone was not. Ramone had been with him all his life, since the day he abandoned Mama and me and followed Padre back to Mexico. I struggled not to be bitter about that. My father left us, and his abandonment included his no longer support-ing us. As if his move back to Mexico City somehow absolved him of his duty. Then Ramone was accused of murder, and he vanished. Shortly afterward, Madre died of a broken heart. So long as the Don was here, his name protected her. And foolish though it was, she cared for him and sacrificed everything to be his woman."

Every last detail of the story was hard for Sadie to believe. She'd never imagined such a thing. All three of these ladies were pillars of faith. For the first time, she wondered about all of them. What had brought them to this life of pure self-sacrificing service?

"With him gone, Mama was left to be nothing but a fallen woman. She couldn't bear to be such. But she was very beauti-ful, so the men came. When she rejected their advances, the men turned to me, assuming I was no better than my mother. Mama protected me until her death, selling the finery Padre had lavished on her when he was with us. After her death, and with a town that considered me little better than *la prostituta*, though it was never true, I fled my home and came here. Sister Margaret took me in. She saved me, and even more precious, she led me to a faith in God that has given me peace."

Sadie was so taken aback she could barely think of all she needed to ask. Yet she had to find out if Ramone was behind the attacks. Despite his sister's loyalty, Sadie needed to talk to the man. Each word seemed weighty and heavy, deep in Maria's soul, like stones that weighed her down. Maria was a woman of melancholy temperament, and this explained so much.

That helped Sadie to remember what was most important. "Maria, I know you well, and I believe what you've said about your brother. Even back when Grandfather died, there was talk that Ramone had run out of fear, that maybe he witnessed something. Or maybe he was involved somehow, tricked into going along with some plot. We think Grandfather held his silence for the same reason. He saw something that—" Sadie stopped, took a deep breath, and frowned—"that he thought was so dangerous, he was willing to take the name of his killer to his grave. . . ."

A tense silence filled the room.

Sadie surged to her feet. "I have to find my brothers. We must speak to Ramone, Maria, and find out what he knows. If he's innocent, then someone may be setting him up to look guilty. Where can we find him?"

Maria told her, and the information tightened Sadie's jaw until she feared it might crack. It was all she could do to speak. "I must go. Thank you, Maria. We will be careful with your brother. We aren't chasing him down to hurt him or arrest him." Unless he needed arresting, of course, but Sadie didn't say that out loud. "We just need to ask him some questions. And there's a very good chance his life is in danger."

Maria had an expression of such sorrow on her face. Her shoulders slumped, but honor shone from her eyes. She looked like a woman who'd spoken the truth and knew it was what she was called to do by her Father in heaven. She wouldn't regret it.

⁓❧⁓

"Heath, come quickly."

Heath wheeled around, reaching for his gun. The urgency in Sadie's voice had him looking for who was harming her.

She was alone, riding her horse hard, straight at him.

"What is it? What's happened?"

"Where are Cole and Justin and Rosita? We need to get back to the CR right away."

It was getting mighty late. Heath had gone door to door with questions and had come away with nothing. In the last few houses he woke people up.

"Cole took the east, Justin the west, and Rosita went toward the north part of town where most everyone speaks Mexican." It wasn't like Skull Mesa was a huge city. "We can find 'em—"

"We need to get home," Sadie snapped. "Let's find them. And we should stay together."

That shocked him. Sadie was always trying to be tougher than her brothers, tougher than anyone. But suddenly, after a visit at the orphanage, she didn't feel it was safe for her, or any of them, to be alone.

They were a while finding Cole, Justin, and Rosita. It had to be near midnight before they hit the trail for home.

"What is it, Sadie?" Cole asked as they reached the edge of town. "Tell us."

"I want to get back to the CR, and I want to ride hard. No time for talking. I think the danger may be coming closer to home every minute." Sadie steered her horse for the trail out of town and spurred it into a flat-out gallop. They all had good mounts. Heath's buckskin was an equal to Chance's big bay,

233

and Justin was riding that one. They were big men, though, and Sadie's little palomino mare was quick as a flash. Cole rode fast along with them on his black stallion.

Bent low over his stallion's neck, Heath turned to Justin. "If she's so all-fired worried about staying together, we really oughta make her stop leaving us behind."

"I agree," Justin said. "But we've got to catch her first."

Heath started to grin, but then he thought of the fear in Sadie's voice and her near-frantic demand that they all get home, and his grin disappeared.

This desperate ride reminded Heath of the day Chance had been injured. Heath had come for Sadie. It had started everything—his closer acquaintance with the family, his longing for home.

Before long, they were charging into the ranch yard. Sadie reined in and sat up straight in the saddle. Heath was close enough to hear her deep sigh of relief, and he wondered what in the world she'd learned.

Men came boiling out of the bunkhouse in response to the thundering horses. Guns in hand, ready to fight for the brand. It stirred something deep in Heath's heart to see their loyalty.

John and Alonzo led the rush to meet them when it became clear the group was headed for the barn.

They all dismounted.

"Take care of the horses, but leave them saddled," Sadie ordered with the authority of an owner.

Rosita swung down and strode for the house without a word to anyone.

Justin added, "I want the watch doubled tonight. There could be trouble."

"Pay special attention to the east," Sadie said.

That surprised Heath, as the mesa was to the west. He thought any trouble would come from that direction.

"No, we need to ride out again. The horses stay saddled or get us fresh ones. And leave a man to watch the house." Sadie plunked her hands on her hips. "The sentries should plan on taking shifts. It'll be a long night."

A long night? What was Sadie talking about?

"No," Justin snapped. No one forgot he was the real boss of this outfit. "Unsaddle these horses and then get on with guard duty. Anyone free should get some rest."

Sadie spun on him. "We have to go. Right now!"

"Inside, Sadie." Justin looked at John. "Get a guard posted. You men, strip this leather and rub down the horses."

Sadie's mouth closed hard. Her jaw looked to be clamped shut to keep the words in her mouth.

It reminded Heath that they weren't sure who they could trust among the hands. Suddenly she left, storming toward the house.

The rest of the group rushed to keep up.

Once inside, they found Rosita with the lanterns lit. She was busy preparing food.

Sadie turned to the others in the kitchen. She wasn't waiting until they could settle in at the table or find a comfortable chair in Chance's office.

Justin tore his hat off his head and tossed it at a hook on the wall. "If you want to go galloping off in the cold and dark, when we're all exhausted and half starved, you're gonna have to convince me of it."

"I rushed back here because I feared an attack, and soon. I thought we might get here and find everything in flames. Justin, we have to go."

"Sadie," Cole barked, "start talking."

With a jerk of her head that spoke volumes about her impatience, she nodded and swallowed hard.

Rosita moved to get her a cup of water.

"Ramone is back."

Rosita gasped. "Ramone, the old Don's son?"

"Yes. I found out at the orphanage. Maria knows where he is."

"Maria? From Safe Haven?" Justin's brow furrowed.

"Ramone is her brother. She said he returned to the area not that long ago."

"I never heard of Ramone having any more family." Justin, impatient and unable to be still, began helping Rosita put food on the table. "When Grandfather was shot, and Ramone took off, he headed straight for Mexico. He was protected by his father there. Why leave his sister behind?"

Sadie took a long drink of water. "His sister and mother, you mean. He abandoned them both. It only makes sense that he ran because he was guilty."

"Did Ramone come back before Pa was hurt?" Cole asked, furious.

"Yes, but Maria doesn't believe he's behind the attack."

"What sister would?" Justin brought a plateful of biscuits that Rosita had made into ham sandwiches to the table. He set it down with a hard clatter. Everyone helped themselves.

Heath had barely eaten today. He gulped down the food without taking his eyes off Sadie.

Only Sadie put off taking a bite. "I don't know if she's right, but she was adamant that he isn't a man to harm anyone. What she's afraid of is, if someone knows he's back, the same someone who shot Grandfather, hurt Pa, and shot at us will attack and pin the blame on Ramone. Then kill him to silence him. I think Ramone may have witnessed Grandfather Chastain's murder."

"Maria told you all this?" Heath asked between bites. He barely knew the quiet older lady from the orphanage. Had she kept these secrets out of malice toward the family?

Rosita set a pitcher of milk on the table, along with a bunch of tin cups.

"We need to get to him and find out what he knows. If Maria

is wrong, then Ramone is behind Grandfather's murder, Pa's accident, and the shooting. If she's right, his life may be in danger, and the men who attacked us will be tired of sneak attacks and may descend on us at any time. Killing Ramone will be the final part of their plan. If he dies, the truth of Grandfather's murder dies with him. And the men who tried to kill Pa will be free."

"So you want us to get to Ramone." Justin took a bite of his biscuit with barely controlled violence, his every word and motion revealing impatience and anger. "How do we do that, Sadie?"

"I know where he is."

That brought everyone to frozen stillness.

Then they all started talking at once.

Sadie silenced them with her reply. "He's staying in Don de Val's house."

"He went to his father's house. Of course," Cole said.

"The Don's hacienda is in ruins," Justin said. "It's been abandoned for thirty years. Every bit of wood and many of the adobe bricks have been carted off to use in other places. Some homesteaders have tried living in it through the years, but they never lasted. Last time I saw it, the roof and most of the walls had caved in. It's little more than rubble."

"According to Maria, the back of the house, what was once the servants' quarters, is mostly standing, although the roof has fallen in. He's living in those rooms."

"He sounds like a madman," Cole said.

"He may be exactly that," Heath agreed. "Keep it in mind when we try to catch him."

"Let's go." Sadie grabbed a couple of biscuits and shoved them in her pocket. She finished her milk with two big gulps.

"No, not yet," Heath said.

"But we have to. We need to capture him and hold him before someone kills him. We have to question him, find out the truth after all these years. We can ride in quietly and grab him while he's sleeping. If we scare him into running and he slips away, it may be thirty more years before we can get the answers to our questions."

"Two good reasons why we wait." Heath had finished his sandwich and reached for another. The plate was emptying fast.

Sadie hesitated. "And those are . . . ?"

"First of all, if you want to take a man unawares, you go in later, just before dawn. If he stays up at night, standing guard—"

"He's only one man, so how can he stand guard? He has to sleep."

"Yes, but he's more likely to be alert now. If he's alone—and we know one other man was involved in the rockslide that hurt your pa—but if he's alone, more than likely he'll be sleeping or at least have lost his sharpest attention in the hours just before daybreak."

Sadie crossed her arms and tapped her foot, but she was listening, and Heath appreciated that. "You said there were two reasons. What's the other one?"

Heath gave a little shrug. "Your men are alert, too. Are you sure you want them to know we're going? Can you trust them all?" He knew the answer to that, even if the others didn't.

"No, we can't," Cole said and looked behind him as if he could see through the door.

Justin said, "Everyone get some sleep. In four hours we ride out and take this coyote prisoner. Then we get some answers."

Heath started heading for the back door. It'd been a brutally long day and a few hours of sleep would keep him sharp.

"No, Heath, you stay here." Cole moved to block the door in a way that struck Heath as odd.

"You . . ." Heath almost couldn't get the words out as he realized what Cole was implying. "You don't trust me." His voice went flat. It wasn't a question; it was a statement of fact.

"You think I'm going to go out there and warn whoever's behind this trouble."

"We trust you!" Sadie's voice was first and loudest.

"For Pete's sake, of course we trust you." Justin turned, his fist clenched, and looked like he wanted to take a swing at Cole. And knowing these two, he just might.

Heath made a mental note of where the lanterns were just in case the two numskulls started fighting and got too close to one of them again.

"I trust you, Heath," Cole said. "I do. What I'm worried about is you going to the bunkhouse and—"

"And saying the wrong thing to the wrong person," Heath said, cutting him off. "So you don't think I conspired to kill your father—you just think I'm stupid."

"That's not what I meant."

"It sounded like it to me," Sadie snapped. "He saved Pa. He took a bullet for me. He—"

"That's not it." Cole raised both hands as if in surrender. "Yes, maybe I was afraid you might say something, but what I really think is, if you go out there, the men are going to have questions."

Heath glared without responding. It *still* sounded like Cole didn't trust him.

"And you're either going to have to lie to them or stay silent, and either one will put the men on edge. Then they're going to see you leave early. It'll be easier to slip away, or at least to let the men see us at the moment we're leaving, if you sleep in here." Cole's dark blue eyes glinted with irritation. "I trust you, Heath, and frankly, all your questions and the way you took offense make me think you don't trust me."

It was a pure fact that Heath could handle someone pushing back hard better than someone meekly apologizing or dodging direct answers. Cole was pushing, and Heath liked it that way.

"That's all right, then. I'll sleep in here."

"No one's in Pa's bedroom," Justin offered.

Sadie gasped, and Rosita made a sound not unlike a cranky cougar.

Justin had the sensitivity of a razorback hog.

Heath said, "I'll sleep in front of the fire. I'd take a blanket if you've got a spare."

He left the room before he could hear any more opinions from the Bodens. And before he started thinking that Sadie oughta give him a good-night kiss.

As soon as this was over, which seemed like it was taking forever, Heath was gonna ask for permission to ride out with Sadie.

Then he thought of Cole and Justin and decided he wasn't asking—he was telling.

25

Justin had a quiet word with the sentries so they wouldn't shoot. Beyond that, the Boden brothers didn't tell a soul where they were going.

Not counting Heath, of course. He got to go.

And Sadie couldn't be stopped.

But no one else.

Except Rosita, who'd fed them all breakfast.

Confound it, once he started counting, Heath realized they'd pretty much told everyone. These Bodens didn't know how to sneak worth a lick.

They'd been on the trail just under an hour when Justin said, "We ride real quiet from here on out."

A short time later, in the starlight, he saw the pretty curve of the Cimarron River running near a crumbling mansion. With the whole place washed blue in the night, the green grass was black, like a moat surrounding the long-neglected hacienda. Years of work were evident in the spreader dams that kept a hundred acres green, even in the winter.

A sharp hiss from Justin had them all dismounting well away

from the house. An old, collapsed gate told them this was de Val land. The gate's base was sturdy enough they could hitch their horses to it.

They headed the rest of the way on foot, Heath staying close to Sadie.

"Let's try and catch him asleep. I don't want him shot. We need to talk to him. Fan out," Justin ordered with a whisper that still carried the weight of his authority.

They approached the run-down house from the west. The remaining servants' quarters were on the east side. Justin took Sadie and circled to the north. Heath and Cole took the south side.

The wreckage of the house had a ghostly quality to it, as if the past now haunted them all. At least it sounded as if it haunted Ramone.

Heath let Cole lead the way until they reached the corner of the house. Then Heath's hand shot out and grabbed Cole's shoulder. He leaned to Cole's ear and, in a barely audible voice, said, "Wait."

Cole turned, scowling, but he waited.

Heath slipped past him and rounded the corner, the first to expose himself to someone keeping watch from inside the building. He moved fast enough that Cole had no chance to protest. No sense letting a nervous man with a grudge against the Bodens see one of his main targets step into his line of sight. If Ramone had shot Frank Chastain, he was a man who'd killed before.

Once Heath slipped around the corner, a familiar calm iced his nerves. His hands became steady as stone, his vision and hearing razor sharp. His heart slowed, and each breath was deep and silent.

As a boy, he'd helped keep himself and his ma fed by learning to hunt. Pa was gone all the time, and Ma tended their garden, cooked, and did a little hunting herself. They also kept a few cows and a flock of chickens. Heath took their old rifle into the woods and over time developed the know-how of sneaking around as silent as a ghost. He learned how to distinguish the sounds that were normal and belonged from those that warned of approaching danger. It became second nature for him to move soundlessly, to go still instantly.

Even knowing Justin would see to Sadie's protection, he prayed that no harm would come to her. There was more, too. Plenty to pray for as he inched forward. He had never killed a man, and he never wanted to. But a man didn't go armed in this wild land without knowing the moment might come when he had to pull the trigger.

Heath rested his hand on his Colt revolver. His stomach twisted. There might be shooting trouble. Heath would do everything in his power not to harm Ramone. They needed him alive.

If Ramone started firing, Heath wouldn't let anyone die under the gun of an embittered, jealous lunatic.

Heath reached the nearest wall and flattened his back against it. What the Bodens called the servants' quarters were in much better shape than the rest of the house. Even so, it was badly damaged, the windows shattered, the roof mostly collapsed. But the walls still stood, and that had the main part of the hacienda beat.

Cole was right behind, so Heath kept going to stop Cole from taking the lead. As he moved along the side of the structure, Heath came to a window with no glass, no shutters. He eased himself to his knees. No light came from inside, but with the roof gone, Heath hoped the starlight would help him to see. He went on past the window, nearly crawling on his belly to stay low enough that he wouldn't be silhouetted. He got to the far side and looked back. Cole had stopped at the window, his gun drawn, and pointed upward.

Their eyes met. Heath studied what he could see inside the structure from this angle. Cole did the same.

Slowly, Heath stood and eased forward until he saw all there was to see of the servants' quarters from where he was positioned. Since the wall across was solid, Heath figured the quarters must be a double row of rooms. Justin and Sadie were no doubt right this minute peeking in the windows on the opposite side of the house.

The room was empty except for the debris from the fallen ceiling, and there wasn't much of that. This part of the house had been used to a lesser extent for building supplies. Plenty had been stripped away, but the scavengers seemed to draw the line at actually tearing the house down. They'd taken what fell off, but the walls that remained were left alone.

It was just as well that the remnants of a whole collapsed ceiling weren't lying on the floor. It'd give Ramone too many hiding places.

Heath turned to move on, keeping low. He reached the end of the building and poked his head around. Seeing nothing, he looked again more carefully. He was in time to spot Justin looking around from the north side.

Heath made sure Justin saw him, then straightened and came around the corner. A doorway, its door long gone, stood in the center of this side of the building. Heath approached Justin until they met on either side of the door.

"Nothing," Justin whispered.

"Let's see what's inside." Heath leaned forward to peer into the room. He resisted the urge to check on Sadie, leaving her in the protection of her brother. He tensed his muscles to spring, knowing he'd make a perfect outline if someone had concealed himself in a shadowy corner and now waited to kill any and all who trespassed.

Drawing in a deep breath, Heath threw himself in, low, rounding the corner to get out of the meager light.

Justin shot through on the next step. Cole was right behind Heath, and without even looking, he knew Sadie came next. She moved like no man he'd ever known.

There was no sign of life.

Where was Ramone? Had Sadie heard wrong? Had Maria been lied to, maybe deliberately so in order to pass on false information?

And then Heath noticed a black square in the floor, near the far side of the room. It was too perfect. It had to be a cellar. They had more places yet to search.

Heath gestured to Justin to get his attention, then pointed at the opening in the floor. Justin nodded.

Heath made a rush for the cellar opening, doing his best to stay quiet, though he stepped on plenty of squeaky floorboards, so his best was mighty poor.

He reached the cellar opening and dropped to his belly just as Justin dropped on the other side. Cole stood a few paces back, gun drawn, ready to do what needed doing. Heath noticed that Cole had Sadie tucked firmly behind him.

No light down there, no sound, not even breathing. Someone could be asleep, but everything Heath knew about tracking told him the cellar was empty. "There's no one—"

The metallic *crack* of cocking guns wrenched Heath around. *"Alto!"*

Halt. Spoken in Mexican in a heavily accented voice.

"I kill next *hombre* who moves." The silhouette of a man standing in the open doorway to the outside was all Heath could see. He had a pistol in each hand, one aimed to the left at Justin, the other to the right at Sadie and Cole.

Heath would have made a move, but he didn't dare. Sadie stood closest to the intruder, right in the line of deadly fire. The first bullet would hit her.

"Is that you, Ramone?" Cole spoke from where he stood next

to Sadie. He made a very subtle move, a mere shifting of his feet. He eased forward and leaned so that his shoulders blocked Sadie, putting himself between his sister and those guns.

"*Alto!* No move."

Heath's eyes had adjusted to the dark. He could just make out Ramone's hands; they were trembling. Did this show of nerves mean the man wasn't a killer? And did that make them safer? Or did it make him more dangerous? A nervous man might accidentally twitch and pull the trigger.

They all stood, frozen in place.

"I live in my padre's hacienda. You no belong here." The words sounded like a mix of anger and despair, each in equal measure. "You have taken all from me."

The guns lifted slightly, as if his distress were more than he could bear, and all he had left was to hand out death and destruction.

"Padre, no!" Out of the dark the words rose, making no sense to Heath. And then he recognized the voice.

The CR ramrod Alonzo. Calling Ramone his padre. Father.

Heath's thoughts began spinning as he listened to a man he thought he knew well admit to being someone completely different.

Not Alonzo Deval, but *Alonzo de Val*.

"It is me, Padre, your son. I can't let you shoot." Alonzo centered himself in one of the gaping windows, his gun leveled.

Heath saw the darkness was fading, the distant sky turning a faint gray. The dawn was upon them. He could now make out Alonzo's features in the window. His gun was pointed at his father.

It twisted Heath's gut to think of a son shooting down his own pa. Even worse, Heath could hear the affection Alonzo held for the man. But a resolve was there, too. Alonzo was set on protecting them.

"Put down the gun, Padre, and talk to me. The Bodens mean you no harm."

A taut silence followed. Ramone's guns were still on them. His hands still trembled for what seemed like several minutes. As the light increased a bit, Heath saw Ramone's face a tad more clearly. He appeared to be handsome, very much an older version of his son.

Alonzo spoke calmly, reminding Heath of the gently flowing waters of the Cimarron. "I know your goodness, Padre. I know what they accuse you of. And I know you are innocent. You are safe if you put down the guns. I have worked for the Bodens and heard them say they mean you no harm. But they want answers. That's why they are here."

Ramone's pistols remained leveled and cocked.

"I have no wish to shoot you, *mi padre*. It would break my heart. But I will not let you kill these good men and their good sister. Please talk to the Bodens. Tell them—and tell me—what happened that day. You are not a killer. But if you pull that trigger, all that was done to Señor Chastain will be blamed on you."

In a broken voice, Alonzo went on. "I watched the direction the Bodens went, and it took me only moments to know where they were headed and suspect they had found you right here. I'm a fool to not have thought of it and come to check on you. Like you, I came to try to regain our land, Padre, but I have failed."

"Deval, instead of de Val," Sadie said. "Don Bautista de Val. His son, Ramone, who worked for us without speaking of who he really was, who vanished the day my grandfather was killed. And now Alonzo Deval."

Heath sure wished Sadie would shut up. Why draw the attention of these men to the lone woman in their midst?

"It is Ramone Alonzo de Val Jr., Miss Sadie." Alonzo said it as if he were formally introducing himself.

"You all came here in secret in *la noche*." Ramone's harsh

answer echoed in the room. "And my own son rode with you. My own son is a traitor."

"Ramone," Heath said in what he hoped was a tone that didn't make the man's trigger finger itchy, "we came to talk with you, not hurt you. We believe that you had no part in Frank Chastain's killing, but we think you know who did. Or at least know something about that day that will help us find out who did. Whoever killed that fine old man is still here, still aiming to kill more Bodens and hang that killing on you. We need to find out what you saw that day so we can stop the men who shot Chastain and set that rockslide on Chance Boden."

"*Nada* can stop them. *El hombres* are powerful, with *mucho amigos* even *mas* dangerous than *el diablo*."

"Please put down the guns, Ramone," Cole said. "Like Heath said, we will not harm you. In fact, we want to save you—and in the process save ourselves."

"That's right. And step out of the doorway," Justin added. "We think the men after you could be coming at any time. We came in the night because we hoped to catch you asleep. So we could avoid drawn guns, like we have now."

There was a long hesitation. Ramone glanced over his shoulder before finally lowering the pistols. He stepped inside and put a wall between him and whatever terrors were held in the breaking dawn.

Heath watched the man move about, then a scratch ripped through the silence and a light popped into view. A single match was almost blinding.

Ramone rustled around, and then a lantern's blue light danced. When he put the glass chimney in place, the room lit up. It seemed as bright as day after the long hours in the darkness. Heath saw Ramone's face clearly for the first time.

It was ruined. An ugly scar deformed the whole left side. Ramone had been looking at his son when Heath had first made out his handsome features. But now, looking straight on, Heath saw the brutal scars on the left side of his face. His eye showed white in its socket. The scar was wide and thick—as if it'd never been stitched—and ran from his forehead to his chin. For all that, Ramone moved easily, with grace, despite the trembling.

Heath then saw the rest of him.

Ramone was filthy, his clothing in tatters. His fingernails were caked with dirt. He had long hair that hung down in greasy coils. Beyond the filth, he was skin and bone. Suffering and want were etched on his face.

"*Mi papa*," Alonzo said, then disappeared from the window. His footsteps pounded as he rushed around the house. Seconds later, he was inside and pulling his father into his arms.

After a long hug, Alonzo pulled back from his father with such gentleness, Ramone's emaciated body looked even more fragile.

"I came to do just as you had planned," Alonzo said to his father. "To marry the daughter of the household." Alonzo gave Sadie a longing glance. "I wanted to regain at least a portion of the land for the descendants of Bautista de Val." His eyes shifted to Heath. "But it was not to be."

Heath saw Justin and Cole react to that, but he didn't have time to deal with them right now.

Alonzo asked his father, "Why didn't you speak to me, tell me you had come back?"

"I could not. They kill you if they know you are *mi hijo*."

Cole approached the son and his pa. "I don't know if you remember me, Ramone, but I remember you—just barely and I heard your name for years. When you left, there were plenty that suspected you of killing Grandfather Chastain, but my mother never did. She always thought you'd been chased away. While you may not have won her heart, she believed in your decency." For just a moment, Cole hesitated. He then asked,

"Is that scar of yours left from the day my grandfather was murdered? Was Ma right? You were forced to run?"

Ramone's knees gave out. Alonzo reached out and caught his pa and held him. The man would have ended up flat on the floor if his son hadn't braced him up.

"Has anyone got any food?" Alonzo asked frantically.

"No, we came in on foot." Sadie frowned, glanced at her brothers. "Do any of you have jerky or anything left in your saddlebags?"

They all shook their heads.

Justin said, "Let's get him back to the CR. We can take care of him there."

Ramone seemed to relax some. "You're really not going to kill me?"

Sadie rushed over to Ramone's side. Heath followed, still wary of the man and mindful that someone was definitely after the Bodens, including Ramone maybe. Killers who might even now be waiting to dry-gulch them. They were by no means safe, and he didn't intend to be too far away from Sadie until they were.

"No," Sadie assured him again, "we're going to protect you, Ramone, and stop the men who are after all of us."

"That's right," Cole said.

"Thank you." Ramone gathered his strength. "Yes, Cole, I remember you. You tagged your padre day and night. We all liked having a little one around. The new *niño* with the handsome father who turned my Veronica's head. I remember it well. From the moment your father came to the Cimarron Ranch, Señorita Chastain had eyes for no one but him. More than that, she loved you. I think she would have married your father just to get you for a son."

Heath was jealous of Cole being surrounded by that kind of family.

He'd had it with his brothers and his ma before she died. But Cole had it his whole life. Of course, Mrs. Boden was Cole's stepma. So Cole had lost a mother, too.

"Before you and your padre came," Ramone said, "I had hopes that I could win her heart. I never meant to hurt the beautiful señorita. I had no bad wishes for her and would have been good to her all her life. But along with wanting her, I wanted a piece of what I'd been denied."

Ramone swallowed hard, and Heath almost asked if they could carry him to the Cimarron for a drink of cool water. But they'd be exposed. Once they moved out of here, he wanted to go fast.

"Even with a new beau, I believed I had once found favor in Veronica's eyes, so I did not give up my pursuit of her. The day Mr. Chastain was shot, I was there. I deliberately waylaid him on the trail to ask for Veronica's hand or at least be given permission to court her. Your grandfather had just come from a meeting with one of the governor's men. Señor Frank was very upset. When he saw me, a man he trusted, he told me much of what had happened. They were going to take the Cimarron Ranch. They were using Señor Frank's French-Canadian heritage against him, adding in his years of Mexican citizenship. He was American by then, and that had satisfied Señor Dantalion for a time because he'd been busy pushing all the other land-grant owners off their lands."

"Dantalion?" Cole's voice was intense, and Heath was struck by how smart he was. Cole wasn't a man of the land, not fully, but he had a fine mind and he knew the law. "I don't know that name. But you say he worked at the governor's behest?"

"I only heard your *abuelo* say Dantalion, no first name." Ramone used the Mexican word for grandfather. "Your *abuelo* said this man used power allowed him by being close to the governor. He said the governor was a decent man and didn't know the things that were being done in his name. And Señor Frank had tried to see him, but was always blocked. He had been paying bribes for years and that had kept the wolves from the door. But Señor Dantalion had finished with his other schemes. He had stripped away land grants, driven owners away, and handed the land over to his *amigos*. He shifted his attention to the Cimarron Ranch. Dantalion had told your *abuelo* that the governor wanted the land to be held by an American. Beyond that, the governor turned a blind eye and let Dantalion do as he pleased."

"And when you heard that," Sadie said, "you knew you had no hope of gaining Grandfather's permission to court his daughter."

"No hope. He had to have a fully American son-in-law. And he needed to find such a man fast. Your padre was right, so I did not ask. To reveal my interest in Veronica would lead to being cast from *el rancho*."

"But how did Grandfather die?"

"We had dismounted. Your grandfather's horse was weary from a long ride. We walked along the trail, letting our horses rest, and all of this poured out—his worry, his anger. That is when three men with rifles stepped out in our path."

"Dantalion," Cole said in disgust.

"Yes, your *abeulo* spoke his name. He had a look of wealth about him. A black suit, a flat-topped black hat with Mexican trim. He had eyes black as night and hair just as dark.

"Señor Frank had said he was just returning from a meeting with them. He knew it ended badly, but he expected thievery of his land, not an attack. There was no hope we could win a gunfight with our weapons holstered and their *pistolas* aimed and cocked. Dantalion began threatening Señor Frank, telling him he had to leave the CR. But I saw *muerte* in his eyes. I knew he had not come to talk, but to kill. His words were taunts as he approached us. When he got close, I took a wild chance and jumped for his gun. I managed to shove it upward so that when he fired, he missed. Your grandfather had his gun out and fired. He shot one of the men while the other ran. For a moment I thought we would win. But then Dantalion came around with a knife and slashed my face and knocked me to the ground. He then shot Señor Frank at close range."

"Why did he leave you both alive?"

"He thought your *abuelo* was dead, so he paid him no mind. He knelt on my chest as I lay there, half blind and bleeding. He said he was a respected man and no one would believe he'd done this crime. He'd be the man sent to investigate, and he'd make sure I was blamed. I'd hang."

Ramone hesitated for a long moment before he spoke again. "He gave me the option to run or die right there on the spot. I ran. I know that makes me a coward, but he was right. I could tell by the way he spoke and moved that he had power and I had none. I got on my horse and rode for Mexico. I heard much later that Señor Frank had lived for a short time, and that Veronica had married Chance and held the *rancho* somehow."

"Why did you come back now?" Cole asked.

"My padre died. He left me nothing. His *esposa* always hated me, and though she was cruel to me, in many ways I could not blame her. I was proof of the Don's infidelity, and I knew it went on long after he had abandoned my mother. I was run off like a cur dog. My own beloved *esposa*, Alonzo's mama, is long dead and probably glad to be done with me."

"Don't talk so, Padre," Alonzo said. "*Mamacita* loved you. You gave me and my sisters a good home."

"Thank you, *hijo*. Yes, your mama was a fine woman. My daughters have married and are happy. My only son had gone wandering, and I suspected he came here." Ramone glanced again at Sadie and looked sheepish. "It had been so long, I believed the danger would be past. And then my horse stepped in a rabbit hole in the desert and broke his leg. He died and I went on, on foot. A rugged journey. And I've learned to stay away from strangers because of my terrible scars. When I finally got here, to my padre's hacienda, it felt like the end of the road. A ruin fit for the son of an immoral man. I managed to see Maria once, and she gave me food. But I haven't the strength to go back to her. I knew Alonzo was here somewhere, but I didn't have the will to hunt. My food ran out days ago. Still, I have lived on by fishing in the Cimarron. Yet I could never catch enough to satisfy. I didn't want to show myself, so I've been sneaking around in the dark. Like a nighttime creature, I've lived mostly in a hole in the ground."

Heath glanced at the cellar.

"Those days are over, Ramone." Sadie rested her hand on the man's bony shoulder. "You will come home with us. We will protect you, and what you've witnessed will help protect us. We will face whoever is after us, be it Dantalion or someone who is under his influence. And we will make the CR safe for my father so that when he returns, it will be to peace."

The sun was fully up now. Heath knew it was safer to ride in the light of day, though he didn't fool himself that the danger was over. "I'll go fetch the horses." He rounded the small crowd gathered around Ramone. When he reached the door, Justin snagged his arm.

"Hold up. You're not going alone."

"It's all right. Whoever's out there is after you Bodens. And it looks like Ramone, too. They won't waste any bullets on me because you're under cover and that would warn you. If we all went together, it might be okay as well, because they could see me and be warned. But Ramone can't walk—"

"No, Kincaid, and stop trying to take care of us. You and I will go together."

Heath had a wild urge to laugh. "Fine, boss, risk your neck. But I'm right."

"I tied my horse near yours," Alonzo said. "I'll come too."

"Let's go." Justin rushed out the door ahead of him, the idiot. The three of them ran for the horses.

26

Sadie was so relieved to see Heath come back, it took her a second to realize she was happy to see Justin, too. Alonzo also, mostly.

Justin and Heath, their guns drawn, stayed out to cover the horses. Cole and Alonzo got Ramone to his feet again. They each slid one of the ailing man's arms around their neck and helped him to a horse.

Sadie brought up the rear. Once they got Ramone on Alonzo's horse, he looked steady enough to ride on his own.

Heath grinned. "Sadie can ride with me, and Alonzo can take her horse."

The explosion wasn't long in coming. Sadie found herself snatched up and plunked in front of Cole, and they rode out. Sadie leaned around her brother and smiled back at Heath.

"Stay sharp," Justin hissed, as if annoyed with anyone daring to smile.

He was probably right.

They set a good pace, and the trail, winding around clumps of aspen and through lush winter grass pastures, was quiet.

"We should go that way." Ramone pointed to a spot ahead that was nothing more than thick woods leading to a steep incline.

"What's up there?" Cole rode up to the right side of Ramone.

Alonzo was on the left. He'd rarely left his father's side, only when they reached a stretch of the trail too narrow to ride two abreast.

"It's a shortcut to *el rancho*."

Sadie tried to imagine the way the trail might go, but she'd ridden over in the dark, and the trail—one she'd traveled only a couple of times in her life—twisted and turned until all she did was follow it without any idea which direction they were going.

"There's a way over that mountain?" Justin pulled his horse to a stop, and they all followed suit and turned to face the thick stand of trees.

Ramone pointed toward the mountain. "Yes, not far, although I have not used the trail in many years. It is *muy peligroso*."

"If it's so dangerous, then why in the world would we take it?" Sadie fought to keep from rolling her eyes.

"Because otherwise it's nearly a two-hour ride, and we could be at the CR in half an hour if we went that way. But the trails are narrow up there; they may have caved away and become impassable. They are more suited to a good mountain-bred mustang ridden by a skilled *caballero* than a fine thoroughbred."

"It would have the advantage of being a surprise move," Heath said.

"When Señor Chastain and Don Bautista lived here, the trail was well-traveled. They weren't exactly friends. It was said that Señor Chastain knew of the Don's unfaithfulness to his wife and disapproved. Even so, they were two strong men and made a good team running the huge land grant. They saw each other often, and hired hands went from one place to the other daily, working the herd together."

"This trail's never been used in all the years I've lived here," Justin added.

"There was no use for it after Padre left."

Heath reined his horse around and surveyed the terrain. "If there is someone looking for us, they'll be watching the trail we rode over on, not this one that Ramone knows."

"This is a poor place to stop and talk," Justin said to Heath. "I don't want to get caught on a trail that might have caved away over the years. We can explore it later. Let's go on the trail we rode on to come here."

Justin turned his horse, and the rest of the party did, as well.

They moved out. Heath brought up the rear, behind Cole and Sadie, with Ramone and Alonzo next. Justin took the lead.

The loud crack of a rifle split the air. Cole's horse reared. He wrestled it under control. The bullet had come from ahead of them.

The rifle fired again, then once more.

"Up the short trail!" Justin shouted as he wheeled his horse around.

For a time, the horses fought their bits, reared up, and snorted. Ramone was the first to charge into the woods. He knew where he was going. His reaction was so quick that Sadie had to wonder if they'd been led into a trap.

Bullets whizzed past. They came from overhead somewhere, someone centered on the twisting trail to get them dead-on. She heard shots from right behind them, Heath returning fire.

With the horses bucking, Cole went flying off.

Sadie clawed at the reins, but the horse twisted and reared so high she was afraid she was going over backward. She threw herself sideways and slammed into a stout tree. There was shouting, gunfire. Hooves slashed only inches from her face. In the blur she saw Justin grab Cole and nearly throw him onto the rearing horse. "Can you hang on?"

"Yes, get Sadie."

"Move!" Justin slapped the horse on the rump just as a hand sank into the front of Sadie's dress and she was on horseback again. More shouting. She realized she was dazed from hitting the tree, and the world was spinning in a way that had nothing to do with the panicked horse.

Heath was close, and he was roaring something at Justin. It was when Justin yelled back that she realized Heath had her and they were riding fast.

She made herself small and held on tight so as not to make things harder for him. For all the chaos, they were on the new trail just a minute behind Ramone.

Justin yelled ahead, "Ride fast! Get to the ranch."

The gunfire quit as they left the main trail. This new one was a hair-raiser, the first leap nearly straight downhill. Ramone had pointed up, a trail over a canyon wall, but it appeared they'd have to go a long way down before they got to climbing.

Ramone had told them the truth that this route was a dangerous one.

It looked as if no one had been on it for years, maybe decades. Deer and elk must still use the trail, though, because the woods hadn't completely swallowed it up. But shrubs grew tight to the sides of it, and any horse not being goaded would have turned up its nose at a trail with branches slapping at its face as they charged on.

Of course, the bullets had helped convince the horses to run.

"I'll block the branches as best I can." Sadie held up her arms to protect her face and hopefully Heath's too while she was at it. That left his hands free to guide the horse. Whipping limbs tried to knock her back, but Heath's solid presence gave her the support she needed to hang on.

They plunged down and down and down until finally they reached a level stretch. The trail was wider here, though not by much, and they started making good time.

Still dizzy, Sadie gathered her thoughts enough to ask, "Is Cole hurt? Was he shot?"

"He's bleeding, but he's hanging on." Heath's voice settled her, and his strong arm around her waist reminded her of the day he'd come to tell her about Pa.

An unwooded stretch allowed her to fold both of her arms across his to hold him the only way she was able.

"Are you all right?" Heath whispered the words, his lips nearly touching her ear so she could hear him.

"Yes, I hit the tree and it shook me up for a few minutes, but I'm fine."

His arm tightened around her just a bit, and his face pressed against her. "Thank God, Sadie. When you and Cole fell, I was sure you'd been shot. I was afraid . . ."

He lapsed into silence. She held his arm tightly and treasured a brief moment of closeness in the midst of the madness—and of hope that they would survive to get to the bottom of this.

"Here we go. The trail starts heading up now." Heath shifted her around so instead of straddling the horse, she was sitting sideways on his lap. She looked up and he looked down. Since he was only inches away, she kissed him.

"Settle down, Miss Sadie." Heath's smile did something to her. If she didn't know it was impossible, she'd've thought her heart was melting. "Hang on tight. It looks like the trail could get mean."

Sadie wrapped her arms around him, glad of an excuse to hang on with all her strength.

Pressing one strong hand to the back of her head, he urged her to bury her face against his chest. She wasn't sure if he wanted her close or if he was somehow protecting her, but it didn't matter because she wanted to be as close as humanly possible to him.

The uphill side was as steep as the downhill. They wove back and forth, riding sideways along the face of the canyon wall, then turning to climb again.

They'd climbed a long while when Justin, who was bringing up the rear, called out, "Keep going. I hear someone on our back trail. I'll try to slow 'em down."

After a quick hug, Heath said, "Keep going, Sadie. I'll go and help Justin." He was gone from the back of the horse before she could say anything. But then what would she say? *Stay with me and let Justin face them alone?*

Wanting to scream, Sadie swung her leg around so she straddled the horse again and pressed forward. Cole was ahead of her, wounded. He looked back, saw her, and nodded. He must not have noticed she was alone, because he turned forward and rode on. She saw blood low on his back and knew his body had protected her. He'd taken bullets that would have hit her if he hadn't shielded her. Far beyond Cole, Alonzo and Ramone rode hard, following orders, and she was glad they were. Cole was slowing them down, and there was no need for everyone to be trapped. Alonzo followed Ramone, who was the only one who knew the way and was badly weakened.

She caught up to Cole, desperate to send someone back to help Heath and Justin. Cole and Ramone weren't up to helping. If she yelled for Alonzo, Cole would hear her and insist on going back to help. And anyway, if there was trouble ahead, Alonzo needed to be with the wounded.

With a clenched jaw, Sadie realized how many times she'd fussed about being protected, treated like a delicate flower, kept from danger and trouble and any kind of risk.

Well, no one was stopping her now. She looked back at the torturously winding trail and could see no sign of Justin and

Heath. But there weren't any gunshots, either. That had to be good.

There was a long way left to climb and she kept at it, her mind made up. She needed to pick a spot. She'd lie in wait, hoping Heath and Justin would come. And if they did not and an enemy did, she'd fight for the CR just as her brothers were doing. Just as her father and grandfather had done.

That moment she finally saw what it was Pa had been trying to teach her with his demand that she give up her job and move home to the ranch. He wanted her to feel the Chastain blood that flowed in her veins from Ma. He wanted her to feel the love and effort and sweat he'd poured into building them a home. He wanted her to cherish family and hold tight to the legacy she'd been given.

She understood then how much her father loved her, nearly as much as her heavenly Father loved her. Whether or not Pa had done right by them, it was his love she needed to remember, and it was just as Heath had said on the day Pa had been hurt. They were so blessed to have a father who loved them. And just as Pa fought for them, she would fight for her home.

As she thought of her pa's love, she realized her love of home. It awakened with such force, it was nearly painful. And part of that was a willingness to fight for it. Stand against anyone who'd try and take the CR away. Add to that, she was flooded with a determination that no one was going to murder her grandfather, nearly kill her father, shoot Heath and Cole, and get away with it.

Anyone who attacked one Boden attacked them all. And this evil man had indeed attacked them all.

They'd stand and fight as a family. Yes, even the females.

Justin and Heath were protecting all of them at a terrible risk. She could do nothing less.

She would make a stand.

And then she saw it . . . and her moment came.

27

The trail was lined on both sides by a dense forest that was next to impenetrable. Those spots where it became clear, the land was likely to slide away so steeply that no horse could walk it. Or instead it'd head straight up with the same result.

Heath was still searching when Justin caught up to him. At the same time, Heath found a gap big enough to hide in. He took it. Justin rode up and must've been doing the same as Heath, because before he came level, Justin nodded, then vanished to the far side of the trail.

Heath waited, controlling his breathing so that not a sound escaped. Then a hoof fell with a soft thud. Whoever was coming was riding slow and cautious.

Well, that was a pure shame, because if he was really cautious he'd have run for California.

Justin would get first chance at him. Was there one man? Heath knew that more than one was involved. But were they both here today? There'd been only one gunman. Heath knew weapons well enough to be sure of that. And if they hoped to waylay and kill the Bodens, why would only one man come? If there were more, why didn't more than one of them fire his gun?

The man came into view. Heath recognized him as a layabout he'd seen in Skull Gulch a few times, loitering outside the saloon. The man's clothes were worn and dusty, his skin darkly tanned and weathered like everyone in the American Southwest. Yet Heath had no idea who he was.

Heath pulled his gun, but he didn't intend to shoot, not unless he needed to save a life. And even then he wouldn't shoot to kill. They needed to talk to this *hombre*.

Justin lunged out of the woods as quick and quiet as a striking snake. He grabbed the man and yanked him off his horse. It was so silent it was almost like the man just vanished in the blink of an eye. Heath rushed out and caught the horse's reins in time to see Justin land a brutal punch on the outlaw's chin that knocked him out cold.

His eyes met Justin's. Justin jerked his head down the trail. Did he mean someone else was coming, or was he just worried there might be someone?

Justin dragged his prisoner out of sight.

Heath took the horse and led it away, then tied it up well off the trail. He rushed back to stand watch. The whole thing had taken a minute, maybe two. If someone was coming, thanks to all the twists in the trail, they wouldn't notice their lead man had been taken out of the fight.

Heath crouched, waiting, watching. He saw a movement across the trail. Justin was waving a hand at him. Before Heath could figure out why, Justin stepped out onto the trail with the unconscious shooter slung over his shoulder, leading his horse.

Heath rushed to get the horse he had hidden.

"I don't see anyone else." Justin spoke barely above a whisper. "And I don't like leaving everyone else alone for so long, with only Sadie and Alonzo at full strength. Let's head on up."

When he put it like that, Heath's stomach twisted. He swung up on the outlaw's mangy horse, only waiting to be sure Justin had his prisoner tied on behind his saddle. Then Heath rode up the trail at a fast clip.

Justin could keep up or be left behind.

⁂

Sadie heard hoofbeats. It sounded like two riders, so it couldn't be Heath and Justin because Heath was on foot.

She drew back to put a thick tree between her and the trail.

Heath appeared, charging uphill. She let out a worried breath. Next she saw Justin rushing from behind. An unconscious man was tied behind his saddle. He moved just as fast as Heath, a look of grim intensity on his face.

They'd caught the man who shot at them. Maybe this madness was finally over. A quirk of humor kept her concealed as they rode past, thinking she would enjoy catching up with them and watching them realize she'd outsmarted them.

But she changed her mind as they vanished around a bend in the trail. Her idea was a foolish one. If Justin and Heath were on edge, and they sure looked it, then she didn't want to make any sudden moves and startle them into an attack.

They were rushing to get to her and the men, worried about protecting them. They'd get there ahead of her and be upset. And if she spooked them, she might end up under their guns.

Shouting after them would do it, but the speed at which they rode made her wonder if they knew trouble was coming. And wasn't that why she'd hidden here to begin with?

She decided to stay put for a few more minutes, to watch for trouble and also to put off the trouble coming with her big brothers.

After a while, a rustling sounded in the woods. Maybe she'd

heard a coyote or even the wind, but it set her on alert and she trusted her instinct. She went absolutely still.

Heath heard Justin closing the gap between them. They were making a racket riding fast, so any sneaking was over. It was safe enough to talk again in a normal voice.

When Justin was right on his tail, Heath glanced back. "Give the horses a breather. The climb is too hard for them at this pace."

Justin reined in, and they settled into a fast walk.

"You did good work there," Heath said. "You think there was anyone with him?"

"I waited for as long as I could stand to and saw no sign of anyone." Justin looked back with disgust at the man he had draped over the saddle. "Why would someone with him lag back so far?"

"I don't know, except that whoever is behind all this has been mighty careful to keep his presence a secret. And you're right that we need to catch up with the others. Now that we've got a prisoner, we can ask him some hard questions, starting with what he was doing shooting at us from cover, and the names of everyone he's working with, especially if it's someone at the ranch."

"Maybe we can finally get to the bottom of this." Justin looked back again, not trusting even an unconscious man.

Heath glanced at the man, hog-tied and out cold. "I hope he knows something that helps. I've seen him hanging around in Skull Gulch, but I don't know who he is. Do you?"

"Nope, but he looks familiar. I reckon he's been watching us for a while." Justin scowled as he faced forward. He patted his horse on the shoulder as if checking for the speed of its breathing. "The horses have rested enough. Now quit jawin' and pick up the pace."

❧

Sadie waited, motionless, every breath coming in and going out silently.

The underbrush rustled again. Whoever or whatever it was, it sounded like it was closing in on her. She fumbled on the ground until her hand rested on a fist-sized rock. She picked it up, ready to fight to protect her men.

The rustling changed directions and headed for the trail. She saw something, a shape. Then the trees gave way to reveal a man, a furious-looking man. He led his horse out, swung up on it, and started forward at a near gallop, way too fast for such a steep and rocky trail. But the horse acted game and sure-footed.

He looked different from the man Justin had captured. That one was dirty, his clothes old and threadbare. His horse, ridden by Heath, was broken down with age.

This man rode a gleaming brown thoroughbred and was dressed sharp. He was clean, wearing a black suit and white shirt, a lot like what Cole wore to work. He had on a flat-topped black hat with fringe on the brim, which reminded Sadie of how Ramone had described Dantalion, the man who'd killed her grandfather. His hair was more gray than black. Was this the same man who'd committed murder decades ago? Was he back to kill again?

She figured out one other thing, too. If these two men were together, then this one was for sure the boss.

What should she do?

With grim determination, she watched him pass by. Should she fight? Should she follow him quietly? Should she hide like a frightened rabbit?

At first she was disgusted that she'd put herself in danger by not staying with Cole. Next, she'd messed up by not coming out when Heath and Justin rode by. But then it struck her that it was a good thing she'd done it. None of her menfolk would know there was another outlaw on their trail, and based on how quietly he moved and how raging mad he appeared to be, this man was dangerous.

Considering that whatever was going on stretched back to Grandfather Chastain's time, their enemy was mighty slick, very determined, and most likely very smart.

Just the kind of man who'd hang back and sneak around like a vicious coyote.

She'd found out there was a second man to capture, and she was the only one who knew it. Reckless or not, she had a chance now to save the lives of the men she loved. And she wouldn't let herself regret it.

She listened to him riding up the trail. When he was well ahead and out of sight, she led her horse from the cover of the woods and fell in behind him, mindful to move slowly, even though that chafed, and to keep her horse quiet. She didn't want to warn the man she was here before she got him close enough to Justin and Heath. Because she needed them to back her up in this fight.

28

Heath spotted the back end of Cole's horse up ahead. "We're catching up."

Everyone else was out of sight, a trail of dust hanging far overhead. Heath hoped that meant they'd crossed the peak of this climb and were well on their way to the ranch house.

At the sound of their approach, Cole whirled, gun in hand. The second he saw them, he relaxed and rode back down the trail toward them. "Where's Sadie?"

Heath pulled his horse to a stop. "I sent her to you, Cole." He paused a moment, then said, "She must be ahead."

"No," Cole said, wincing in pain. "I let her bring up the rear. I hadn't even noticed she was gone." He was all in. One side of his shirt and his pants were soaked in crimson. He had his left elbow clamped to his side to staunch the blood. There'd been no time to tend the wound or even to see exactly where the bullet hit. He was pale as milk. His hand trembled on the reins. Hanging on to the saddle horn was almost too much for him. Heath was shocked by how bad he looked.

Heath wheeled the poor, winded old nag around and headed downhill.

Justin said, "Cole, let me tie this outlaw onto your horse. I'm going with Heath."

"No you're not." Heath turned back, bothered by the delay. "Stay here and I'll find her."

"We've ridden this whole trail. There was no sign of her. You need help."

"Maybe she stepped off the trail to have a moment of . . . of privacy, and we just rode right past her. She's probably coming along right now." Heath didn't believe it, no matter how badly he wanted to. "You've got to keep moving, Justin. Tend the prisoner. Get over that hump to the CR and send someone riding hard for town to fetch the doctor and the sheriff. I'll find Sadie and catch up."

Justin shook his head. "I'm not leaving Sadie out here."

Heath shifted so that Justin's body blocked Cole's view of him, then dropped his voice to a whisper. "Cole *needs* a doctor. He's lost too much blood."

Justin's jaw got so tight, Heath worried his teeth might crack. Without turning to examine Cole, he grunted his assent. He'd already seen for himself the truth of the matter and knew Heath was right.

Never had a man looked so torn. His stared down the trail so hard he might've thought he could conjure Sadie out of thin air.

Justin stuck out his hand. Surprised, Heath reached over and shook it. "There aren't many men I'd trust with my sister's life, Kincaid. But you're one. You're a man to ride the river with."

Heath was stunned at how honored he felt.

"I'll be back as soon as I get everyone home, turn them over to Rosita, and send for the doctor and sheriff."

"Don't forget you can't trust anyone on your ranch, Justin. And don't let this back-shootin' coyote out of your sight for a minute. I wouldn't even turn him over to the sheriff until you get the answers you need."

Justin jerked his head once, spun around, and said, "Let's go."

"No . . ." Cole said, the word coming out slurred. "Sadie . . ." He drooped so far forward over the saddle horn, it poked him in the belly.

Justin grabbed the reins out of Cole's hands and led them up the trail. He moved out fast, as if he had to go before he started hollering. After his one single protest, Cole went silent, which told Heath just how badly hurt he was.

Heath headed down the trail at a pace that liked to break his neck.

Where was Sadie? *Where?*

Where should she attack? *Where?*

Sadie did her best to close in on the man ahead of her. He was a good distance ahead, so she didn't dare gallop. The noise of it would surely give her away.

How long had she lingered here? How far ahead had Heath gotten? Once Heath and Justin reached the others, they'd know she was missing. Unless they'd reached the top and crested the canyon wall. Then who knew? If the woods were thick over the hill and the trail twisted, they might not notice she was gone for a long time.

Her stomach lurched to think of being left out here alone with that furious, fancied-up man. He wasn't anyone she wanted to face. Yet she knew he was the enemy and had to be stopped. And if the job fell to her, so be it.

She saw the whipping of a horsetail far overhead. The motion drew her attention. She realized the trail had twisted back on itself, and though she was a lot lower, she wasn't too far from the man if she could somehow cut through. She studied the tail and was sure the horse wasn't moving.

Why not?

Sadie decided to go find out.

❧

Heath rounded the trail and came face-to-face with a man holding a rifle. He was waiting. He'd heard Heath coming. Heath saw how he was dressed and thought immediately of the man Ramone had called Dantalion. The man who'd terrorized Ramone and was behind all that had happened at the ranch.

And now one wrong move and he'd be riddled with bullets and of no use to anyone.

The man smiled and kept the gun dead center on Heath. "Turn around. We're riding right back to where you came from, and if you say one wrong word or try to warn them, I'll let loose with this rifle."

With a sickening twist of his belly, Heath figured this man already had Sadie. She might well be dead, though there'd been no shooting lately, so he clung to hope. *God, please don't let any harm come to my sweet Sadie.*

And if he led the man to the Bodens, they might all end up dead, not just Heath.

All Heath could think of to do was to buy some time. Time for the Bodens to get home to the ranch where they could defend themselves. To give this vermin time to make a mistake.

"You've finally stepped out in the open," Heath said.

The man smirked. "No, I didn't. You may have found me, but you won't live to tell anyone about it."

"That gives me precious little reason to lead you to my friends."

The man shrugged a shoulder, looking smug. "I know how men think. You want to stay alive. You'll do what I say because you'll think it's not betraying your friends. You're hoping I make a mistake so you can get the drop on me." The man laughed. "But I never make a mistake."

Heath took a chance that he was right about the man's name. "Sure you do, Dantalion."

The man's eyes narrowed. "How did you know my name?"

Heath managed a laugh to match his enemy's. "You honestly think I'd tell you that? Give you more folks to hunt? You don't give me much reason to cooperate with you. And if you think you can shoot me and that ends things, then you're a fool, Dantalion. Even now, your name is out and the story is spreading that you're a killer and a coward. You look too slick not to be an important man, but before the Bodens are done with you, you'll be in prison and all your powerful friends will avoid you like you're carrying the plague."

The man's cool sneer twisted into something malevolent. His hands tightened on the rifle. "I don't need your cooperation. The Bodens can't get off this trail, and you're the only thing standing in my way."

"If you pull that trigger, they'll have all the warning they need."

"No one beats me," Dantalion growled. "As you lay dying, remember it's not just the Boden men I'll kill. Their sister has to die, too. Only, once I have her, I might keep her alive for a bit. She's a pretty little thing."

Words that should have sickened him instead made his heart soar. Dantalion *didn't* have Sadie. That changed everything. He had to get out of this alive so he could spend the rest of his life with a woman he now realized he loved more than life itself.

And considering he was facing death, he thought he was a pretty good judge of what he loved more than life itself.

His finger itched to go for his six-shooter. At this range he couldn't miss, but neither could Dantalion. And with that rifle raised and leveled, Heath wouldn't get his shot off first.

He was fast, he knew that. If this low-down coyote could be distracted for just a second, Heath might have a chance of getting his gun into play.

As he tried to think of what might throw the man off from his single-minded aim, an object flew out of the forest and smacked the rump of Dantalion's brown thoroughbred. The horse reared. Heath drew his six-shooter, aimed, and fired.

Dantalion tumbled off the back of his horse, and his rifle went flying. The horse blocked Heath from taking another shot for a crucial second, then the frightened animal sprang out from between Heath and his target. The horse charged up the trail, and Heath had to jump out of the way or get run down.

Another rock struck the back of the outlaw's head.

Dantalion lunged for the side of the trail, looking for cover. Heath fired, then fired again, and Dantalion reeled back and landed in a cloud of dust flat on his back, his head bleeding, and two bullet wounds in his chest.

Sadie charged into view with another big rock in her hand, and three more cradled in her non-throwing arm.

Seeing her unhurt and heavily armed, Heath almost laughed. No time now, but he'd get around soon enough to telling her she was the finest woman he'd ever known.

Heath rushed for Dantalion before Sadie got close enough that the man could grab her. He lay on the ground, unmoving, but with his teeth bared like a rabid wolf.

"Heath, I'm so glad to see you!" Sadie ran to his side. He hugged her and smiled, not taking his eyes off Dantalion for long.

Dantalion made a move for his sleeve, but Heath dropped to his knees and stopped him cold.

"We need to search him for hideout weapons, Sadie."

Sure enough, Heath found a gun up the man's sleeve. There was a knife in his boot, another in a sheath under his waistband at the small of his back. There were also some papers in the inside pocket of his coat, along with a leather pouch of gold coins, and something wrapped in oilcloth in the pocket of his pants. Heath took it all.

With a feeble swipe of his hand, Dantalion tried to reach for Heath's pistol.

Heath dodged the effort easily and said in disgust, "Do you see where my bullets landed, Dantalion? You're dying. You'll stand before your Maker before this day is out. Do you want your last act on this earth to be murder? You have a few minutes before you reach the Pearly Gates. I suggest you spend those minutes confessing your sins and trying to make right all that you've done wrong in this life. You can start by telling me why you're trying to kill the Bodens."

"You think your troubles are over?" The man smiled, and the evil of it sent a chill up Heath's spine.

Heath stuffed the papers and gold in his own pockets to study later, then looked at the gray in the man's hair and asked, "Did you kill Frank Chastain?"

The man laughed and it set off a fit of coughing. Blood tinged his lips, but finally the coughing ceased. He breathed raggedly in and out. "I did indeed kill that arrogant old man. And I ran that coward Ramone out of the country so I could blame him."

"You mean after you cut his face open? Blinded him in one eye? You call him a coward for not staying to fight when he was wounded and disarmed?"

"Stopping me won't keep any of you alive. Your days of having the Cimarron Ranch as your legacy are over. My death stops nothing because more will come. It'll take time to find someone as helpful as me, but they will. You'll regret not letting me run you off."

"Don't die with a monstrous sin on your soul." Heath wondered how a man could face death while spewing evil. The devil truly had a claim on this man, but didn't the moment when eternity was in front of you force you to turn to God?

Sadie caught the man's arm. "If you're afraid of the others who want to harm the Bodens, they can no longer harm you. You're beyond that. Why aren't our troubles over? Are there more men in this with you? Who sent you? Does this have to do with the Bodens' land grant?"

"You're the worst kind of invaders. I will tell you *nada*."

Heath glanced at Sadie. He had no idea what he meant by invaders. He saw confusion on her face that matched his.

Then Sadie, being kinder than Heath would have managed, told the man, "Then don't tell us. But won't you please ask God to forgive your sins? No matter what you've done in this life, all God asks is that you believe in Him. God loves you, and He doesn't want any of His children to spend eternity in flames. It's not too late to repent."

The man shook his head. "God wants no part of me, and I want no part of Him."

"That's not true. He's your heavenly Father."

Heath was afraid she was wasting her time. "The shots look bad, but let's get him to a doctor. I've seen men survive some terrible things. Maybe we can patch him up and ask our questions a little harder."

Dantalion moved then and got to his hands and knees. With a wicked laugh, he dove for the trees in a desperate attempt to escape. The laugh turned to a scream of terror.

Heath leapt toward the woods and plunged into thin air.

He caught hold of a narrow aspen that bent down, completely in half, its roots clinging to the edge of a cliff that was concealed by the thick trees. His grip held solid just as Dantalion's scream ended with a dull thud.

Heath glanced down to see that his legs dangled over some sort of cliff. How far down it dropped, he couldn't tell.

"Sadie! Stop!" He looked up to see her skid to her knees and throw out her arms to let the trees stop her.

Steadying herself, she called down to him, "Hang on. I'll get a rope from your saddle."

But Heath had spent a good portion of his childhood dangling, mainly in the cavern on the Kincaid property. He climbed hand over hand up the aspen tree, bent over like a rainbow. He got himself over the arc of it, then back down, and swung his feet to solid ground.

He landed right next to Sadie before she could get busy saving him, which no doubt she'd have done. Then he dropped to kneel at her side, and as long as he was in the proper position, he said a prayer of thanks.

Sadie hurled herself into his arms, and they clung to each other. Heath had never been so happy to be alive.

Heath turned to the cliff and pushed the branches aside. "He didn't know there was a cliff here." Heath looked at Sadie. "If he's still alive, we need to get him. We need to question him."

Heath, with Sadie beside him, inched forward. About a foot past the trees was a ledge, held there by the roots of the aspens and the underbrush, and then a sheer cliff. Heath gazed a long way down.

Dantalion lay sprawled, faceup on a pile of jagged stones over a hundred feet below. A pool of blood ran from the back of his head. His neck was bent at an unnatural angle.

Heath turned back and pulled Sadie away. He regretted that she'd seen it, because it was a sight she'd have to live with.

"He can't be alive." Sadie swallowed as if fighting the need to empty her belly.

"No, he's dead. There's no point in climbing all that way down."

"I don't know how we could get down there even if we wanted to."

They stood there staring at each other, neither one saying anything. The silence stretched on, and then Sadie's eyes filled with tears.

"I killed a man," she said.

Heath pulled her into his arms again. One hug wasn't near enough. He'd been dying to hold her ever since he'd caught sight of her, but he'd been sidetracked by having a man to shoot.

"Neither one of us killed the low-down varmint. He bought into more trouble than he could handle, and when things went bad, he ran like a yellow-bellied coward and fell over a cliff. If one of my bullets or your rock hit a spot that might end a man, he was alive enough to jump. I'd say that means neither of us killed him, no matter how hard we tried."

Sadie had a grateful look on her face, which didn't at all match the woman who'd come charging out of the woods, slinging rocks at an armed man. But her ability to be the softest kind of female one minute and a warrior the next was a big part of why he never wanted to let her go.

Just in case she didn't know that, he moved to kiss her. She must've had the same thing in mind, because she was already pulling his head down.

The kiss went on until Heath's head was spinning. Finally, with the worst regret in the world, he eased her away. "We have to catch up with your brothers. It about killed Justin to let me come back for you alone."

"Because he doesn't want us being alone together?"

"Nope." Heath thought of the words of respect he'd heard from Justin, and his heart warmed. "He was mad with worry about you, thinking about outlaws and shooting. He was scared to death. I'm sure if he'd had more time, though, he'd've gotten around to not wanting me to get you alone."

Then Heath's head cleared enough that he remembered what he'd known the minute he heard Dantalion threaten her in such an ugly way. That she was alive and he had too much to live for not to survive himself.

"Sadie, there are a lot of reasons there's trouble ahead for us."

Sadie's pretty brow furrowed.

"I want to go home—to Rawhide. So bad I ache."

"I can't leave here, Heath, without costing my brothers everything."

"I don't want to take you with me for fear I'll find myself taking orders from the bossy big brothers I love. It'd make me feel like a failure."

"And I've found a restless spirit in me to see more of the world, and at the same time a deep love for this land—my land, the Cimarron Ranch. I want to be part of the legacy Pa is handing to us. But that will ruin my brothers and not get you to your brothers."

"While you stand to be part owner of a vast ranch, if I stay with you, your part will become mine. But I'll have in no way earned it. And that's shameful to a man."

Sadie scowled. "All in all, I'd say most of our troubles come down to having way too many big brothers."

Nodding, Heath said quietly, "No matter how many brothers we have, that isn't reason enough to stop me from saying . . . marry me, Sadie."

She smiled at him, and suddenly all their reasons meant nothing. To be able to wake up next to that sweet smile every day for the rest of his life made whatever needed settling worth whatever effort it took.

"None of this is big enough to stop me from wanting to spend my life with you. Marry me. We'll figure everything out."

She cradled his face in both of her rock-wielding hands and kissed him so gently it hurt, but it was the best hurt in the world. "You're right, Heath. There are no troubles big enough to stop me from marrying the man I love. It would be the greatest honor of my life to marry you."

He kissed her deeply, and then they turned together and headed up the trail.

29

"You need to go back and get him," Justin insisted. "At least search him. Dantalion might have carried notes or . . ."

That reminded Heath. He pulled the papers and gold from his pockets. "I did search him. He did carry notes."

Heath and Sadie had told Justin their story, including their plan to get married. Justin had been trying to come up with a way to make Heath disappear ever since. In the rush to get to the CR, his worrying over Cole and Ramone, and Justin's nonstop nagging, Heath had forgotten all about the papers.

He handed half of them to Justin. "I'm not climbing down there. If you want to, go ahead. But you'll miss the wedding."

Justin's eyes narrowed.

Heath unfolded the papers in his hands. His brow furrowed. "Mills Dantalion. There's a note here with that name."

Justin looked between Heath and Sadie. "Who is he? And what grudge does he have against the Bodens?"

Heath handed Justin the note. "What does it say?"

Justin looked the note over and replied, "Says something about a thousand dollars in gold."

Heath held up the fat pouch filled with gold. "Do you suppose there's a thousand dollars' worth in here?"

Justin hefted the bag. "Yep, I'd say that's a good guess."

"You think someone was paying Dantalion to attack you?"

Justin went back to reading. "There's not much here that makes sense. Something about us being farthest south."

"Is he talking about our property?" Sadie asked "Because it isn't. There's a lot of New Mexico Territory south of us."

"That's true, but maybe he's not referring to the territory." Justin stood there thinking for a while. "So what is the CR farthest south of?"

"And if they paid Dantalion a thousand dollars in gold, does that mean he was a hired gun?" Sadie wondered. "Did someone pay him to kill Grandfather, too?"

"We keep thinking up new questions, yet no one seems to have any answers. Is there anything else?" Heath started paging through his papers.

"Nothing that looks important. A mention of some meeting. The dates are over a month ago."

"Right before your pa got hurt?"

"Yep, long enough ago that he had time to plan the rockslide."

"One of these is a bill of sale for a saddle, another for a horse, both bought back in Santa Fe. There are other papers too just like those."

"Maybe he's keeping his records because whoever hired him said they'd pay for whatever costs mounted up while he hunted Pa." Sadie looked over his shoulder, and Heath had to fight to keep reading. Her warm presence was distracting him.

Justin looked up and scowled at Sadie, then looked back at Heath. "I think you need to go climb down that cliff right now—it won't take all that long."

Heath held on to the papers in his hands extra tight to keep from strangling Justin. The man wanted to get rid of him, no doubt about it. "No amount of mountain climbing is gonna make him less dead, and no one else around here is going to climb down there and search him. So, if he did have something else on him—and he didn't because I checked—it'll still be there a day from now."

"You don't know that."

"Listen, I want to marry Sadie. On our ride home we decided to get married right away. The only other choice is we send Sadie's ma a wire and ask if she has permission to step her delicate toes away from the holy ground of the Cimarron Ranch. If they say yes, we could get on a train and ride up to Denver to get married with them looking on." Heath didn't want to bother with that, and he was pretty sure Sadie didn't either, but he mentioned it to torment Justin.

Sadie slid her arm around Heath's waist.

He caught hold of her and pulled her close. What a woman to have by his side for a lifetime!

"Will you get your hands off my sister?"

Heath smiled at Sadie. "Nope. And you got the sheriff out here and the doctor. Now let's get the parson to come out too and perform the wedding. I have no interest in a long engagement."

"Nor do I," Sadie said. "I want permission in the eyes of God to claim you as my husband, and permission in the eyes of my grouchy big brother, too."

"Well, you're never gettin' that, not even if you end up being married for fifty years."

Though Justin kept on complaining, Heath didn't think his heart was in it anymore. Which to Heath only made this moment sweeter.

"Speaking of the doctor," Sadie said, "he said Cole's bullet wound isn't dangerous as far as where it is. But he rode too long and bled too much, and there's always a chance of infection. He's not out of the woods yet."

Justin turned to face the hallway that led to Ma and Pa's bedroom, where he'd left his ailing brother. "Cole's going to need a lot of care, Sadie, and for way longer than he's likely to want it. You should put the wedding off until he's not going to need you night and day."

"Heath is moving into my room right upstairs. There'll be no trouble tending Cole and being married at the same time."

Justin flinched, his eyes darting between Sadie and Heath. "You should wait until Ma and Pa are back home. You know it'll break Ma's heart not to see you get married. She'll want a fine dress for you and a fancy wedding, with all the neighbors included."

"Considering all she's gone through lately, she'll thank me for relieving her of so much work. And our folks won't be back until spring. Heath and I aren't waiting until spring to get married—that's just out of the question."

"Don't you want Sister Margaret to come? Don't you want all the ladies at the orphanage here, Louisa and Maria and Angie?" Justin seemed to linger over his guest list for some odd reason.

Heath had never seen a man so eager to plan a party.

And then Parson Gregory walked in. "I was told your family needs prayers. Cole is hurt, and also another man. I heard the name Ramone, but I don't know him."

"Who told you to come out here?" Justin barked.

Parson Gregory took a step back in alarm.

"Justin, you behave yourself." Sadie turned to the parson. "He's just overwrought about Cole."

"I am not overwrought. You make me sound like some delicate maiden wringing my hands. I've never had one moment in my life where I resembled that."

Barely suppressing a laugh, Heath said, "I'll bet that's nothing but the pure truth."

Sadie frowned at them both. "We do need prayers for Cole, Parson. You can start by praying we find a way to keep him in bed long enough to heal."

The parson smiled. "I know Cole well. I can imagine he's a restless patient."

Justin took up the story, calmer now. Heath might even go so far as to say Justin was resigned.

"And Ramone we found hungry and exhausted, so we brought him home." Justin was giving a version of events that could only be described as *cleaned up*.

"That's very scriptural of you, Justin." The parson looked humbled. "'I was hungry and you fed me. I was thirsty and you gave me to drink.'"

"I've heard that verse, Parson. Thank you. And thank the good Lord Ramone wasn't naked because we didn't have any clothes to spare."

"Ramone is Alonzo's pa," Sadie added.

Heath decided they needed to get back on the subject, which was performing a wedding, and they hadn't come anywhere near that subject yet.

"Alonzo, the CR ramrod?" the parson asked.

"Yep," Justin said. "Alonzo's got his pa all taken care of. Ramone has a hot meal in his belly now. He'll heal up fast."

Heath had to speak up. "The reason Justin reacted like he did when you came in is that he was surprised to see you because Sadie and I had just been talking about sending for you. We're getting married right now, today. We'd like you to speak the vows."

The parson smiled. "I'd be more than happy to do that. I love performing wedding ceremonies."

Justin glowered at them from behind the parson's back,

but he kept his mouth shut, something that surprised Heath a little.

"Is Cole awake?" Sadie asked. "I'd like him to witness our wedding."

"Nope." Justin looked smug. "He doesn't need another shock today anyway."

"Cole is awake." Rosita came out of the downstairs bedroom at that moment. "He is weak, but he seems to be recovering."

"Rosita, Heath and I are getting married and we want the parson to marry us at Cole's bedside. You and Justin can come. I'd like John to be there, too."

Rosita nodded calmly. "I'm happy to run out for John. I'll be back with him before Cole settles down."

"Settles down from what?" The parson stared at the closed door to Cole's bedroom, which was the same room Chance had lain in not that long ago. Also hurt. The parson looked as if he thought he'd better get in there and start praying hard.

"He'll just be surprised by the wedding is all." Heath decided blaming everything on surprise was a decent plan. "We just decided today to marry and we haven't told Cole yet."

"Maybe we should have the wedding in Pa's office." Justin was still cranky. "Cole might not be up to this big a surprise."

Sadie rested a nervous hand at her throat.

Heath said, "We'd hate for our announcement to kill your brother. I think Justin's right."

Rosita returned with John close behind.

"What's this about a wedding?" John asked.

Rosita insisted Cole would survive, so they went to Cole's room to start the ceremony. Cole took the news exactly like Heath figured he would.

"Angie, I didn't know you were here!" Sadie gasped out.

The young niece of Sister Margaret was at Cole's side, taking orders from the doctor with a befuddled expression on her face. "The doctor's wife usually helps him care for patients, but she just had a baby. Doc Garner came to the orphanage hoping Aunt Margaret could help. She couldn't so they picked me."

"Please stay for my wedding." Sadie clapped her hands together and held them to her chest as if she'd just been given the best gift in the world.

Heath kind of wished Angie and the doctor would wash the blood off their hands before his wedding began. He wasn't sure he wanted Sadie to remember the ceremony including bloody hands.

"Wedding?" Cole was pale as a ghost and shaky, yet he became alert enough to be annoying. "There's not going to be a wedding."

"Oh, yes there is." Sadie plunked her hands on her hips.

Cole started badgering her. The doctor was trying to get him to rest.

Angie said, "He is going to make it, isn't he, Doc? He's got great color in his cheeks."

Yep, color. The color red, put there by fury. Heath didn't think that was healthy.

You had to give the Boden brothers credit where it was due. They were united in being idiots when it came to letting someone marry their sister. Heath couldn't fault them for wanting to protect her, but they weren't going to protect her from marriage to a man who loved her, so they should just quit being knotheads.

"We can get married here with you as witness," Sadie said, "or we can get married in Pa's office."

Cole had either exhausted himself or come to terms with the marriage. He looked at Heath with a sad smile. "It's not personal, Kincaid. You're a good man, and one I'm proud to call my friend." He shrugged. "It's just I had this picture in my head of the man who'd marry Sadie, and he was a mixture of a Yankee general, the president of the United States, a kindhearted parson, and the marble statues you see of ancient Greek gods. And you don't measure up to any of that."

"Well, he's a lot warmer than a statue, so that's in his favor." Sadie kissed Cole on the cheek and gave him a tight hug.

Heath felt a little choked up. Justin and Cole had now said more friendly words to him than he'd ever expected. It was only fair he say his piece before he joined the family.

"I've talked with Sadie about where I come from, but never with you two much. I've got three older brothers back in Colorado. Fine, strong men who love me. I didn't realize how much I missed them until I came to the CR and met you Bodens. One of the reasons I've been drifting for a while is because I could never find my place at the Colorado ranch we all ran together. Being the little brother, all I ever had was three bosses, and I blamed them for that. But since I've been here, working beside you, Justin, and your pa, and then when I got to help with the troubles surrounding your family, I started to find my own backbone.

"I never thought I could work for my brothers, and I can't. But I can work *beside* them, just like I've worked beside you. I want to go home. I'm not sure when and I'm not sure if it'll be for a visit or to take charge of my land, but now I know I can do it. I can stop being a pest of a little brother and instead stand strong with them. I found that here on the Cimarron Ranch and I'll always be grateful to you for it.

"I hope Sadie and I have your blessing, because I am a lucky man to join this family. I'll do my best to never give you a moment of regret that you were witness to Sadie's marriage to me. That's the vow I make to you."

Justin and Cole both nodded. Then Justin said, "Let's get on with the promises, Parson."

The Boden brothers survived witnessing their little sister getting wed to a lowly cowhand, who with a few vows made before God and man became one-third owner of their Cimarron Ranch. Except he wasn't really, because Chance Boden owned every inch of it regardless of his nonsense about ruling his children's lives.

But better than the ranch, Heath had become one hundred percent husband to the most beautiful, courageous woman he'd ever known.

They'd managed to use up most of the day, and the sun was setting now. Rosita went off to fetch a meal for everyone. Angie settled in at Cole's side. The doctor asked if there was enough food and a place for them to sleep for the night. He didn't think Cole was out of danger and wanted to be close at hand as a precaution.

For some reason that set Justin to grousing about heaven knew what, and then shortly afterward he left to make sure the beds were prepared.

Cole fell asleep, or maybe he passed out, but whatever happened he needed some peace and quiet to recover from it.

The parson headed back to town.

The sheriff came in with Justin and wanted to talk about their prisoner, who was locked in the cellar under the kitchen floor. Heath wanted to sit in on the questioning.

Sadie dragged him into her pa's office instead. "You're not going anywhere, husband."

"But we need to get to the bottom of this. There's still a threat to your family." Heath saw the papers and gold he'd taken from Dantalion. Justin had left them on the desk. Heath reached for the papers to study them closer.

Sadie stopped him with a kiss.

"What we *need*, Heath Kincaid, is to be man and wife. Whatever ranting Dantalion did, we have stopped the threat for now. If there are other forces against us, we'll meet and defeat them, only we won't be doing it tonight."

"But we should—"

She cut off his protest with another kiss—a longer, more passionate one. When she finally pulled back—and his arms were wrapped so tight around her that it was no small accomplishment—he decided they needed to be man and wife indeed.

"I have an idea, Sadie." Heath was no longer thinking of anything but his new bride, and truth be told, he had a lot of ideas.

"What's that?"

"Let's write to your parents and ask permission to visit them."

Sadie's eyes lit up. "I'd love to go see them."

"All these rules of your pa's, well, there's nothing saying he can't change his mind and say it's all right for you to take a train ride to visit him in the hospital."

"That's true." Sadie's hazel eyes sparkled in the lantern light as if made of spun gold. "If he's agreeable to a visit, then there'd be no problem. I'd like the chance to tell him I understand now what he was trying to do with his demand that we all live together at the CR. Cole and Justin and I had gone down different paths. Pa was heartbroken by that. He wanted us to understand the legacy he was leaving to us, but all I thought he meant was the CR—the land and gold and cattle."

"You don't think that's it now?"

"Not at all. And I started to realize that the day you told us we didn't know what we had in a father's love. I realized it more when I climbed a mesa that had no way up.

"As I've worked and fought by my brothers' sides, with it in my mind that I was fighting for our ranch, I started to see the true legacy was love. Ma and Pa's love for us. Our love for them and each other. *That's* the Cimarron legacy."

"While we're there, I want to ask your pa if it's all right to take you to meet my brothers and their families. It's close along the way to Denver. We could get off at Colorado City and ride to my ranch in a few hours' time."

"It really would be rude of my pa to dictate to a daughter when she's got a husband."

Rude wasn't the word Heath would have used. More like a stubborn old bull with horns long enough to run Heath right through.

"I don't know if we can settle all our troubles about me going home and you needing to stay here, but wherever we end up, we can always travel between our families. It's not that long of a train ride."

"We can, can't we?" Sadie brightened even more.

"If you get any more beautiful, I'm going to lose my eyesight like a man who's stared too long at the sun."

The sweet look of love on Sadie's face made him want to sweep her away, be alone with her—truly alone—away from both families. They could travel by train, and he would show her the world. Which reminded Heath of their biggest obstacle. A mighty serious one.

"But what about the trouble here? Cole's injured, and if we leave, Justin will be on his own," Sadie pointed out.

"I think whatever trouble is out there has been driven back for a while. Dantalion said it would take time. I'm sure he was organizing it, and they—whoever *they* are—will be a while finding a new troublemaker. That gives Cole time to heal, Justin time to investigate Dantalion and any traitors on the staff, and us time to enjoy being married."

"Are we being selfish to want time alone?" Sadie's pretty brow furrowed with worry.

"Suppertime!" Rosita called from the kitchen.

"Heath, you need to ask this varmint a question," Justin shouted from the far side of the house.

"Sadie, can you come in here?" Cole sounded weak, pathetically so. Even though he had the doctor and a nurse at his beck and call.

Heath smiled, then laughed. "We're going to be lucky to have one second alone. We don't have to worry much about selfishness."

"Family is a burden and a joy."

"And between us we've got five big brothers, so there's no escaping the burden, and so much joy I'm up to my eyeballs in it. We're gonna be surrounded by family no matter which family we live with."

Sadie smiled. "And that's a good thing."

"Heath, get in here!" Justin didn't need one speck of help and everyone knew it.

"Let's go eat." Heath took her arm. "Rosita is the only one who's even close to happy that we got married."

"Do we have to?" Sadie asked.

"Sadie, the doctor needs another pair of hands in here." Cole was sounding mighty healthy.

"No, I don't." The doctor was sounding overly grouchy.

Heath rolled his eyes.

In the hall, Cole fussed from behind Sadie, Justin hollered from behind Heath, and Rosita kept calling them to the meal.

"Yep." Heath ignored Cole and didn't bother responding to Justin, but Rosita got his attention. They headed for the kitchen. As they sat at the table, all by themselves, he whispered to Sadie, "Eat fast and don't even think about staying for dessert."

About the Author

Mary Connealy writes romantic comedies about cowboys. She's the author of THE KINCAID BRIDES, TROUBLE IN TEXAS, and WILD AT HEART series, as well as several other acclaimed series. Mary has been nominated for a Christy Award, was a finalist for a RITA Award, and is a two-time winner of the Carol Award. She lives on a ranch in eastern Nebraska with her very own romantic cowboy hero. They have four grown daughters—Joslyn, married to Matt; Wendy; Shelly, married to Aaron; and Katy, married to Max—and four precious grandchildren. Learn more about Mary and her books at:

maryconnealy.com
facebook.com/maryconnealy
seekerville.blogspot.com
petticoatsandpistols.com

More From Mary Connealy

Visit maryconnealy.com for a full list of her books.

Disguised as a man, Kylie Wilde is homesteading for profit so she will be able to live comfortably when she moves back East. But both love and danger threaten to disrupt her plans.

Tried and True
Wild at Heart #1

Ruthy MacNeil nearly drowned before being rescued by Luke Stone. But is she in any less danger with this handsome cowboy than she would've been if she'd stayed on her own?

Swept Away
Trouble in Texas #1

Tucked away on a remote Colorado ranch, can controlling cowboy Rafe Kincaid and feisty free spirit Julia Gilliland overcome their differences before they lose their sanity—and their chance at love?

Out of Control
The Kincaid Brides #1

⬙BethanyHouse

Stay up-to-date on your favorite books and authors with our free e-newsletters. Sign up today at bethanyhouse.com.

f

Find us on Facebook. facebook.com/bethanyhousepublishers

Free exclusive resources for your book group! bethanyhouse.com/anopenbook

If you enjoyed *No Way Up*, you may also like . . .

When a fan's interest turns sinister, young actress Lucetta Plum takes refuge on a secluded estate owned by her friend's eligible yet eccentric grandson. As hijinks and hilarity ensue, and danger catches up to Lucetta, will her friends be able to protect her?

Playing the Part by Jen Turano
jenturano.com

To impress the politician courting her and help her family, Lydia King is determined to obtain a donation to the Teaville Moral Society from the wealthiest man in town, Nicholas Lowe. But as complications arise, Lydia must decide where her beliefs—and heart—truly align.

A Heart Most Certain by Melissa Jagears
TEAVILLE MORAL SOCIETY
melissajagears.com

When a wedding-planning gig brings single mom Julia Dare to the Caliente Springs resort, she's shocked to discover that her college sweetheart, Zeke Monroe, is the manager. As they work together, Zeke and Julia are pushed to their limits both personally and professionally.

Someone Like You by Victoria Bylin
victoriabylin.com

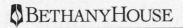